PRAISE FOR SHERLOCK MARS

"An undeniably fun tale with a protagonist who can apparently handle anything..."
—*Kirkus Review*

"A consistently compelling and entertaining read from beginning to end, "Sherlock Mars" is a blending of humor, action adventure, and mystery/suspense that will have a very special appeal to science fiction enthusiasts."
—*Midwest Book Review*

"Kingon blends history, science, popular culture and social issues with imagination and a large dose of humor."
—*Readers Favorite*

"Outstanding, Fun, Informative!!! A terrific read. It is entertaining, surprising and fun."
—*The Space Show*

"The book is well-written and the characters and situations are innovative and fresh... a light-hearted mystery and over-the-top science fiction."
—*Online Book Club*

"Brimming with comedic double-entendres and cultural references, the writing is polished and light-hearted. Sherlock Mars is an out-of-this-world success..."
—*Laugh Riot Press*

"If you like SciFi, and even if you don't, this is a fun read which will give you some good laughs. If food is your thing, there's plenty of that in this comic novel. Try this cross genre delight."
—*Netgalley*

Sherlock Mars

Sherlock Mars

Jackie Kingon

GUARDBRIDGE BOOKS
ST ANDREWS, SCOTLAND

Published by Guardbridge Books,
St Andrews, Fife, United Kingdom.

SHERLOCK MARS

Cover art © David Stokes
with images from: © dreamstime.com and © NASA.

ISBN: 978-1-911486-00-8

For Al with love.

1

SUNRISE: BANDS OF PALE PINK LIGHT peek over the horizon of Mars' eastern sky, a remnant of the days before terraforming created another blue marble in the solar system. Communities once under protective domes, looking like giant paperweights surrounded by dry, red earth in an oxygen poor atmosphere, are now thriving without them. Come and see for yourself; my husband and I did over twenty years ago. Come to New Chicago, Mars' capital at the base of Olympus Mons, and enjoy a meal at my restaurant, Molly's Bistro. Mars Media gave it its top rating: four spiral galaxies.

But not today. Definitely not today, even though it's a balmy forty-five degrees Fahrenheit with thin cirrus clouds overhead, almost no chance of a dust storm, and New Chicago Boulevard is filled with strolling shoppers. Don't come today. It's the one day of the week we're closed. Besides, my husband Cortland and I have been invited by Rick Frances, my new neighbor and owner of Virtual Vittles—a virtual restaurant where holographic smoke and mirrors recreate the experience of dining in a fine restaurant—to a virtual meal a week before their grand opening.

When my headwaiter, Frank Carol, hears the news that Virtual Vittles will open next door, he asks, "Is having a virtual restaurant nearby going to be good or bad for good food, Molly?"

I turn the box of Chocolate Moons upside down and shake it. Nothing. Empty.

"We'll soon find out."

When we first got the invitation, Cortland, a successful music producer, protested. Said he didn't want anyone messing with his perceptions and would feel ridiculous thinking he was drinking wine and eating delicious food while swallowing nothing but air. But after weeks of cajoling and saying I wanted to check out the competition and Cortland saying they don't serve real food, ergo no competition, he agreed.

So here we are, standing outside VV's tall wood paneled door second guessing if we should go in. We pause, watching the sky dim, knowing it is eclipse season, a few days each year when the orbit of Mars' moon Phobos is inclined so that it partially covers the sun for about thirty seconds twice a day. It always makes me realize that although I don't miss my earlier life on Earth, I do miss seeing its large moon pass through its phases.

Then, before we can change our minds, Cortland nods, and we go in. A tall man with slicked-back brown hair in a navy blue uniform with gold buttons buttoned to the neck greets us. "Welcome to Virtual Vittles," he says with a slight bow. "I'm Avery Spelling, head waiter. Rick apologizes for not being here. He had to take a call. Please follow me."

We walk through a very quiet white room. I hardly dare breathe. It doesn't help when Cortland says, "This place looks like it was plastered in the stuff used for death masks."

Avery turns and says, "We want no distractions."

"Better to fry our brains," Cortland says.

Avery makes a subtle diplomatic cough that is neither subtle nor diplomatic to show that he heard.

The room is divided into cubicles. Each cubicle has people seated around tables covered with white linen cloths, white china, and crystal glasses. Most are poking at floating colored menu pallets in front of them and talking in hushed voices. Avery stops at an empty cubicle and gestures for us to step inside. He pulls out a white French provincial chair near me. I sit. Then he walks to the other side and does the same for Cortland. A moment later, floating screens appear at eye level in front of us.

"We have over fifty thousand choices on the menu," Avery says. "If you don't find what you want, we can create it."

I ask, "Any recommendations or specials?"

"Everything is special. Study the menu and touch the screen to make your selections. In a moment, someone will come and assist you. Any questions?"

We say nothing.

"Enjoy your meal," Avery says, turning away.

"I wish I had brought crackers or something," I say.

Then after a long delay, Cortland leans forward conspiratorially and says, "Why do I feel like we're in a horror movie?"

"Because maybe we are," I whisper.

2

I JUMP WHEN A WAITER APPEARS and pours water into my glass.

"Is this water real?" I ask.

"Yes. We thought real water added a nice touch." He turns and leaves.

I sip the water. Gather my thoughts.

Cortland's brows knit. "How does it taste?"

"Like water."

"Anything special about it?"

"Not that I can tell."

"Well, who knows what's in it?" He pushes his glass away.

A few moments later, Rick Frances, in a crisp white dinner jacket, white shirt with ruffles, black trousers, and black patent leather shoes approaches. Accompanying him is an attractive woman with long dark hair and Asian eyes in a white lab coat. Keys dangle from a chain around her neck. One hand holds a small black case.

"Molly! Cortland!" Rick says, arms outstretched as though we are old friends. "I'm thrilled you're here." He gives me an air kiss on both cheeks, grabs Cortland's hand, and shakes it vigorously. "Sorry I wasn't here to greet you. Meet Lena Fermi, my chief engineer and the brain behind VV. She makes sure everything runs the way it should."

We smile at Lena.

"What did you think of the menu?" Rick asks.

"Overwhelming," I say. "I thought I knew food, but you have food I've never heard of."

Lena smiles and says, "That's because we can combine taste combinations and foods even if they physically don't exist, like a chocolate peach."

Rick turns to Cortland. "You're president of Molawn Music, and The Lunar Tunes are your twin daughters, right?"

"Right," he says. "Becky and Lois. Really Quebec and Los Angeles, but no one calls them that except us."

"Loved their rendition of 'Moon Rover.'" He sings, "Two drifters, off to see the moon..."

Cortland clears his throat.

Rick stops. He turns to me. "And it's an honor to have *the* Molly of Molly's Bistro. I hear that your food is full of soul and sensation."

I smile, say nothing.

Rick says, "Now let me explain how VV works. Everything is electronically coded. We scanned you when you sat in these chairs."

Cortland jumps up. "You scanned us?"

Rick puts his hand on Cortland's arm. "Relax. Sit. The settings are deleted every time you get up so we can use the chair again."

Cortland sits.

Rick continues. "Items on the table are keyed to the virtual experience through haptic holograms. The tactile illusion is generated by the pressure of sound waves. Each piece of cutlery, each glass, each plate is connected to our main computer. When the virtual experience is engaged, you'll feel sensations that mimic the push and pull of a knife and fork cutting food. When you lift something with your fork or spoon and put it in your mouth, you'll have the sensations that mimic the real thing. In fact, Molly, you can have the experience of eating your own restaurant's food. We programmed your menu as well as the menus of many other restaurants. Want a Jovian burger? Saturian slider? No problem."

"No problem?" I say.

"We're not stealing recipes; we're electronically reinterpreting food. We credit each restaurant. In fact, several restaurants said I brought them business. Want to try your honey maple spare ribs? One of my favorites."

Cortland lifts a tablespoon and examines it. "So this thing is rigged? Feels like a regular silver spoon."

"It was once," Lena says. "We use the best sterling. That pattern is crafted to resemble Gorham's Strasbourg."

Then Lena puts the case she holds on the table, removes a headset and gloves, and demonstrates how the equipment is used. Cortland says the demonstration reminds him of a flight attendant giving instructions for an emergency. Lena winces.

"May I?" she asks, holding a headset in front of me.

"Does it hurt?" I ask.

"Of course not," she says. She places the headset on my head and adjusts it. "How does it feel?"

"Hardly know I'm wearing it."

Then she does the same for Cortland, who looks like he is tolerating a medical exam.

Lena says, "You'll be so engrossed in what you see and feel that you won't be aware of anything artificial." She holds up the headset. "The frames on these send signals to your taste buds so the perception of 'eating' will be coordinated with what you do with your eyes, hands, and mouth."

"What if we don't like what we're eating?" Cortland asks.

"Say 'new menu' and a new menu will appear in front of you. Then say 'new selection.'"

Cortland nods. "What happens when I say the word 'help'?"

"Say 'stop' and the program will disengage."

When the "meal" ends, or, more accurately, when the program ends, Cortland and I sit for a long time and say nothing. Then Cortland picks up his water, drains the glass, and says, "Was that as good as I thought it was, Molly?"

"Better."

Cortland says, "If that were a real experience and not a virtual one, VV would put Molly's and every restaurant I know out of business. The garlic bread alone was so delicious it could redefine garlic, butter, and bread."

"Good thing nobody can reproduce that in reality without drugs. Did you have the butter cookie cone filled with white chocolate gelato with thick hot chocolate sauce poured into the bottom tip?"

"Three," Cortland says. "I hate to admit it, but Rick Frances deserves a lot of credit, because diabetics can eat sweets, those with food allergies can gorge on foods that would be dangerous, and alcoholic beverages can be drunk with impunity. But I've never been so hungry in my life. I can't wait to get home and eat something solid."

Our house, with the exception of the brightly lit elevator that opens as we near, is dark. When we came to New Chicago, an expensive city on the base of Olympus Mons, and before Cortland made it big producing hit music, he worked for his cousin, who owned a chain of Little Green Man Pizzas. He found this run-down factory in a then-marginal neighborhood. He transformed the four lower levels into offices and a recording studio, the middle two floors into apartments for Becky and Lois, and we live in the duplex penthouse, complete with wraparound terrace, full gym, and pool. The entire building rotates, maximizing views and light. A few years later, the neighborhood exploded into expensive 'left bank' trendiness. Cortland said, "Lucky guess."

When I first arrived in New Chicago, I didn't know what to

expect. I knew it was the capital of Mars and a bustling mega metropolis at the south eastern base of Olympus Mons: a shield volcano, meaning its cone is not steep. And that the mountain was three times as high as Mount Everest and wider than the entire Himalayan range. It was made from overlapping lava flows that flowed from top to bottom like melted wax from a candle. The controversy as to who discovered it in 1879 is still raging today, as some are certain it was Schiaparelli Marinara but others insist it was Spaghetti Bolognaise.

Huge cliffs surround its enormous base; one of which dominates New Chicago's western view. There is no place I can go, no single vantage point from the ground where I can see its huge shape, which is frustrating knowing that I'm only seeing a small part of the cliff. But I've enjoyed hiking among twisted motionless torrents of lava on its gentle slopes in the many natural preserves, especially those on the north side where a wide ramp was built over the last active lava flow. Cortland promised me that we will take a copter to the summit rim for my birthday, so I can view the ringed caldera which is large enough to enclose a city as big as New York and out onto the Tharsis plains and see Arisa Mons, Pavonis Mons and Ascraeus Mons three great volcanic peaks from on high.

As soon as the elevator rises and the door opens to our apartment, the house lights turn on. We push past the service bot that greets us, arms outstretched for our coats. We drop our coats on the floor, rushing into the kitchen. Then we eat everything. Everything! Including tomato paste straight from the can, frozen vegetables straight from the freezer, vanilla extract and Worcestershire from the bottle. Don't say *ugh* until you know what starving feels like.

The following week, VV officially opens. When the first "meal" ends and people are as hungry as we had been, those who never pushed or shoved in their lives—even if someone yelled fire—run into Molly's Bistro as though they had heard the words "free beer."

So regarding my headwaiter Frank's question: "Is having VV next door going to be good or bad for good food?" I would have to say, having VV next door was very good indeed.

3

THREE WEEKS LATER, in the lull between lunch and dinner, Frank buzzes my office. Rick is here and wants to see me. I zoom in and rotate my life-sized holo; I do a comb, brush, lipstick, and go into the dining room to greet him.

Rick is standing in the middle under the colored glass ceiling, giving the room a 360-degree scan. He stops when he sees me, gives a big open smile, and bursts, "It's been a long time since I was in a good restaurant. I'm enjoying the cooking smells so much that I feel like I'm gaining weight inhaling the aromas. Is it true that you have the finest prime meat grown from stem cells?" He extends his hand. "Nice to see you again, Molly."

I meet his eye. "Nice to see you too, Rick. You've done your homework. How can I help you?"

"I want to book a party."

"A party? Seriously?" I am more surprised than if he had handed me a ghost orchid.

"I don't do all my living in virtual reality."

I laugh. "Would you like some coffee? We can talk in my office."

Rick nods.

I turn and call to Frank, who is sitting at a table near the kitchen checking the dinner menu and stroking his goatee. "Bring two coffees and a dish of our new Gran Couva Valrhona chocolate cookies to my office."

I sit at my desk. Rick sits in an armchair opposite me. Frank brings the coffee and cookies, puts them on my desk, pours two hot cups, and turns to leave.

"What kind of party did you have in mind, Rick?" I ask, pushing a steaming cup toward him.

Rick ignores my question. His eyes are riveted on Frank. He says, "Forgive me for staring at you, but you resemble someone I once knew. You could be her brother."

"Really?" Frank says, turning away. "I don't have a sister. Need anything else, Molly?"

"No, Frank. Thanks."

Rick continues to look at Frank. "Sorry, she was pretty. Very pretty." Then, as Frank puts his hand on the doorknob, Rick says, "Did you ever live near Elysium Mons?"

"Never," Frank says, stepping through the doorway and closing the door with a sharp click.

Rick turns to me. "I don't usually forget a face. Names, yes, but I have a very good visual memory."

"Can't help you on that one," I say.

"Maybe it will come to me later."

"Happens," I say. Then I wait. When Rick says nothing more, I say, "In the past I thought liquid food substitutes like soylent that keep you nutritionally healthy and feeling full and pills that temporarily alter your taste buds would make significant dents in my business. But people still wanted to socialize over a good meal in a pretty environment. When VV first opened, I wondered again if my business would suffer. But the opposite happened because people left VV hungry."

Rick chuckles. "We're a good match, then."

"Yes, guess we are."

Rick leans in. "Rumor has it that a McMoons is planning to open on the other side of me with flashing neon lights and booming their theme song 'It's a Big Burger After All.' Now, I love good food. Real good food. I once owned a restaurant with my ex-wife." He pauses. Then his jaw drops and his eyes grow wide.

"What?" I say.

"Nothing. Just a hunch. A fleeting thought."

I wait.

Rick eats a cookie. "These are delicious." He looks me in the eye. "So, I would rather have my patrons stream into Molly's after they've been to VV than people streaming into McMoons. Places like McMoons could compromise our property values. This area has upscale, trendy boutiques like those on Rodeo Dive. You could consider opening a gourmet take-out shop on the other side of me."

So Rick and I plan a round-robin dinner. Diners would arrive at VV, have virtual appetizers and virtual cocktails, then stream over to Molly's Bistro for real appetizers and real cocktails, then head back to VV for the next course. This would be repeated until the meal ended at VV with entertainment provided by Virtual Virtuosos and everyone by that time filled with good food and good wine.

What could go wrong?

4

THE DAY ARRIVES. Starting at VV, Avery Spelling, spiffy in a black tuxedo, checks gold embossed invitations against a guest list. When waiters escort them to their tables and help those who had not been there before don the VV equipment, the room fills with electric nervousness. But slowly, everyone relaxes, and it becomes more festive than priests discovering that the wine at the eleven o'clock mass is Chateau Laffite.

I remember how my hands sweated before the headset slid over my eyes and the gloves went on. But like me, when the first virtual appetizer arrives, this one being fresh lobster chunks on homemade buttered pesto toasts accompanied by Champagne Orange Royals with Lillet, all you hear is "oohs" and "ahhs." And when the next course appears, a warm Saturian potato pocket topped with cool caviar, there is only rapt silence that continues until the appetizer experience ends and everyone is told to go to Molly's Bistro for the real thing.

Frank Carol stands under Molly's red and blue awning in a short white jacket and watches people exit VV. They walk in an orderly manner until inside when they see waiters holding silver trays filled with real Champagne Orange Royals. Then civilized behavior falls into a black hole.

Most guests are seated in the main dining room at tables

covered with pale peach cloths and napkins and fresh flowers in glass vases. Late responders are seated on oversized buttery stools in the Rosewood bar in front of antique-looking mirrors with shelves displaying exotic liquors like Jupiter Red Spot brandies. To compensate for the complaints we knew would come for being seated beyond Pluto, Rick and I begin our greetings there.

Frank brings us ginger ale with a thin orange slice to make it look like we are drinking Orange Royals while working the room. Almost immediately Rick spots an attractive woman with short brown curly hair sitting at one end of the bar sipping her Orange Royal through a Day-Glo straw. He threads his way over, embraces her, and begins an animated conversation that I can't overhear but wish I could. This lasts until he spots a slinky looking blonde wearing a glowing Lurtex dress that pushes everything over the top. He pecks the brunette on the cheek and scoots away, greeting the next woman in the same effusive manner. Then I am distracted by other people.

I catch up with Rick as he heads toward the dining room. "Didn't know you were such a ladies' man."

He holds his glass high over his head, avoiding an elbow knocking it. He puts his other hand over his mouth and whispers, "Fun after a painful divorce."

A waiter passes a tray of real Orange Royals in our direction. We swap our ginger ales for one and clink.

I find Cortland and the twins sitting on the side of the main dining room in a gray upholstered booth. I raise my glass. "Love you guys," I say over the din.

"And Burton?" Becky asks, squeezing her fiancé's hand so tightly her knuckles turn white.

"Of course I love Burton." I blow a kiss.

Loving Burton Ernie took a while, but it was finally true. When I first met him, Becky said I had to see him for himself—whatever that meant—and not for what he did or how much money he made and taunted that he came from fortunetellers on Venus, astral projectors, prosthesis makers for octopuses, or he was a rocket scientist.

Finally, when she was satisfied, she said rocket scientist. Then she added that he was a descendant on his mother's side of the Vilna Goan, a Jewish sage whose commentaries on the bagel hole are in the crib notes to the Talmud, and on his father's side, descended from Michael Jackson, whose Moonwalk dance is now the national dance of Earth's moon. However, all Burton was left with though the intervening generations that had juggled his genes was a predilection for the polka and a love of kosher knishes.

Jody, a pretty young waitress who smiles often and gets big tips, walks nearby carrying a tray of used glasses. "I'll never make it through the night if I drink too much of this," I say, adding my half-finished glass to her tray.

"No problem," Cortland says, retrieving my glass, draining it, and putting it back on Jody's tray.

When the last appetizer is served and everyone is ready to return to VV, Ruby, owner of Ruby's Spa, who once wouldn't let me into her spa because when I first came to Mars I was very overweight, rises and booms: "I've had so much food I can hardly face any more. At least at VV we can eat without suffering."

Hearing this, I vow never to go to her spa again and instead give my business to a small struggling establishment run by a new Mars immigrant, Elizabeth Arden VIII.

And so the meal progresses, alternating between VV and Molly's Bistro. But suddenly, before the dessert at Molly's is served—a decadent chocolate orange soufflé—there is a loud crash in the kitchen. Rick and I stop what we are doing and rush in. Frank freezes, then joins us. Most of the soufflés had slid off a serving trolley onto the floor.

My chef, Mario Bugatti, with his chef's hat tilting over one eye and red face perspiring is waving his arms at Vanna Georgia, his sous chef and screaming, "What's the matter with you? Got a power outage like an android? Can't you do anything right?"

Vanna raises her hands in defense and sobs, "It's not my fault. I did what you asked."

"But not in the way I wanted," Mario booms slamming his hand on the counter's marble surface.

"So in addition to my culinary skills that you never seem to recognize, I'm supposed to be a mind reader?

"Stop immediately!" I say pushing them apart and standing between them.

Mario looks at the mess on the floor and huffs. "I'll need time to make new soufflés."

Rick and I look at each other and try to think of a way to stall for time while Mario makes the soufflés.

"How about having Becky and Lois sing?" I say.

"No way," Rick says. "I went to a great deal of trouble orchestrating some great virtual entertainment. Don't want Becky and Lois outshining it."

"You have a point. But you can't beat live entertainment."

Rick rolls his eyes.

Frank says, "It might be possible to insert a surprise course."

"Surprise course? I ask. "What do you mean?"

Frank turns to Mario. "Do we have any Saturns—balls of frozen pistachio mousse with pink meringue rings, in the basement freezer?"

Mario eyes widen. "We do. I just made enough a few days ago for a Cereal Box Character party that booked the entire restaurant for next Thursday."

"Cereal Box Character party? That's a new one," I say.

Frank says, "The guests dress as cereal characters. You know, Snap Crackle and Pop, Tony the Tiger, the Lucky

Charms Leprechaun."

"Seems undignified but you never know what appeals to people and business is business," I say.

"There's plenty of time to make more before that event," pipes Mario visibly relieved.

Frank turns and heads down the basement steps and says, "I'll check to see if there are enough Saturns."

We wait.

"Do we have enough, Frank?" I yell.

"Almost finished counting, Molly." We continue to wait. Finally. "Yup more than enough. Tell Vanna to come down to help me load the dumb-waiter."

When Frank and Vanna come up, Vanna puts a spoon into one of the Saturns and holds it out to Mario. "Taste this, Mario, and see if it's perfect. Perfect," she repeats louder.

Mario turns his face away glares at Vanna and says, "My taste buds are too refined to taste anything under such pressure."

I reach for the spoon and say, "I'll taste it." But Rick grabs it first, tastes it, and says, "Delicious."

Then Frank and Vanna put the pistachio mousses onto the trays, and the waiters carry them into the dining room.

Rick circles the room laughing and chatting. Then he sits with Sandy Andreas, CEO of Congress Drugs and Drugstores and San Andreas Foods, supplier to all Flying Saucer supermarkets, and his wife Solaria, head of the Culinary Institute, and their friends, who booked two tables.

I greet others in the opposite direction. Suddenly, I hear a lot of activity coming from the Andreas' table. Rick stands, hand to throat, gasping. I go to help him, but he waves me away and goes toward the kitchen. After ten minutes when he doesn't return, I become nervous and go into the kitchen to see if how he is. Vanna points to the back door.

At first I see nothing. Then I see a leg near the recycling bin. "Rick," I call. No answer. I walk closer. "Rick," I repeat. A garbage can has tipped, covering his face and much of his upper body. "Rick?" I push the garbage away. He doesn't move. Not at all. His eyes are open and pupils fully dilated. I scream so loud I can feel the little bones in my inner ear readjust. The kitchen staff comes running. Mario bends over Rick and gives him mouth-to-mouth resuscitation and pounds his chest. No response.

I push on my palm. A red light flashes and a mechanical voice says, "Please charge." I can't believe that with everything I had had to do, I forgot to check my charger. I shake my hand vigorously, activating the piezoelectricity stored in my clothes to give it a boost. Then I click Mars Yard: Emergency!

5

I WAIT AT THE FRONT OF THE RESTAURANT, peering through a window for chief detective Lamont Cranshaw and his partner Sid Seedless. We've known each other a long time and worked together when I first came to Mars and worked as a security guard at the Culinary Institute. I had solved a murder with the help of my co-worker Jersey and her husband Trenton, a brilliant scientist and Bunsen Burner Prize winner. Before I knew him, Trenton had crashed his Porsche-Aquila XXX racing car coming out of a double S curve, and most of his body was destroyed. When he was offered the choice of being a brain in a bottle or becoming the first human android, Trenton chose android and said the choice was a no brainer.

Back then, Jersey, Trenton, and I not only helped Lamont and Sid discover who poisoned the Culinary Institute's most popular product, Chocolate Moons, but also found a delicious antidote. Cortland hoped that it would be the last time I played detective, but he had to admit I was good at it.

I see Lamont and Sid arrive. Lamont puts his weight on one of the double doors and pushes it open. He enters with a roll to his shoulders, jingling change, smelling of fabric softener. His ice blue eyes widen, making him look like one of his Irish policeman ancestors. Sid follows behind holding a sandwich.

"What's that?" I hear Lamont say.

"My lunch. I had no time."

"If you want a sandwich, I'll show you a sandwich." Lamont punches Sid's arm so hard that the sandwich goes flying. "Move it."

The restaurant is filled with hushed buzzing voices. Lamont waves his badge over his head and booms, "Police, I'm in charge. Secure the perimeter!"

"But this isn't a military operation," Sid says, hand to the side of his mouth.

Lamont glares.

"Does 'secure the perimeter' mean everyone can go?" a visibly shaken diner asks.

"Definitely not. It means you can't leave until I say you can leave." He gives a thumb point to Sid. "Sid will answer any questions while you wait."

Everyone groans.

Three other officers arrive. Lamont says, "One of you stand at the door and help Sid to make sure no one leaves. The rest of you see that no one touches anything." Lamont looks at me with a face like a thundercloud. He is about to say something when the door opens again and the coroner enters with several assistants. They stride over.

The coroner says flatly, "Where's the body?"

I point toward the kitchen.

I see the coroner give his assistants a serious nod. He says, "Get started collecting samples of everyone's DNA. No one leaves until you finish." They walk away.

They follow me through the kitchen into the back yard. Mario and Vanna join us while a pale and jittery kitchen staff moves to the side.

Lamont says, "Anyone touch the body?'

"I did," I say. "I tried to find a pulse."

"I did also," Mario says. "I tried to give him mouth to mouth resuscitation."

Lamont looks at us. "You shouldn't have done that. I have to put that in my report."

"We thought he was sick." I sigh. Mario sweats and nods.

The coroner puts on protective gloves and does a quick exam. "Can't tell much until I do an autopsy," he says. He taps his palm in several places and presses it to Rick's palm. After he studies the result, he and Lamont press their palms together.

Mario glares at Vanna and growls. "Maybe something you put his food?"

"He had the same thing everyone else had," Vanna snarls. "All the mistakes are my fault; all the successes yours. Right, Mario?"

I roll my eyes. Unfortunately, I was doing this more. When Mario and Vanna worked as a team, their creativity was unsurpassed, but they nit-picked almost everything: was soft ice cream a liquid or a solid, was cotton candy a solid or a gas? They almost came to blows when I said I wanted to add ethnic foods to the menu starting with the Jewish holiday Passover. Mario insisted that it was a dinner held once every four years and everyone asked questions.

But Vanna said Saturn's Ringing Brothers Media interviewed Elijah Prophet who said that, unlike Santa Claus, who visited every Christian kid's home on Christmas, left toys and left, he was to visit every Jewish child's home once a year on Passover and drink a cup of wine. But when the mothers see him, they grab him and say, "No wine unless you stay and eat dinner." So there's only time to visit three families and the rest are passed over. And that is why that holiday is called Passover, according to Vanna.

Lamont raises an arm and yells, "Can we have some quiet, people?"

Mario with clenched fist and Vanna with clenched napkin

stop looking like two pit bulls ready to pounce at each other.

The coroner removes his gloves and says, "Done here." He motions to the paramedics to load the body onto a stretcher. He turns to Lamont. "Let you know as soon as the toxicology report comes back." He walks into the dining room, says something to one of his assistants, and leaves.

Lamont points to the door and says, "OK everyone, out of the kitchen." He removes a small yellow box from his pocket, taps a code, and a yellow laser with blinking black letters that says CRIME SCENE floats across the kitchen door. My head feels like a bowling ball striking ninepins.

"Come with me, Molly," Lamont says, making me more nervous.

Eyes follow us through the dining room. Someone shouts, "Hey, Molly, do we get our money back?" I sigh. Lamont points to two corner chairs. We sit. I study a speck of circling dust suspended in the air, hoping it will distract me from the tension I feel, but it only makes me dizzy.

"Rewind, Molly." Lamont thumps the table and says, sharp as a knife, "What you remember?"

I tell him how Rick Frances and I had planned the Good Food Makes Good Neighbors dinner and how diners would alternate going from VV to Molly's Bistro for each course. "Rick thought having a dinner like that might generate a neighborly feeling and stop McMoons from opening next to VV."

"And what's the matter with McMoons? Mars Yard practically lives on their burgers. Sounds elitist. You downed plenty of them before you lost all that weight. Two ninety-five Earth pounds right?"

"No, 287 Earth pounds or, for your information, about 108 Mars pounds." I stand and put one hand on a hip. "But as you can see I'm less than half of that today. In fact, close to fifty Mars pounds. Whatever." I scowl and sit.

"Whatever? Whatever? What do you mean? That word takes up half the definitions in today's dictionaries."

"Oh God," I sigh.

"Can't deflect my questions with that, Molly. Unless you're hiding something. Are you?" He narrows his eyes and gives me the once over. "How well did you know Rick Frances?"

"We met before the official opening of VV when he invited me and my husband to a meal that demonstrated how VV works. It was very impressive."

"How impressive? I heard you were starving when you were finished. What good is that?"

"It was good for me. My business tripled after they opened."

6

LAMONT SNIFFS LIKE A BLOODHOUND. "What do you know about your chef?" he prods. "He's not an android, is he?"

"An android? Why do you ask?"

"Since the process that transforms people into androids has become easier and cheaper allowing more people with health issues to live disease free, the population has grown. But not public acceptance. There is a serious backlash. People fear being pushed out of their jobs, being displaced."

"Really? My best friend Jersey is married to Trenton, the first human android, and has been for over ten years. She never told me of having problems. They still live, as we did, when we first came to Mars, in Pharaoh in Arabia Terra."

"Well that's just the point. Then there was one living in Arabia Terra, a rather remote area. No one cared. Most people who heard about the process thought it was unique and limited. No one thought it would appeal to a significant number of the general public. Things are different today: many more live in every major city and their numbers are growing."

I say nothing.

Lamont scratches his head and continues, "Someone named Trenton applied to Mars Yard as a forensic scientist, but there was no mention of him being an android."

"Would it matter to you if it turned out to be my friend's husband?"

"No, not as long as he could do the job." Lamont jots some notes then looks at me. "Now tell me about your chef."

"I was at a fundraiser at Sang Sang prison and mentioned to the director that I needed a new chef. Mario Bugatti was a star in a culinary rehabilitation program. I hired him because the director said watching Mario cook was like watching alchemy at work. He was so talented he could be channeling recipes from Jean George Vongerichten, the great chef who lived long ago in New York."

"New York, Earth or New York, on Uranus's moon Miranda?"

"Miranda. There's a Statue of Liberty holding an ice cream cone standing in the middle of their capitol, Carmen."

"Gelatosphere or Cosmic Crunch?"

"The flavor isn't important, Lamont."

"Truth is in the details, Molly."

"OK, Cosmic Crunch. Ever have their chocolate handcuffs?" Lamont's eyes light up. "Our tax dollars never tasted so good."

Lamont writes: tax handcuffs. "Why was Mario sentenced?" he asks.

"He owned an art gallery and argued with one of his artists. When push came to shove, the artist fell, striking his head on a sculpture of a bull eating a dollar sign, and died."

"What happened to the sculpture?"

"Tripled in price."

"And Mario?"

"Sentenced to twenty-five years for manslaughter. Shortened because of good behavior. My staff says he's talented but moody, a real infant terrible. Vanna's had problems."

"Vanna Georgia, your sous chef?"

"Unfortunately, Mario takes his frustrations out on her.

She's threatened to leave. I think…"

Suddenly we look toward the other side of the room where Sandy Andreas is standing, shaking his finger in Sid's face, and projecting his voice with stage-like quality. We thread our way towards them.

"Why we are being questioned?" Sandy growls. "I didn't know Rick Frances. Never been to VV before tonight and I'm not likely to go again. He sat at our table and started to talk. Then he made a strange expression, said 'excuse me,' stood up, put his hand to his throat, and walked to the kitchen. That's all I know."

Sandy points to Frank. "He served him the pistachio dessert. Look, it's still on the table."

"Did you touch it?" Sid asks Sandy.

"Why would I touch it? Are you accusing me of touching it? Do I need a lawyer?"

Lamont says, "We know where to reach you, Mr. Andreas, if we need anything else. You can go."

Sandy, who rarely acknowledges anyone's presence unless he thinks that they have more money, a higher rank, or he wants something, grabs his wife Solaria's hand, pushes past me, and yanks her toward the door.

Lamont takes my elbow, and we go back to our chairs, curiosity curling his eyebrow.

"About Vanna? You were about to say…"

"She's also talented. Not as much as Mario. She could be head chef at another restaurant."

Lamont says, "Did she and Mario know each other before they worked for you?"

"Mario was hired first. Then I advertised for a sous chef. We got lots of applicants. Mario rejected everyone. Then, finally, after Vanna made a smoked salmon croque-monsieur, a parmesan-crusted chicken, and a crisp strudel filled with candied kumquats and pistachios topped with citron snow and citrus sections in a Riesling jelly, all of which I thought amazing—and why I remember it so well—Mario said she's the best of a bad lot. So I hired her."

"Where did she work before?"

"Nirgal Palace Hotel."

He nods. Everyone knew Nirgal Palace, though not many could afford to eat there, much less travel there; it was on a resort station that orbited the planet.

"That's a place I always wanted to go." Lamont jots more notes. "Why did she leave?"

"After three years, she said felt it too confining and wanted to go back to Mars. My daughter Becky wants to get married at Nirgal Palace."

"Is it true that that they have a swimming pool that gives the illusion that you are swimming outside the hotel in space?"

"Yes. I've never had time to go, but want to next time I'm there."

"Tell me more about Vanna"

"She was born in Amazonis Planitiam; her father's a biologist and her mother a chemist. I think she has a brother and a sister who went into science. She said she always loved to cook, so she attended the CIM..."

"CIM?"

"Culinary Institute of Mars. She got the Bangers and Mash award."

"Hmmm. Love bangers and mash."

"She's professional and easy to work with."

Lamont frowns. "Unlike Mario Bugatti, who is professional and difficult to work with."

The restaurant thins out. Sid stands near the door next to Frank talking to people and checking their names as they leave. The coroner's assistant walks over to Sid, says something, and shakes his hand. They leave. My brow wrinkles. Lamont notices. "What, Molly? What?" he asks.

"When Rick Frances came to discuss having a joint dinner and met Frank, he thought Frank looked familiar, but Frank said that they had never met."

"Anything else?"

"Everyone I see here owns a shop in the neighborhood or is a friend of someone who owns a shop." I point to a light brown skinned man with short hair wearing a red bow tie and white dinner jacket. "I don't know that man with Vanna."

Lamont blinks his eye cam, takes a holo.

"I asked Vanna to call anyone she knew at Nirgal Palace who might help me get a deal on Becky's wedding. She said she knew the banquet manager and would call him. He told her that he would be in town this week because he wanted to meet with Rick and do a virtual restaurant at Nirgal Palace. That could be him. He goes by the name Starr Bright."

"Sounds like an alias for someone working on a space station."

"It is. Vanna said his real name is Sol Brody. She mentioned that he was a champion cereal eater."

"Sol Brody! Sol Brody!" Lamont cries. "That's the name of a serial *killer*, not a cereal *eater*. That Sol Brody left a bowl of Shredded Wheat next to his victim. Mars Yard calls him the Cereal Serial Killer. But he's in a jail on Pluto."

"I'm relieved to hear that because we booked a Cereal Box Character party for next month."

"You did?" Lamont gives me a strange look and makes a note.

"Why? Are you thinking that there could be a connection between Rick Frances' death and this party?

"Probably not. But can't rule out the possibly of a copycat killer emerging. Mind if we plant someone from Mars Yard there?"

"Only if you think it will bring us closer to solving Rick Frances' murder."

"Leave no stone unturned, Molly. Leave no stone unturned. Besides, it's no problem. I'll get Sid. He's a natural. It won't take much to transform him into Shredded Wheat."

I sigh.

Then from the corner of my eye I see the front door open. A team in bright orange Mars Yard vests enter. They wave at Lamont, who waves back.

"Those investigators must go over your place with a micro-sweep, Molly. Unexpected details yield the most clues. So don't plan on reopening soon." Lamont rubs two fingers on his palm and taps once. Words float between us. "The coroner transferred this to me. A virtual note found on Rick's phone. What do you think?"

I read: "Going to call you." It is signed "C." I look at Lamont.

"Any idea who C could be?" Lamont asks.

A frown creases the skin between my eyes. "No idea," I say. But I quickly think: Cortland begins with the letter C. Would they consider him a suspect?

7

WHEN AFTER TEN LONG DAYS I finally get the call that Molly's Bistro can reopen, I get an unpleasant surprise. Tables are flipped, chairs pushed to the side, floors caked with dried spilled liquids. But the mess in the kitchen is worse. I palm my staff: "Get back here for the cleanup or you and Molly's Bistro will be out of business."

One by one, the staff shuffles in.

Mario pushes the kitchen door open and scowls. He sees Vanna, who had arrived before him, squirting a counter with disinfectant. "I hope no one touched my Russian Roulette sauce. It's hit or miss working with some people," he growls.

Vanna makes a nasty finger gesture, raises the bottle of disinfectant, pretending to spray Mario, who has turned away and doesn't see.

Frank moves the vacuum through the bar. Others push chairs and tables into place and wipe them. When the restaurant looks as good as it can without a major overhaul, I tell everyone to go in the dining room and find a seat.

When everyone is seated, I say, "We're all upset. Everyone was here when the murder happened."

Jody wipes her eyes and blows her nose. Mario, red-faced and hands curled into fists, sits to one side visibly controlling his breathing. He rises and says, "If anyone copied my recipe files and I learn that another restaurant is serving one of my specials, I'll sue."

I say, "The police aren't in the cooking business, Mario. They're more interested in individual ingredients rather than recipes. They would probably be looking for something used to camouflage poison, not something that makes a soufflé rise."

Mario stares at me. "Unless they would be one and the same," he sighs. "When it comes to the police, I'm on edge." He slumps into his chair.

I look at the others. "I would like to know what each of you remembers."

No one moves or shows any expression. Finally, Jody pipes, "Everyone was having a wonderful time. But every time the people came back from VV, they were hungrier and less polite. Some people grabbed food from my tray before I served them. Some finished before others got their food."

"Breadsticks were flying from baskets, rolls snatched off tables," says another waiter.

"Did any of you see Rick Frances say or do anything unusual? What about you, Frank?"

"No nothing unusual," Frank says.

"You served Rick and me some ginger ale when we were at the bar. Who poured it?"

"I did," Harry, my regular bartender, says. "I had hired a few friends who had worked here before when we had large events, but each was busy serving other customers. I remember because one of those women that I saw Rick talking to asked me if I was going to serve those deep fried pistachios that she'd heard so much about, and I said I did serve them but someone must have eaten them. So I gave her another dish."

"And you told the police," I ask.

"Yes, of course."

Jody says, "The evening may have been busier than usual,

but nothing we couldn't handle. Having VV next door is great. Since they've opened, my tips have tripled."

Harry says, "Molly's Bistro is the hot place to work."

My palm signals a call. I glance and see that it's my best friend Jersey, who, when we last spoke, said that her husband Trenton was up for a big job at Mars Yard meaning that they would move to New Chicago. I let it go to voicemail. I look at my staff and say, "Thanks for sharing your information. If you remember more, let me know. Now let's have a great reopening."

A roaring round of applause.

8

I GO TO MY OFFICE. Close the door. I sink into my desk chair. Look at Jersey's name and sigh. It must be good news because bad news travels faster than the speed of light, so I would have already heard it.

Years ago when I first came to Mars, Jersey—a typically tall, thin Mars native—and I became best friends when we were security guard partners at the Culinary Institute of Mars.

Before Mars, I was born and raised on Earth. I left to go to college on Earth's moon to attend Neil Armstrong University because back then I weighed 287 Earth pounds, but on the moon—which is still a haven for the plus-sized and called a floating ball of mozzarella by Martians who are the thinnest and most stylish in the solar system—I weighed 47.6 pounds. I could have weighed less on smaller worlds, but none had as many good restaurants.

Today, through a very long continued struggle, as I told Lamont, my Martian weight, is a respectable 50.1 or 133 Earth pounds.

I met my husband Cortland Summers on the moon, and my twins, Becky and Lois, were born there. We owned a large condo in a crater, gave luscious dinner parties, had lots of friends. I thought I would never leave.

But when Cortland invested all our money in a shopping center in a new neighborhood on the side of the moon that the Earth never sees and no one wanted to buy advertising space because Earth would never see their ads, all ended in chapter eleven.

Long story short, Cortland's best job offer came from his cousin Billings Montana, who lived in New Chicago, Mars. Billings owned Little Green Man Pizza and couldn't sell pizza franchises fast enough and needed help. He told Cortland if he came, he would make him a partner. So off we went.

I call Jersey back, and we catch up. "So I'm telling you," Jersey says bubbling with good cheer, talking so fast I barely grasp what she's saying, "ever since Mars Yard called and told Trenton that he got the job as chief science officer and they asked if he could transfer immediately to their headquarters in New Chicago, his eyes spin like whirling targets. Then before I tell him what I think, he calls them and says we're on our way. Molly, we have no place to live!"

"Do you want to go?"

"Well, yes. Great opportunity."

"So don't worry. I know New Chicago neighborhoods. Maybe you'll be my neighbor."

"Not likely to be your neighbor, Molly. You live in a fancy part of town. Even with Trenton's raise and my new bank job at Chase Martian, we'll never be able to afford it."

It was true. Cortland had made it big. Very very big.

After years of working at Little Green Man Pizza, he had enough money to start Molawn, his music agency. He not only landed Neils and the Bohrs and Max and the Planks, whose hit "Particle Wave" became a contender for the national anthem, our twins—aka The Lunar Tunes—had music that Cortland wrote and arranged that made the Solar System Hit Parade.

I say to Jersey, "Do you want to stay with me while you look for a place to live?"

"I wouldn't want to put you out Molly. But yes. That would be wonderful. I'm sure we'll find a place quickly. Trenton's laboratory will be transferred to Mars Yard headquarters. The rest of our stuff will be put into storage until we find a place. I'll only bring a few essentials. You won't even know we're there."

A few moments later, Trenton calls. "Thanks for letting us stay with you while we find our own place. We really appreciate it. I also called to tell you that Lamont forwarded samples collected from your bistro the day of the murder. Also, we found a prescription medicine called Grafton with Mario's name on it."

"He never told me he took any medicine. What's it for?"

"A rare neurological condition that causes premature aging called progeria. Without treatment, people rarely live past thirteen, yet they look ninety. I read about the case of Sam Burns, who died in 2013. He made it to seventeen. It took years, but at last, a product called Grafton controls it."

"Then it's not catching."

"No. But if Grafton is used in combination with other chemicals, it can be toxic to those who have progeria. It is not uncommon for a small amount to be accidently ingested. The person can get sick but recovers. In fact, you have a number of things that are harmless but when combined with other things in the right dosage become toxic. Then there are other things that are commonplace like bleach, ammonia...that are poisons."

"So if you found a book of matches in my restaurant and a building burns down, that's evidence that someone in my bistro did it?"

"Just giving you some background, Molly," he huffs. "Many bakeries and restaurants use Grafton to enhance food coloring. It's harmless unless you have that condition."

"So it's like peanuts. Almost everyone eats them and loves them. But they cause harm if you are allergic to them."

"Exactly. But you should put an asterisk next to any dish on the menu that might have peanuts or Grafton. You never know who might be sensitive."

At five o'clock, Molly's Bistro opens. A few of my regulars return. But even the new background music didn't soften the solemn mood. The next night we are busier. By the weekend, you wouldn't have known anything had happened.

Saturday night, Sandy and Solaria Andreas sit up front at their regular table drinking Martian Marys. Sandy says that he came for lobster thermidor and key lime pie, but against his wife Solaria's protests that it would be too rich, he orders the special: golden calf.

VV was dark. A sign on its door read "Closed till further notice." No one knew anything. Then two weeks later the *New Chicago Times* said that Lena Fermi and Avery Spelling, the new owners, would reopen VV.

9

"WHAT WERE YOU THINKING?" Cortland says. "I'll take the twins to tour satellites in the Oort cloud if Jersey and Trenton stay with us. Jersey is so obsessive compulsive, and Trenton's not much better."

"It's only until they find a place of their own."

"Sure you can't get out of this, Molly?"

I take a deep breath and say nothing.

Jersey pulls up to our home with a larger than I thought van attached to the back of their rover.

"Where's Trenton?

"Dropped him at Mars Yard. He hates unpacking."

I eye the bulging van. "Thought you said that everything was going into storage."

"They are in storage. These are things that I thought I would need just in case."

"In case of what?" I peer inside. "Is that a barbecue grill? Why do you need a barbecue grill?"

"You never know."

Next to the grill is a box marked snorkeling equipment. "And that?" I point. "We're nowhere near a place where you can go snorkeling."

"You never know."

I look further. "Is that a toboggan?"

"It's only a sled. Trenton adjusted the gravity link so it can slide up as well as down hills." She puts her hand on her waist. "Boy, I never thought that you would be so picky."

"You're lucky I have room. Drive around to the back and park in the garage. I can program the door to open from here. There's a big empty space near Cortland's extra recording equipment." Jersey looks more relieved than if a doctor told her to take two aspirins and call him in the morning because she didn't need a lobotomy.

Jersey and Trenton settle in.

Every day Trenton leaves for Mars Yard, and Jersey goes condo shopping. Every day real estate agents show her properties, and every day she finds something wrong.

Some weeks later, VV reopens.

Lena and Avery blitz the media with ads that say, "Now open new and improved VV. Humans and androids welcome." I want see what they did and if I can learn more about Rick. I think I will appear more neighborly if I bring a guest, so I call Flo Montana, Cortland's cousin, a professional taster for Tasters and Spitters Inc., and ask her to join me for "lunch" at VV. I never met anyone as indifferent to food as Flo, so lunch at VV should be perfect.

I know Jersey will welcome a break from house hunting, so I invite her as well. I wonder if they will get along. Flo, a master of ostentatious good taste that screams expensive restraint, shops at exclusive Rodeo Dive boutiques while Jersey bargain hunts garage sales.

Both are in front of VV waiting. Jersey in jeans and a Culinary Institute t-shirt. She sees me and waves. Flo, in a stylish blue suit and pink silk blouse, raises her chin. Her air kisses next to my cheek feel like exclamation points. She must be going somewhere after lunch because she is wearing all her tasting medals. She sees me looking and says, "I rarely wear all my awards because I don't want to risk spitting on them. But there's no problem here."

We enter VV. Avery and Lena greet us. My jaw drops.

Lena says, "We remodeled. Do you like it?"

VV no longer looks like a science experiment but like a luxury restaurant. Gone is the stark white interior. Gone are the cubicles. The room is paneled in wood not too dissimilar from my bar area. Grass green cloths cover dining tables with napkins folded into sharp creases. The gold and white Wedgewood china and Waterford crystal that I remember are still there with fresh lush flowers added to the tables.

"Flo has been here before," I say. "In fact, the night Rick Frances was murdered."

"Totally tragic. We miss him," Avery's long face says.

I turn to Jersey. "Jersey just moved to New Chicago. We were security guards at the Culinary Institute."

"The good old days," Jersey says, pointing to her t-shirt.

"Her husband Trenton is the new head of forensics at Mars Yard," I add.

Avery's eyebrows rise.

Flo puts her hand over her mouth and whispers, "My kind of restaurant."

"Yeah," I whisper back. "No food. Just pictures of food."

"Yes. But look at the table settings, the flowers. It's a feast."

"For the eyes, not the stomach."

"You're always so literal, Molly."

"No, just hungry."

Avery takes my elbow and leads me across the room to a table. I see Vanna and Sol. I pause and wave. They wave back. But when I take a step toward them, Flo says, "Please talk later. I'm on a tight schedule." So we move on.

When we sit, a waiter pours water while another puts small

dishes of olives, nuts, and crackers the size of oysterettes in the center of the table.

Lena says, "We've added new dishes since you were here, Molly. I found if you start with something real, it enhances the VV experience. Real coffee and tea with cookies are served afterwards."

Flo throws me an eyebrow and says, "Well, I would be full on that."

"Me too," Jersey adds.

I think, *Foodies from hell.* I look at Lena. "Ever give tours of the kitchen or whatever you call the area that creates these illusions?"

"We call it the kitchen," she says. "I would be happy to show you after lunch."

Avery says, "We've made the programs more multi-sensory. The flavors and textures of the food trigger sights and sounds that complement the other senses. We call it immersive dining. You'll see what I mean once the program starts."

A waiter brings headsets and gloves. I sip water, eat two crackers, three olives, and several nuts before we begin. Jersey and Flo eat nothing and exclaim in chorus, "You're spoiling your appetite!"

When "our meal" ends, I say, "That was even more fun than when I came with Cortland."

"How so?" Jersey asks.

"More intense. When I ordered poached lobster, the walls around me filled with images of waves crashing on a shore. I felt a moist mist on my face and smelled the salt of the ocean. It was wonderful. Did any of you order the arctic snowball dessert?"

"Too full," Jersey says.

"Right before it appeared, my space went blue, the color of the polar ice caps, and I was sure the temperature dropped a few degrees."

"I thought that is how it always was," Jersey says.

"No, it's much improved."

Flo says, "I finished with a hot fudge sundae. I'm sure I gained weight."

"That's impossible, Flo. Everything is a hologram."

"But my brain didn't think so."

"But your stomach did."

"You're always so technical, Molly."

"Trenton will love this," Jersey says, sipping the real tea that had been placed on the table with a miniscule dish of tiny vanilla cookies. "A great place for our anniversary."

We each take a cookie. Jersey and Flo break theirs in half and eat half. I don't know how they can do that; the cookie is so small. I eat the whole thing. I take another. When I am about to reach for my third, glances get traded, and their eyes narrow.

"What?" I say.

"Molly, you were 287 Earth pounds when I met you," Flo says.

"That's what she weighed when we both security guards at the Culinary Institute," Jersey adds. "Her height and width measured the same."

"It's only one more cookie," I snap.

"That's what they all say," Flo responds. "Well, that cookie was over *my* limit. If I could skip dinner, I would, and add five miles on the treadmill, but I can't. Yesterday I drew the short straw on tasting children's birthday cakes."

What fun, I think.

Then Flo rolls her eyes and exclaims, "Total torture!"

I say nothing.

Flo adds, "This evening I'm going to the Museum of Charity Parties. I'm on the toothpick committee. All the toothpicks in the museum collection are white, pink or yellow; there are no black toothpicks. We need diversity!" She stands; her medals tinkle. "Thanks for lunch, Molly. Gotta run. Ta ta." She scoots away.

The Museum of Charity Parties is always packed. People come to see the collection of "regrets only" cards, the archives of "shortcuts to long speeches," watch an instructional video of "how to pretend to tip a bathroom attendant while really leaving nothing," and stand solemnly with bowed heads before the Memorial to the Uninvited.

Lena emerges from a side door. "Hope you've enjoyed your lunch. Have time to see the kitchen?"

Jersey and I follow her. Vanna and Sol are leaving. We exchange waves.

Everything in the kitchen is white. Two walls are filled with screens. "These screens display individual orders. They are connected to the tables," Lena says. She points to a third wall that looks like an old library's Dewey Decimal System of card catalogues and says, "This wall has the 'ingredients.'"

The fourth wall has screens with numbers and symbols. Keyboards with color-coded keys are on tables in the middle. Farther back are sinks and dishwashers. I see a tiny mouse dart from a corner and streak across the floor. Lena sees me recoil. She says, "The construction for McMoons has unearthed mouse Mecca. We've had no end to problems."

Avery opens a closet. Jersey peers inside. "You could be in the exterminator business with all this stuff," she says.

"I'm obsessive about cleanliness. If this were a real restaurant, we'd be shut down. But since we aren't and don't make or serve any food except what we gave you—all of which comes prepackaged—we're not regulated like a restaurant."

Jersey puts her head deeper into the closet and starts to study its contents. Avery puts his hand on the door and snaps it closed. "If you don't mind," he snarls.

"Do you both own VV?" I ask.

Neither answers.

As I'm thinking the word *motive*, and as though reading my

mind, Lena sighs and says, "Who would have thought anything like this would happen?"

For what feels like a long time, but probably isn't, no one says anything. Then, to break the awkward silence, I say to Lena, "How did you meet Rick?"

"He placed an ad for a virtual engineer in Restaurants Anonymous and I answered it. We hit it off immediately. Avery and I grew up in the same town near Chryse Planitia, and I knew he wanted to be in the restaurant business so I suggested he come and work here as well. Why do you ask?"

"Just curious."

Once outside, Jersey palms Trenton. "Did I get you at a good time, sweetheart? Molly and I finished our lunch at VV and Avery and Lena gave us a tour. Guess what?" Pause. "How did you know?" Pause. "You're right. Too obvious." Pause "Love you, too. Bye."

"What's too obvious? What did he say?" I ask nervously because Trenton's theories often seem outlandish but usually prove correct.

"He said showing the poisons was an obvious ploy to throw us off."

"Interesting," I say, not sure if he is right this time.

Jersey says, "I loved VV, Molly. Thanks for bringing me. And Flo was so nice."

"It was fun, but not really lunch. Gotta go. Frank is helping me replace the plates the police broke when they did their search. He's going to sponsor me at Restaurant Works. It's a wholesale restaurant supply club. He said he got a membership a few years ago when he was a headwaiter in Xanax City. Strange I never heard about that place before I opened Molly's."

"How well do you know Frank?" Jersey asks.

"Not well. But his references were glowing and everyone loves him."

"So why did he move?"
"I never asked."
"You should."
Jersey's palm rings. She answers. I listen. "That sounds nice. I'll meet you there in an hour."
"Real estate agent?" I ask.
Jersey nods then sighs.

10

IT'S THE PRECIOUS LULL BETWEEN LUNCH and dinner. Sol and Vanna are in a corner of the kitchen eating. I pull up a chair and join them. "That looks delicious, Vanna. What did you think of VV?"

Vanna gets up and brings another plate. "Wonderful experience but such a tease. Here, try my lemon pasta." She scoops some onto my plate. "I just threw it together."

I swallow some. "Delicious. Doesn't taste like something thrown together."

"I've asked Mario if I can put it on the menu," Vanna says, "but he says he's the chef, and you are paying him for his food, not my food."

"I'll talk to him."

Her voice rises. "Don't! It's not worth upsetting him. Besides, believe it or not," her voice lowers, "since Rick Frances' murder, he's been less critical, and for that I'm grateful."

I nod. "Maybe he's scared."

Vanna wipes her lips with a napkin. She looks at Sol, then at me. "Sol is the banquet manager at Nirgal Palace where I worked. I told him your daughter Becky wants to get married there."

Sol puts his fork down. "Nirgal Palace is very popular.

Better book as soon as you can. The Dummies for the Dummy Book Series have taken all the key dates in March. I'll send you a questionnaire to get you started. We want to know as much about the happy couple as possible." He pushes a point on his palm. "Done," he says, smiling. "Sent to your office. I also recommend that you hire a wedding whisperer."

"I've heard of a horse whisperer. But a wedding whisperer?"

"The nervous energy brides and grooms have before their weddings could power a medium-sized satellite around Jupiter for two years."

I say nothing but think, *Becky's stress could power a large one for five years.*

Sol checks the time and rises. "I have one more stop before I leave. I want to be on the evening space elevator."

Vanna touches his hand. "Do tell Molly about your idea before you go." She looks at me. "I'm tempted, but I have no money."

Sol sits. Leans in. "I would like to get investors for a project that would shuttle popular foods to crews working on space stations—like a Mr. Softie truck in space. I think there would be a big market because space station food is nutritious but not tasty."

"Interesting idea. I like it."

Vanna adds, "Don't you think you should also tell Molly that you saw Rick Frances the day before he was murdered?"

There is a pause more pregnant than waiting for a baby's head to crown. Then casually as possible I say, "You saw Rick Frances the day before he was murdered?"

"I wanted to ask him if he would like to open a branch of VV at Nirgal Palace." Sol fiddles with his napkin. Twists his mouth. "I also had personal business."

I straighten my back. Say nothing.

"We knew each other. In fact, we're related."

"Related?"

Sol takes a deep breath. "Rick is my brother-in law. Or my former brother-in law. He married my sister Carol. I worked in their restaurant in Chryse Planitia while I was getting my PhD in Hotel Language. Did you know that there are over four hundred and fifty voice inflections when saying, 'I'm sorry. Is there anything else I can help you with?'"

I say nothing because as a restaurant owner I know this and don't want to interrupt him.

"Anyway, three and a half years ago, Carol disappeared. I thought she and Rick were happy. Their restaurant was successful; they seemed to work well together. Then one day, Carol tells me that she wants a divorce. I was stunned. You know there are people who fight all the time."

"Like Mario and me," Vanna says.

"Right. Like you and Mario. But I saw none of that with Rick and Carol. I thought they had arrived at a settlement, but suddenly Carol tells me that she can't wait any longer for a new life. The next day she's gone. Two months later a message-post from Valles Marineris said she was well and don't worry about her. I've not seen or heard anything since. Nor has anyone else that I know."

Vanna asks, "Did they ever get divorced?"

"Don't know. Rick was very frustrated because he had finally adjusted to the separation and wanted to end with a clean break."

I look at Sol. "And when you saw him, did Rick add anything new?"

"No."

"Lamont found a message on Rick's palm that said 'Going to call you, signed C.'"

"Well I don't know anything. C could be anyone. Could even be your husband Cortland."

"I thought of that," I say. "But we hardly knew him."

There is a knock on the opened door. Frank pops his head

through looks quickly around then pulls back from the doorway. "You wanted me, Molly?"

"Meet me at my office, Frank. It'll only take a moment."

Frank closes the door.

I rise, turn to Sol. "Thanks for your input. I'll be in touch about the wedding."

Frank is outside my office. I think, *this case is going to be complicated, but aren't they all?*

We enter. Frank slides into a chair. "Something wrong?" he asks.

"I'm delighted with your work. You're a stickler for details, no spots on glasses, salt shakers always filled; the beautiful flowers you order are timely and never seem to droop. You swirl crepes Suzettes at the table with the right amount of Grand Marnier and butter as easily as stirring a cup of tea. But more importantly, you've trained the staff to treat everyone, even those awkward newcomers, to feel like they're a long lost friend."

"So?" he says, making a quizzical look.

"So I'd like to know more about you. The police are doing extensive background checks. I should learn as much as I can."

Frank thinks for a moment. "You know my physical details: height, weight, age thirty-seven, mother half-black, half-Korean, father half-Irish, half-Italian. They were part of a traveling troop of water dousers and klezmer music performers. We moved a lot. Our last home was where the first Viking lander came down near Chryse Planitia because the site got many tourists. I did odd jobs before I did restaurant work."

"Were you ever married? Have any kids?"

Frank pauses longer than necessary given the simple question. Then when it is impossible to remain silent any longer without looking like he's hiding something he says, "Not exactly."

"Meaning?"

"I have no kids. Do I have to talk about this?" He pauses again then mutters, "I *was* married briefly. OK?"

"OK. But the police might want more."

Mario knocks softly on my door. He looks pale. "Everything OK?" I ask.

"I wanted to show you this picture of a tower made from coconut crusted prawns. I think it would be a wonderful addition to the menu."

"Love it," I say, pausing, hoping he will say more, and he does.

"I have a doctor's appointment. I may be late for dinner, but all the appetizers and some main courses just need to be run under a broiler and plated. It's something Vanna can do."

11

I AGREE TO HELP JERSEY look for apartments. We scroll through real estate listings. There's a picture of a clean-looking building surrounded by a flowering garden. "How about that? It's a half hour on the metro from New Chicago with two bedrooms, terrace, updated kitchen, two bathrooms with a sauna and Jacuzzi."

Jersey peers closely. "Saw it. Not fit for a lactobacillus."

"Really?"

I continue. "Here's half a town house with a separate entrance, garden, twelve hundred starbucks a month. Sounds like a good deal."

"Saw that too. Hated it."

I scroll again. "Look, a penthouse in a new building with two months free rent as an incentive. But it's a little far."

"Yeah, like on a moon of Neptune."

I sigh.

"You know, Molly, with Cortland being a very successful music agent, Becky and Lois rock stars, and you owing a trendy bistro, you're almost a celebrity. Your friends are very upscale. I think when the real estate agents knew that I was your friend, they must have thought I was one of them, even though I told them my budget."

Finally, she agrees to drive by three places.

The first is fifty minutes from New Chicago.

"Don't know what attracted you to this."

"They don't build them like this anymore."

"No, and there is a reason why they don't. Now that you've seen the outside, do you want to go in?"

"No. Forge on."

The next is squeezed between two recycling plants. "Why did you want to see this? It's far from any shopping and the neighborhood is so ugly."

"But it's quiet. And you can't beat the rent. Only six hundred starbucks a month."

"You can do better than this, Jersey. Trenton gets a good salary from Mars Yard, and you told me that the Chase Martian Bank pays double what your old job at the Culinary used to."

"I know," she says in a weary voice. "I know. OK. You're right."

The last one is in an area called Coney Island.

I say, "That's named for an island on Earth that made the first ice cream cone—ergo the name: Coney."

"I should have studied more Earth history. Tried to impress a boyfriend by learning the capitals of asteroids but lost out to Miss Hubble Telescope who didn't even know what an asteroid was."

"Well, she must have had something, Jersey."

"Yeah, big ones."

Fifteen minutes later, we drive through neighborhoods that become progressively worse: broken bottles litter the street, refuse receptacles overflow, swirling dust hits the windshield, unpleasant smells leak into the rover, people with lowered heads turn and duck into doorways. I tap the door lock, making sure it's secure. Then I do it again.

I finally park in front of a chrome yellow building with a faded awning over the entrance that says "Dim Sum Plaza." A bright sculpture of an eggroll in front flashes the words: "Let There Be Light." A sign below says, "First words said by Dim Sum, lighting engineer."

"Thought those words were someone else's first words," Jersey says. "Guess I was wrong."

We enter the building using a passcode given to us by a real estate agent who said I was a saint for going with Jersey and that no one in her office would go there. We descend a few steps and walk in a hallway filled with a strange sallow light and find the first apartment on our right. I insert several cards that release several locks. The last one won't open. Jersey gives the door a swift sharp kick. It creaks open.

A window at the far end of the living room reflects the flashing eggroll. I close my eyes. My retinas are imprinted with its negative image. I feel queasy.

"I like this place," Jersey says.

"What about that flashing light? Don't you find it annoying?"

"What flashing light?"

I point to the wall.

"Didn't notice. My eye beam filters automatically kicked in. And if I don't see it, Trenton never will."

We go into the kitchen. "Total gut job," I say looking at the ancient appliances, worn cabinets, and peeling paint.

"Trenton can spruce it up."

"It's not an eat-in kitchen."

"Don't care. Except for morning coffee, we either eat out or take supplements." She turns, walks down a hall, and calls, "Two large bedrooms and two bathrooms. Want to see?"

"Not really."

"I think if we take this place we'll be getting in on the ground floor of the next real estate boom," she shouts. "Could become a trendy area."

"Well, you are getting the ground floor."

She walks back. "Does the description mention anything about a storage area?

I read, "Large storage area in the basement: fifty starbucks extra."

"Let's see it. We could use that space. That is, if Trenton will go for the extra money."

"Fifty starbucks is not that much extra, Jersey."

"I know, but I know Trenton."

The basement is large and dark. I imagine former tenants up to no good. "Feels creepy," I say.

"Have you no vision? It's big, it's secure, and I bet Trenton could negotiate the price."

Jersey runs her hand over the wall. "Ooh, slime." She takes out a handkerchief and wipes her hand. "Trenton has been working on a new instant cleaner. He can test it here."

I turn away. "I'm leaving, Jersey," I say, flicking an insect off my sleeve.

"I'll show Trenton this place tomorrow," she says.

I check a message from Mario on my palm: "Want you to know I'm back from the doctor. No problems."

Two days later, Jersey says they signed the lease and got the landlord to throw in the storage space for free. I'm not surprised. No one beats Trenton getting the lowest price. Then she adds that they want to have Cortland and me for dinner as soon as they're settled. I've never had a meal in their home—a drink, yes—a nut, yes–but a meal, no way. Jersey doesn't know how to cook and Trenton doesn't care much about food—so I'm relieved, thinking a real invitation not likely.

Becky and Lois are in the living room. Becky asks Lois what she thinks about reciting the poem "How Do I Love Thee" by Robert Browning as part of her wedding vows.

Lois twirls a strand of long blonde hair and says, "Nice idea."

Becky says, I think it goes, "'How do I love thee, let me count the days.'"

"Wrong," Lois says. "It's 'How do I love thee, let me count the lays.'"

"Think it would be OK if I said 'How do I love thee, let me count the days and the lays'?"

"Sure," Lois answers. "Browning would love the upgrade."

The next day I call Sol Brody, a.k.a. Starr Bright, and make an appointment for us to visit Nirgal Palace and see what they do for weddings. Since I have time to relax, I make a cup of hot clam broth with extra herbs. As I'm breathing in its ocean aroma and about to take my first sip, Lamont calls, voice sounding urgent. "Don't want to upset you Molly, but I just learned that the Cereal Killer escaped from Pluto, and I know that the date of the Cereal Box Character party is close. The Mars-to-Pluto shuttle dropped off new prisoners, then it was loaded with license plate chips before returning to Mars. After the shuttle departed, they found one guard dead with his uniform removed and one prisoner gone."

"I would never have booked that party, but now it is too late to cancel. By the way, yesterday twenty-five boxes of Shredded Wheat were delivered to the restaurant. No one ordered them. The delivery man said it was a gift. I was about to call you and ask if you thought it was important."

"Oh, that."

"What do you mean 'oh, that?' It made me very upset."

"They were sent from Mars Yard. Thought it might unnerve the Cereal Killer to show his hand. Also Sid didn't want to be overshadowed by Fiber One. Wait until you see him in his costume; he looks like a scarecrow but with wheat instead of straw spilling out of him."

"Do you seriously want me to go through with this, Lamont? It's bad enough I already had one murder at the restaurant."

"Not to worry, Molly. We'll have plenty of backup in addition to Sid. In fact, one of our new detectives has a special interest in this case."

"Why?"

"She's a former Miss Granola."

Deep breath with eye roll. Better.

Lamont frowns. "I saw that, Molly. Now refresh my memory. Didn't you mention that Sol Brody was the name of the banquet manager at Nirgal Palace and has the same name as the serial killer?"

"Yes. But it's just a coincidence. A lot of people have the same names. Still, if I didn't have Rick Frances' murder on my mind, I might consider getting more involved. But Cortland would go crazy if I did that. He doesn't want me getting more involved."

"But you're so good at it, Molly. Your insights are like a tonic. After the case of the Chocolate Moons, people called you Sherlock Mars."

"I know," I sigh. Unfortunately, Cortland knows too.

12

CUTTING TO THE CHASE, all the worry and all the security preparation for the Cereal Box Character party was unnecessary. It came off without a hitch. Frank orchestrated a raffle with one of the prizes being twenty-five boxes of Shredded Wheat that Sid won and donated to those living at a remote outpost on the plains of Vastitas Borealis near the North Pole. (He assumed they would take anything, but they sent half back because they said they were overstocked. But a case of good scotch would be most welcome.)

When I tell Cortland that Jersey and Trenton have invited us to dinner, Cortland snaps,

"Not going. Count me out! I'm too busy. So many musicians have submitted new music for me to consider that all I have had time for these last three weeks is listen to music. And I'm only halfway through. Besides, the last time we were at their home, Jersey served one food supplement pill on an iceberg lettuce leaf. And their place was so dark. We kept asking them to turn up the light, which was on a two-minute timer. Jersey has high beam implants and Trenton's vision goes from infra-red to ultra-violet, but we could hardly see."

So one week later I go. Alone.

If I hadn't programmed the self-drive directions, I would have been lost. There wasn't one landmark that I recognized. In the short time they were there, the neighborhood had undergone significant gentrification. A former wreck of a warehouse near their home had been rebuilt. A bright sign advertised luxury lofts. Another building I remembered as run down ugly is filled with trendy looking shops. One corner has a seafood restaurant, From Neptune to Neptune, that I would try. There is a bright new branch of Silicone Slings, a chain of bars that caters to androids and famous for serving Mobile Malts in glasses shaped like red horses with wings. Trenton begged me to buy its stock when it went public, and I'm still kicking myself that I didn't because it quadrupled in a year.

Jersey greets me at the door wearing a pretty yellow caftan. As a house warming gift and insurance that I will have something to eat, I have several orders of coq au vin from Molly's. I also have three tart tartans and two bottles of Bordeaux that Trenton could finish alone.

"This is so nice of you," Jersey says. "I'm going to freeze it for another time. But I'll open the wine."

"Where's Trenton?"

"Cooking in his lab?"

After a long surprised pause, I say, "In his lab? I thought you guys never cooked."

"It's something new. I'll give you a tour of his lab in the basement after we eat. I'm starved."

Another surprise. Eat and starved were two words I rarely heard from Jersey when referring to herself or Trenton. I follow her into the dining room that is now partitioned from their cavernous living space. I stop in the doorway. It's beautiful: decorated with light green grass wallpaper, a beautiful new Oriental rug, and the lighting that is flattering and sufficient.

"Sit here," Jersey says, pointing toward a new chair next to a mahogany table set with heart shaped plates, new silverware, pink cloth napkins, and fresh flowers.

"I'm overwhelmed," I say. "I remember what it looked like before. I'm happy to see that your new lives in New Chicago agree with you."

Jersey beams.

"I don't want to pry or be rude, but I can't believe you spent so much on interior decorating. I saw those heart shaped plates in Macy's Mars, but even on sale they were expensive."

"Oh, didn't spend much. The rug was a dirty bathroom mat that we found in the basement, but after Trenton extracted its essence, added some hemp, and put it in the recyclable with a few copies of *Architectural Digest*, voila! A new rug."

"Amazing."

"We did have help. Trenton convinced the Board of Corrective Education to give students extra credit if they would hang the wallpaper as a science project. Trenton made it from bags of rotting mowed grass that were never hauled away."

"More amazing."

"I hope you like filet mignon. Trenton made Tornados Rossini. He wanted to make something old fashioned, classic, and festive because you're our oldest friend." She turns and calls, "Honey, are you ready? We're waiting."

Trenton enters carrying our meal on a large silver tray. His steel blue eyes glow with a hint of humor. He wears an old much-loved copy of a copy of a copy of a copy of a double-breasted Savile Row suit and a white linen shirt.

I cut into the meat. The filet is soft and flavorful, the foie gras buttery, and the Madeira sauce with truffles delicious. As I scrape the last of the sauce from my plate, I say to Trenton, "If I didn't know you were such a great scientist and detective, I would say that you were a born chef. The flavors were strong and well balanced. Cortland will be sorry he missed this."

"Glad you enjoyed it, Molly. But I'm not likely to do this again. This meal took me over two weeks to make. I could have done the autopsies and analysis of fifty corpses for Mars Yard in the time it took me to make this."

"Why so long? A good chef could make this is less than two hours. In fact, *I* could make this in less than two hours."

"Well, I did an analysis of the atomic structures of each ingredient, checking for radiation and impurities. Then I recombined them by making adjustments in my cyclotron so it fit into a barbecue grill. But it took forever to get the right combination for charcoal. I could have blown up three blocks."

Jersey adds, "He almost did."

"You could have gone to any supermarket. They all sell charcoal."

Trenton shakes his head. "Please, Molly, you're missing the point."

I say nothing.

Trenton continues, "After I used the best scientific method, trial and error, I reversed and distilled some procedures to enhance the flavors. I gave each a spin. When it emerged, I put everything in a food container and sent it to Mercury where they cooked it in a sun-powered brick oven pizza machine. You didn't taste any mozzarella cheese, did you, Molly? I was afraid some of it would adhere to the foie gras. Did you know that sunrise takes 16.13 hours on Mercury?"

"No, it was delicious."

Trenton's eyes spin, something I never got used to seeing, although Jersey says that she finds when they spin to the right it's very romantic. I never asked what she thought when they spin left. "Between you and me," Trenton continues, "I don't understand why people like to cook. It takes so long and is so much work. I think I'm going to continue living on food supplements."

Just as I think, *Why are so many easy things hard for Jersey and Trenton and so many hard things easy?* Trenton says, "I'll bring dessert." He goes into the kitchen and returns with a Grand Marnier soufflé. "Remember that helium chamber that I invented so a person's voice rose and anyone could be an opera soprano? But only Alvin XII and the Chipmunks wanted it?"

"Not chipmunks," Jersey says. "Cheap monks. When Father Alvin started his choir, he found that it was less expensive to sing in the chamber than revive castration."

Trenton huffs, "Well, it makes perfect soufflés."

Jersey rises and says, "I'll serve coffee in the living room. Come."

Jersey and Trenton sit on a beige velvet sofa. I sit on a striped club chair opposite them. I point to a corner of the room where there's a hologram of a floating brain. "I see you were able to set up your favorite game, Pin the Tail on the Cerebral Cortex. Looks better in this room than it did back in your old home."

Jersey smiles.

I turn to Trenton. "I'm glad you're enjoying your work at Mars Yard. Has working with Lamont been stressful? Sid told me that he became moody after he went undercover and arrested The Hyperactives, that gang from Syrtis Major, and overdosed on Mexican jumping beans."

"Lamont's moods are never a problem," Trenton says, adding three spoons of sugar to his coffee. "I simply lower the setting on my emotional receptor."

"So what do you think happened to Rick Frances?"

"I've been going through the DNA samples, including those on plates, silverware, napkins, and glasses. And I did find something strange."

"Strange?" I say, leaning in. "How strange?"

"I checked a list of guests and staff who were at the restaurant when Rick Frances died."

"And?"

"There's the same number of people, but one more woman and one less man."

I wrinkle my brow. "It was so crowded and noisy. It would be easy for someone to leave and no one notice, but harder for a new person not on the list to enter."

Trenton stirs his coffee. "But not impossible. If it was a person people knew, no one could tell if they were in the restaurant all along or just arrived."

We all say nothing.

Jersey refills my coffee cup. I take a hot sip. "I just learned that Avery and Lena come from Chryse Planitia."

"A lot of people come from there," Jersey says.

I add, "And Frank, my head waiter, and Rick Frances also came from there. Coincidence or clue, Trenton?"

Trenton doesn't answer right away. I sense the thought travel through his circuits as he processes the angles trying to find the haystack amongst the needles. Then he says, "I'll do a background check on all of them."

13

CORTLAND THROWS THE CORE OF THE APPLE he just finished through the holo of *Sound of the Spheres* magazine. He's in a bad mood. For two weeks, he's had writer's block and then he over-tuned his pianolyn, damaging its hard drive. When he tried to print a new one, his 3D printer crashed. "I had hoped to compose something wonderful for Becky's wedding," he says, plopping into the chair. "All I'm getting is a rehash of 'You Light Up my iPad'."

"Give it time, sweetheart," I say picking up the apple core. "Here, take a look at this guest list from the night Rick Frances was murdered. Trenton told me that according to the DNA, there was one extra woman and one less man." I hand him the list. "Any names jump out? Anything you remember?"

Courtland scans the list. Shakes his head. "Rick headed toward the kitchen after he was sitting at Sandy Andreas' table. Maybe it was that new singer Merck Manual who sat next to Sandy's wife. He didn't sign the recording contract I offered, but signed with Higgs Boson."

"I doubt if he knew Rick Frances," I say in a soothing voice. "I could pay Sandy and Solaria a visit and ask them about their other guests."

"I don't want you to get involved, Molly. I thought that

when you solved the case of the Chocolate Moons a few years ago that would be the end of your investigating, not the beginning."

"But I'm so good at this."

"Be careful," he sighs.

I take the guest list from Cortland's hand. "I'll look this over in the kitchen while I make a strong cup of coffee. Want some?"

Cortland doesn't answer. He's put on earphones and buried himself in *Sound of the Spheres*.

I sit at my butcher block table in the kitchen and sip from a cup that says "Best Mom this side of the Horsehead Nebula." Among the names on the list I don't recognize are the women Rick had been with in the bar. I keyword Holly Wood and Beverly Hills and think, *Obviously not their real names.* Each has a palm code and an address.

I start with Holly. First ring engages. "I'm Molly Marbles, owner of Molly's Bistro. I'm calling everyone who attended the Virtual Vittles/Molly's Bistro event last week when Rick Frances died. Could I come and jog your memory about the evening's events?"

Holly says, "Don't recall that much. You sat me at the bar? Remember?"

"Sorry, we were overbooked. We had to seat our regulars who sent in early acceptances in the dining room. Some have returned many times, bringing friends," I say, hoping I have concealed my irritation.

Holly says nothing.

"So how about later this afternoon? I have an address." I read it from my palm. "Is that correct?"

"Yes. But ring the apartment for Marjorie Hickenlooper. It's my real name."

Marjorie answers the door. She is very attractive in bare feet, a black t-shirt, and jeans. I think she must be forty but must have been a knockout in her twenties. Her one bedroom apartment is furnished in a sparse modern style. She offers a cup of tea that I decline. As I walk over to the sofa, I see a book I've wanted to read.

"Are you enjoying that book?" I ask pointing to *Carol's Christmas* by Ebenezer Pickens.

"I was enjoying it, but it got to be too scary when Carol turned into a ghost."

I make a face.

"Ooh, sorry, spoiler. Thought you knew."

I frown. "Well, I know now." I sit on a straight-backed chair that's not very comfortable and ask, "How well did you know Rick?

"Depends on what you mean by well. We met at a singles bar years ago when I was at the top of my modeling career. He told me that he was separated from his wife, who disappeared before they were divorced and he had stopped looking for her—but legally he was still married. Then he asked me if that was a problem and I said no because I was not interested in marriage.

"He had a good sense of humor. Said he once owned a restaurant. Knowing I couldn't eat much and keep my modeling figure, he let me try early versions of the virtual foods he was developing. He asked if I thought such a place would be a hit with the modeling community and I told him that I thought it would be a sensation! We had good times until he met Beverly Hills. I can't stand her."

"Beverly Hills, the other woman at the bar?"

"Right."

"Her real name?"

"Polly Pox."

"Sounds like a disease. No wonder she changed it."

"I don't keep tabs on old relationships, mine or anyone else's. Aren't you married to Cortland Summers, owner of

Molawn Music? And your twin daughters Becky and Lois are The Lunar Tunes?"

"That's right."

"Just a minute." She flutters out of the room. I hear a lot of drawers opening and banging closed. Then I hear, "Got it!" She returns to the room, flushed. "Would you give my demo of Star Spangles to your husband?" she coos. "I think it will be a hit if I sing it before a baseball game."

The next day I call Beverly Hills. I tell her I visited Holly Wood to try to learn more about Rick Frances and asked if I could drop by so she might fill me in on anything else.

Beverly lives in a high-rise that, like Beverly herself, had seen better days. After retiring from modeling, she became the hostess of the show *Guess the Pedicure*. When I say I never watch it, she shows me a wall lined with bottles of nail polish, including some that look like they have nothing in them.

"Oh those," she says. "They glow in the dark. Some people want secret symbols and messages painted on their toes."

I see a small cute sculpture of a foot on a table. I pick it up. "Where did you get this?

"It was a gift from Rick. He gave it to me a few years ago."

I return the sculpture to the table.

"Why don't you take off your shoes? I'll give you one of my special pedicures."

"Don't think I have the time," I say.

"Nonsense. Indulge yourself. I won't charge you for the first one. And I'll give you a half price coupon for the next one. Take off your shoes."

I roll my eyes, take off my shoes, and sit in one of her pedicure chairs.

"Any foot fetishes?" she asks squinting at my feet.

"No. None."

"Sure?"

"I'm sure."

She narrows her eyes. "I can tell, you know."

"I'm sure."

"Put your right foot into the warm water."

I submerge my foot in the warm bath of water while she drones on about why the vibrations in pink are better than the vibrations in red. Then she rubs, files, cuts and scrapes until my foot looks like a baby's foot. Then she airbrushes my five toes five different colors.

"There, all ready to go."

"What about my other foot?"

She reaches into her pocket and hands me a coupon. "I said I won't charge you for the first one, and here's a half price coupon for the other foot. Shall I proceed?"

I check the time. "Actually, I'm running late. I'd better go."

Beverly frowns. "Don't forget to wear open toed shoes to show off my work."

"I will."

"Just a sec, want to give you some free samples." She goes to a row of shelves on the back wall and removes two small silver shopping bags. One is filled with nail polish samples and foot creams; the other has ten demo tapes for Cortland.

14

I CALL SOL BRODY AT NIRGAL PALACE.

"I'm sorry," a clipped voice that I can't tell whether it's a person or a program says, "we have no Sol Brody listed."

Then I remember and say, "Starr Bright."

After a brief pause and much clicking I hear, "Starr Bright. How may I help you?"

"Sol, or should I say Starr, this is Molly from Molly's Bistro."

"Great to hear from you, Molly. How can I help you?"

"We want to book a weekend so we can see what you offer."

"You won't be disappointed. How many will be coming?"

"Four. My husband and myself, Becky, who is the bride, and Lois, Becky's sister."

I wait a moment, then he says, "Adjoining suites available on outer ring five in two weeks."

"Perfect. We'll take them."

"Lots going on that week: a Policeman's Ball, and I think this says Buddhist convention. But they won't affect you. They're held in other areas. Do you know anyone else who'll be here when you'll be here? I ask because we can arrange joint events, or, on the other hand, help you avoid them."

"Don't think we know anyone else that will be here."

"Well, two names put a link to your name if you called."

"Really? Who?"

Sol scrolls reservations. "Ah! There. Jersey and Trenton. They booked a small inner court room on ring three."

Inner court room? Nice way to say cheapest room in the cheapest area. I remember the first time Cortland and I went to Nirgal Palace and stayed there with its industrial furnishings, no view, and minimum bathroom accessories. But I know none of these things will bother Jersey and Trenton as long as they know they are getting a rock bottom price.

When I tell Becky about Jersey and Trenton, she becomes a hissing tangle alternating between giving me a fish eye and a disapproving glare. She tilts her head and thrusts her lower lip the way she did when she was a child then explodes. "You can't be serious, Mom! Jersey and Trenton will ruin everything!"

Lois sputters, "They might not want to book Becky's wedding if they think we're related to Trenton."

I look at them wide-eyed. Then after a long moment, "Where is *this* coming from? You've both known Trenton most of your lives. Yes, he's an android, but he's kind and loving and funny and brilliant."

Becky face darkens like a nimbus cloud ready to release its rain. "I know, Mom, but he looks so strange."

"Especially when he spins his eyes," Lois says, rolling hers.

"Since when did his looks matter?"

"Well, Burton's parents don't like androids."

Without missing a beat, Lois adds, "That's putting it mildly!"

Becky twists her long blonde hair until it looks like it will snap and lowers her eyes. "Burton's father was part of the march protesting the rise in the android population. He was the one who carried the sign that said 'Go Back to Oz, Tin Men.'"

"You're sure?" I ask, trying to put my prospective new in-laws into a context that isn't negative and not succeeding.

"I'm sure," Becky says. "Burton showed me the holo."

I shake my head in consternation. "A third of the population has replaced 50% of their bodies with android parts and the number is growing. You do know that your right elbow that you broke crater sledding came from an android parts catalogue."

"I know, I know," Becky singsongs. "But Burton doesn't know."

"Well, don't you think you should tell him?"

"I guess."

"I guess is not an answer."

"Elbows don't count," Lois blurts in Becky's defense.

"Says who? At what point is a person considered a human android?"

Becky jumps up, points, and waves a long red fingernail at me. "You just never liked Burton. You're just looking for an excuse to break up my engagement."

"That's not true sweetheart." I put my hand on her arm. She yanks it away. "Jersey and Trenton rarely go anywhere, and it's their anniversary."

"Yeah, they rarely go anywhere because they're so cheap," Lois says.

The twins give each other a hand signal that I know means "let's leave." Becky says, "Come, Lois, we have to rehearse Dad's new music."

"What did he finally write?" I ask.

Becky puts her hands dramatically on her chest and says, "My Heart Is a Black Hole."

15

CORTLAND LICKS ORANGE TEQUILLA SAUCE from a spare rib and says, "I used to consider Jersey and Trenton only your friends, but I've grown fond of them even if they are a little…"

"A little what?"

"Different. A little different. But Becky is out of line. Did you remind her that she has an android elbow?"

"Of course. But love is blind." I wipe my mouth with a pink napkin and signal for our service-bot to clear the table.

The bot arrives and stacks our dishes onto the tray that had slid from its abdomen. "Any dessert?" it asks.

"Just tea," I say.

"Tea," Cortland adds.

"Lemon or milk? Regular or decaf? Flying Saucer Supermarket Blend? Tea leaves from Titan? San Andreas Farms vitamin enhanced…"

"Stop," I say. "Tea leaves from Titan. We always say tea leaves from Titan."

Cortland says, "Can't it be reprogrammed to stop asking that?"

"We got a good deal on this model because its central processing unit has advertising. I'm told if I remove it, every program crashes. Do you know how to do it?"

"No," he sighs.

Sharing the same thought, we say, "Let's ask Trenton." We laugh.

Cortland says, "So Jersey and Trenton's neighborhood has gone from industrial ugly to interesting trendy. Strange I never saw ads in *The New Chicago Times* for new luxury buildings there or anything about a real estate explosion." He scrolls his palm.

"What are you doing?

"Just a hunch."

I wait.

"Yup, plenty of ads in *The Android Times*."

"Really?"

Cortland says, "I think when a builder scouting new areas to develop saw Jersey and Trenton living there, he realized there was a potentially lucrative market: androids."

The bot returns with our tea and four spice cookies that we never requested. Last week I reprogrammed it to "show more initiative." If I send the cookies back, I'll have to answer questions about returning them and risk ruining the program, so I take one.

I blow on the top of the tea, sip, and say, "Lamont had mentioned how much the android population had grown, but until I visited Jersey and Trenton, I never realized how much. Since opening the restaurant, I've been so busy that I haven't paid as much attention to the news let alone paid attention to changes in the population. Molly's Bistro gets a fairly regular crowd. Come to think of it, I don't remember seeing any android couples. One or two delivery men who were androids but no patrons."

Cortland takes a cookie. "You know, Molly, they are probably taking their business to Silicone Slings near Jersey and Trenton's rather than your bistro."

"But I have much better food."

Trenton smiles. "Also much higher prices and no silicone milkshakes."

"You have a point."

"Not only has their population grown, they're impacting society, opening new businesses, and contributing to the economy. Some might fear that they're after their jobs."

I separate the two sides of my spice cookie and lick the cinnamon cream center. "Jersey mentioned that some of Trenton's friends had trouble finding housing and were rejected by co-op boards for reasons—some of which made no sense unless…"

"Unless," Cortland says, "unless they were being discriminated against. Maybe it was more than their unusual cheapness that made Jersey and Trenton choose that area to live. Could our new in-laws feel threatened? We don't know much about them."

I sip my tea, consider my options. "Maybe I should have Elvis and Lulu to dinner. Good food soothes the savage beast," I say.

"Isn't music the thing that soothes the savage beast?"

"Then we'll have music and food."

Cortland pats my hand.

I had met Burton's parents, Elvis and Lulu Ernie, once briefly. It was at my restaurant the night Rick Frances died. Burton's father owned Club Mood, a virtual travel agency. Burton thought his father would like to meet Rick Frances as both were in the virtual reality business. I had time for the briefest greeting, and Cortland's meeting was even briefer as there were so many wanting his attention. I never learned if Rick and Elvis met.

Burton's father was short for a native born Martian: six foot one. People and animals conceived and grown in gravities lighter than Earth's are taller and usually thinner than their Earth counterparts. Becky and Lois were conceived and grew on Earth's moon. They fit in, unlike me—born and raised on Earth and a very Earth average of five foot six.

Louisiana Ernie, whom Elvis calls Lulu, is six foot seven—average for Martians. I never got used to seeing so many tall thin women wearing push-up bras with plunging necklines, which is what Lulu was wearing the first time I met her. I barely escaped being hit in the face with her boobs as she said in a voice that made sarcasm sound like a compliment, "Well, excuse me!"

I get up from the table and palm Elvis and Lulu. I hear, "You have reached Club Mood, the finest in virtual travel. Want to surf through the rings of Saturn? Want to stand on King Kong's palm and sail through the solar system? Want to go over Venus Falls in a barrel? We make it happen. Can't take your call right now because we're on a virtual underwater safari to Enceladus. At the sound of the dolphins, please leave a message. And remember, why go anywhere when you can stay here and go there?"

I leave a message with an invitation. Then I think, *Wouldn't it be something if they killed Rick Frances?*

16

A WEEK LATER, BURTON and his parents step from the elevator into our apartment. Their eyes widen, seeing wrap around windows, sixteen-foot skylights, and stunning views. The greenhouse connected to the side sends out the aroma of orchards and roses. They inhale deeply and smile.

Good start.

I say, "Cortland bought this building after 'Like a Floating Stone', a song he wrote and the twins recorded, made number one on the hit parade. Back then the city couldn't wait to unload it."

Now it resembles a tinted glass and steel box draped like a fishnet with thousands of photovoltaic cells with computerized leaves that turn in any direction to capture light. Once the sun comes up, the light doesn't simply stream through the windows, it invades from every angle. At night, the cells glow in varying colors depending on how much sunlight they absorbed during the day.

The interior is a series of free flowing connecting spaces. The central area has a gray and pink boulder flaked with bronze-colored chips that sits in a pool. There are recording studios and offices on the four lower levels; each twin has her own apartment on the middle two floors. We live in the penthouse complete with wraparound terrace, full gym, and indoor swimming pool. The entire building rotates, maximizing the views and the light.

"Lulu, Elvis, welcome," I say, giving my perfected restaurant greeting. "So glad you've come." I point to the service-bot next to me. "Take their coats, Stephen." They remove their coats and give them to Stephen, who walks away.

"That's the most human looking one I've seen," Elvis says, wrinkling his nose. "You talk to it like it was a person. I won't let Lulu buy one for our home."

Lulu frowns.

"Hardly a person," I laugh, "just a service-bot. Our friend Trenton made a few adjustments in the old one that I had and..." Cortland puts his hand on my arm. I stop talking.

"Burton said that your home was spectacular," Lulu says," but I had no idea how beautiful."

Cortland says, "It took over two years to renovate. Wasn't it worth it, sweetheart?"

I don't say anything because I still remember the pain. First the estimate that we thought reasonable. Then after paying a third of the money, they did the demolition, and we got a revised estimate about needing pipes lined with a material only found on Ganymede, toilet seats from Ceres, aka the toilet seat capital of the solar system—who knew? Hinges made by a company (which we later learned was owned by the contractor's brother) from Neptune's moon Despina because they said when it came to hinges, they couldn't trust anyone else unless you didn't mind doors slamming and windows sticking. Plus the time for my big toe to grow back after some heavy equipment fell and crushed it.

I say, "Show them around, Cortland. I'll put some finishing touches to dinner."

I had made a traditional American Thanksgiving dinner because when you're finished, you'll have entered a soothing opiate state, and I thought everyone might need that.

I knew about Thanksgiving because I took a course in college called Black Friday Freedom Fighters. I learned that the Thanksgiving meal was created by a man named Macy Pilgrim to celebrate the fortune he made on Mayflower Rocket derivatives. Once a year he sat in a hot air balloon that was paraded before a cheering crowd and ate roasted turkey, mashed sweet potatoes, and stuffing and threw cranberries at the cleavage of his girlfriend Zelda Pocahontas, an Indian from Turkey.

A college education—worth every starbuck.

Dinner is a success. I had basted the turkey in hard cider, roasted a tray of root vegetables, made a sweet potato mousse. After my dinner at Jersey and Trenton's home, Trenton invented a food printer. He gave me a small one that printed desserts. I printed a pumpkin pie, mince pie, and an apple pie. Good thing it wasn't around when I weighed 287 pounds.

Cortland puts his fork down and says, "Those desserts from Trenton's printer were as good as the ones you make from scratch, Molly."

Elvis says, "Trenton sounds like quite a scientist. I would love to meet him and ask him about ideas I have for Club Mood."

Becky glares at me. Lois looks down. Then Becky says, "He's head of forensics at Mars Yard and is very busy. He's very boring. I know you wouldn't like him."

"A serious introvert," Lois chirps. "Very temperamental. Becky and I avoided him whenever we could when we were growing up. Isn't that right, Becky?"

"Right," Becky says in a small voice.

Cortland jumps in. "Tell us about Club Mood and that new underwater trip. Sounds like fun."

"Have you ever been on a virtual reality trip?" Elvis asks.

We both shake our heads no.

"It's not like a virtual restaurant where you're sitting all the time. There's physical interaction. I suggest you start with something easy like a trip to a beach. Advanced trips can be exhausting—feeling as though you surfed in Hellas Planitia Ocean. You'll need a doctor's OK to go on one of those."

Intrigued, I say, "Would I burn any calories? Eating at VV burns nothing."

"And leaves you hungry," Cortland adds.

Elvis says, "Some virtual trips burn lots of calories."

I say, "Sounds better than a gym. But if it's all virtual, how do the calories get burned? Thinking doesn't make it so, even though I wish it did."

"Depending on the trip, we use eye and ear enhancers, spray your skin with nano-haptic receptors to maximize the interface processing, and/or have you wear a garment that has micro-sensors embedded in the fabric."

"Stop being so technical, Elvis. You're spoiling the fun."

Elvis nods and continues. "We have something that looks like an elongated treadmill for walking, running, jumping, kicking. Chairs that move and spin and saddles that make you feel you're riding: a flying tiger, a shark, a dragon." He winks. "Or a composite of several animals."

"A lot of women want to be mermaids," Lulu adds. "We also get a lot of people who would love to climb mountains but, in reality, are afraid of heights."

Elvis continues, "Those thinking that they are on a ship during a storm can get sea sick. I can't think of any experiences that we can't create in any skill level. Isn't that so, Lulu?"

Lulu answers, "Few want extremes. Most just want to have fun."

Elvis says, "How about a complimentary membership for a year? After all, you'll be family." He looks at Becky and Burton and raises his glass. "To Becky and Burton."

Burton stands. "To Becky, my beautiful fiancée." Then he looks at his parents and says, "But we want to go to a real place on our honeymoon, not a virtual one."

Everyone laughs. The evening is going well.

I signal Stephen to clear the dessert dishes, bring coffee to the living room, and add a dish of Chocolate Moons. Elvis watches, poker faced.

We go in the living room. Elvis and Lulu sit on our pale blue sofa. Becky and Burton sit on the love seat. Lois plops into a winged chair, and Cortland and I sit on two barrel-back chairs.

Lulu reaches for a Chocolate Moon from a dish that Stephen had placed on the coffee table between us. "I love these," she says, taking three. She pauses, wrinkles her brow, and looks at me. "Were you the one I read about in *The New Chicago Times* that solved the case of the poisoned Chocolate Moons a few years ago?"

"Yes. But I did have a little help from Trenton and his wife Jersey."

"There," Elvis says, lifting a finger, "you've mentioned Trenton again. I don't care if he has a terrible personality. He sounds like my kind of guy."

"He travels a lot," Cortland says. "Always on the run."

Elvis takes a Chocolate Moon and puts it in his mouth. "Hard to find good talent in the virtual reality business," he chuckles. "Everyone jokes that we'll pay them in virtual money." He reaches into his pocket and hands me his card. "Please, give Trenton this."

I take the card. "I'll give him the card, but I doubt he'll call," I say. Then, I change the subject. "What do you remember about that terrible night at my restaurant when Rick Frances died?"

Lulu says, "When Becky told us about the dinner and sent us an invitation, I regret I set it aside and didn't respond until the last minute. Then the only seats available were in the main room, but near the kitchen or in the bar area. Becky said that the main dining room was so pretty and everybody important would be seated there, so we sat there. I remember seeing Rick stagger through the kitchen door clutching his throat. I thought that something went down the wrong way."

"And you, Elvis? What do you remember?

Lulu and Elvis lock eyes. "Same as Lulu. Saw him stagger through the kitchen door. We were upset seeing this, not only because Rick was in obvious distress, but we had hoped to meet him." Lulu says, "Then we saw you go in. Isn't that right, Elvis?"

Elvis pauses a little longer than necessary, as though distracted.

Lulu repeats: "I said, isn't that right, Elvis?"

"I think so. Yes. Yes. That's right."

17

FRANK SHOWS ME SEVERAL CRACKED PLATES and says, "You never replaced the dishes the police broke during their investigation. Do you want to go to Restaurant Works and buy new ones?"

I stand and check my schedule on my palm. "Let's go after the lunch crowd leaves."

I wave at Frank who is standing next to his smart rover that has a sign on the back that says, "My other car is an Aston Martian." I don sunglasses—still needed, even though the golden disk of the sun is smaller than when seen from Earth. It's a clear day with wispy thin cirrus clouds typical in Mars' low humidity. Sometimes I miss the beauty of the grand cumulous ones, but I'm not likely to see any unless I go back to Earth. Before Mars, I lived on Earth's moon and grew used to living in windless enclosed spaces. It's nice to be outside again. But Mars is very windy. As Earth Eskimos have over one hundred words for snow, Martians have almost as many for wind.

Frank wears a navy blue t-shirt, chinos, and short, well-worn Cordovan boots, a nice change from his headwaiter's uniform. I never noticed that his arms rippled with muscles because he always wore long sleeves. They were either the product of hard physical work—which he did not do—hours at a gym, steroids, or both.

He opens the rover's door. I'm about to get in when an out of breath Jersey rushes toward me.

"Got the afternoon off and thought I would come and take out some of your delicious chicken soup. It's Trenton's favorite. His food printer keeps printing black bean soup. Boy, does that use up ink!"

"Lots of good chicken soup recipes out there, Jersey."

"Yeah, but he wants to be historically correct. He traced the first authentic recipe to the index in the back of the Book of Genesis called Torah Treats." She looks at the sky. "In the beginning, God created the first matzo ball that floated an infinite sea of chicken soup."

"You're kidding, right?"

"I never kid about religion. The writer of the book I read said it was in the tenth book of the Torah."

"I thought the Torah had five books."

"No. There's one written on the back of ten tablets. The writer's mother said that they were commandants and swears that she heard God say, 'So delicious that from this day forth your people will not be called the People of the Book, but The People of the Cookbook'."

I sigh and look at my watch. Jersey sees and says, "Did I get you at a bad time? Where are you going?"

"We're going to Baguette where there's a professional restaurant supply company. The restaurant needs new dishes and they have a wide selection at good prices."

"Really? I need a fork."

"This is for restaurants, not individuals. They may not sell one fork."

Jersey frowns. "Business is business."

I sigh. "OK. Hop in."

I sit in the front next to Frank. Jersey sits in the back. The doors lock automatically. Frank taps the controls and keys Baguette.

A flat, automated voice says, "Baguette on the northeastern side of Ascraeus Mons—program complete. Arrival time: forty-seven minutes."

Frank says, "We're going to be passing through some of Tharsis' beautiful desert landscape on our way toward Ascraeus Mons, Mars' second highest mountain."

Jersey says, "We don't need a geography lesson, Frank. Let's just enjoy the trip."

"I'm only saying that the scenery is so beautiful we could holograph our own Lawrence of Arabia." He swivels his chair away from the controls, looks at us, and stretches his legs.

The automated voice announces, "Dust storm fifty-seven miles ahead. Grains of sand and assorted dust may reach ten feet high. Time estimate passing through the storm: nineteen minutes."

We pick up speed. I peer out the window and say, "I haven't been out of New Chicago in over two years. I never realized there was so much construction." I look at tractors, dump trucks, graders, front loaders, bulldozers, and more at work building new developments.

Jersey says, "The thicker atmosphere in the lower lands makes it an attractive place to live."

Frank adds, "So many roadways are now enclosed. I wish this was one of them. When I used to come to Baguette from Chryse Planitia, it took me over two hours."

"Are you sure you never met Rick Frances?" I ask, braced, remembering how sharply Frank answered the question before. "I learned that he had a restaurant in Chryse Planitia. And you know the restaurant business."

Frank's voice strains, his tone challenged. "Chryse Planitia is a big place. And lots of people know the restaurant business."

"You're right. Mars Yard did a background check. Avery and Lena come from there, too."

"Never met them either." Frank's eyes narrow, clearly annoyed. Then after a long delay, he adds, "Like I said, Chryse Planitia is a big place."

I change the subject. "Vanna and Mario seem to be getting along better. When I went into the kitchen recently, they were have a quiet conversation."

Frank nods. "Are you aware that Mario saw a doctor two weeks ago? He said that the doctor couldn't find anything wrong. I told him he should get a second opinion."

A gray wall of dust is rushing toward us. It didn't matter if we turned right or left, so we zoom into it. Frank checks the instruments. I clutch the seat rail. Dust and debris are striking the rover with machine gun precision. We rock from side to side. I hope we are not blown off course. There are no compasses on Mars as there is not magnetic pole, so I hope the rover's automated navigational system is not affected. Suddenly, the lights go off and everything goes black, but just as quickly, the lights go on again. Then they flicker, stabilize, flicker again, and die. We sit in the dark.

"Lighting malfunction," the car voice says.

"We know that," Jersey whines, a trace of fear in her voice.

The car voice says, "Auxiliary power will commence in 3, 2, 1 seconds." The lights come on. We exhale. Then there is a high-pitched sound. "Rover cover pierced," the automated voice says. We hear the high-pitched sound wail louder and louder. Protective helmets drop from ceiling cases. But before we have a chance to put them on, the wailing stops, and we hear a swishing sound. "Plasteel jelly plugging the ruptures," says the automated voice. Then a moment later, "Ruptures repaired." The helmets automatically slide back. We slowly let ourselves relax.

Frank touches a button. Music plays.

I lean back, close my eyes. My mind speeds into a review: planning the VV dinner with Rick Frances, Jersey and Trenton moving to New Chicago, plans for Becky's wedding, dealing with prejudiced in-laws. Then I must have drifted off because the next thing I know the car's automated voice is saying, "Arriving Baguette; please resume manual drive."

Frank says, "Baguette kept its protective dome that was built when the atmosphere was not thick enough to sustain life so they could continue controlling the weather inside."

We drive over a small arched bridge, enter an airlock. Jersey reads a sign. "Welcome to Baguette. Sunny and 72 degrees, today and every day."

We exit onto a street that has rows of willow trees with hanging flower baskets and two splashing fountains in the center divider. Shops are filled with sophisticated and expensive looking merchandise.

"Slow down, Frank," I say. "Baguette is so pretty." I point to a bakery with a blue and white striped awning. "Let's have coffee and a pastry there before we go to Restaurant Works."

Frank parks. We get out. I straighten my skirt and cinch my tan jacket. Frank says, "If you wouldn't mind, Molly, I want to go on ahead and say hello to an old friend at Restaurant Works. There have been a lot of changes in my life since I was here."

Jersey and I wave good-bye to Frank and walk to the bakery. Lusciously decorated caloric treats are artfully displayed in the window. There is also a sign that says, "Annual Pie Eating Contest Today: Former pie eating champion Greg Heinz, descendant of Duncan Heinz, challenges reigning champion Molly Crocker, descendant of Betty Crocker."

"I'm not a big fan of pie eating contests," Jersey says. "Maybe we could find another place."

"But lots of people love them." I turn away, glance across the street, and freeze. "Is that who I think it is, Jersey?"

"Who? Where?"

"On the corner. The two women carrying shopping bags? Is that Holly Wood and Beverly Hills?"

18

BEVERLY LOOKS IN OUR DIRECTION and pivots away. She says something to Holly that we can't hear, then they duck into a nearby shop.

We wait for the light to change, cross the street, and follow into a shop called Supportive Secrets. Up front are racks of conservative white bras. Farther along are risqué styles in dramatic colors ending with black ones.

A saleswoman approaches; she looks at me with the intensity of a doctor about to deliver bad news and says, "May I help you? You look like a light pink."

"Light pink?" I say.

"Almost no one buys white. We only stock them so mothers with thirteen-year-old daughters can have something to fight about. I bet you're wearing light pink right now." She reaches out. "Mind if I check?"

"Yes, I mind. What difference does it make?"

"People who buy pink don't spend as much as people who buy black."

"So who buys light pink?"

"The same mothers that want their daughters to wear white: pink is their compromise color. But their daughters return them and get black. She looks at my chest. But you look like an authentic light pink to me. Very rare."

She turns to Jersey and looks down at her chest. "Are you even wearing a bra?" she asks.

"As a matter of fact I'm not," Jersey answers. "Not much to put in it."

"How about a training bra, the type twelve year olds wear to get ready?"

"I'm comfortable the way I am," Jersey snarls.

"Thanks for your help," I say "but we're both just looking. Right, Jersey?"

"Right," Jersey says in a serious tone.

We walk toward the back, fingering skimpy items smaller than their high price tags.

"You're not going to find anything you like there," she calls after us. "Hey, you're not the bra tag police are you? They're worse than the mattress tag police."

"Just watch it," Jersey calls, twirling a black lace garter belt over her head.

When we reach the dressing area, Holly pops her head from behind the curtain. "Oops!" she says, looking at us.

"Holly, what are you doing here?" I ask.

"I could say the same thing," she says.

Beverly's head pops from the other dressing room and looks. "Aren't you Molly from Molly's Bistro? What are you doing here?"

"Holly just asked me that."

"You girls having fun?" the saleswoman asks, seeing us talk to Holly and Beverly. "Want to try a nipple pasty? I'm great at putting them on."

"No thanks," Beverly says, "have a drawer full of them."

"Tried one once. Too invasive," Jersey says.

"On you, yes," the saleswoman grumbles. She looks at me. "I'm downgrading you to the white category." She turns and walks away.

Holly gives Jersey and me the once over. "You girls seriously need our help."

"I wouldn't let a salesperson talk to me like that," Beverly says.

"I thought you and Holly couldn't stand each other," I say.

"We didn't when we were models and dated Rick Frances," Beverly says. "But after your visit, I called Holly to compare notes. We decided that now that Rick Frances is dead, we should bury the hatchet. We have a lot in common. Don't we, Beverly?"

Beverly nods.

"Nothing more?" I ask.

They smile and say nothing.

I convince Jersey to go back to the bakery. Now it's packed. We push to get in. I blink because think I see Lena.

I poke Jersey. "Is that Lena from Virtual Vittles?"

Before she can answer, Lena spots us. "Molly! Molly! What are you doing here?"

"I can ask the same thing, Lena."

"I came to do research. I don't think anyone has done a virtual reality food contest, and I needed to see the real thing before I can program one. Why are you here?"

I tell Lena why I'm there. Then I look about the room more closely. There are two tables, each with pies, in front. A man with the nameplate Greg Heinz sits at one, opening and closing his mouth as though chewing air. I assume it is a warning up exercise. The other chair is empty. We turn to leave, but a man approaches. He wears a badge that says "Pie Eating Judge." "Your name is Molly? Isn't it?" he blurts, slightly out of breath.

"Yes," I answer.

"Where are you going? We've been waiting for you."

"Me?" I ask pointing to myself. "My friend and I only came for coffee and a snack."

"Nonsense! You just said that your name was Molly." He points to a picture of a woman in a tan jacket with brown eyes and brown wavy hair. "That's you!"

Jersey peers closely. "Could be you, Molly."

"Not helping, Jersey."

"That's not me. My name is Molly, but not Molly Crocker."

"Modesty. Modesty. We know who you are." And louder, "Don't we, people?"

The audience claps and chants: "Molly! Molly! Molly!"

"This is a big mistake," I say.

I see Lena waving and pushing toward us, but there are too many people blocking her way.

"Let's get out of here, Jersey." We bolt for the door.

Greg Heinz, who has gotten up from his table, yells, "This isn't over, Molly!"

Frank is in front of the bakery waiting next to his rover. "I was about to come in and see if you were ready to go," he says. "What's going on?"

"They confused me with some other Molly..."

"Bakeries get rough crowds," Frank says. "A lot of frustration drowned in cream puffs."

Restaurant Works is so close that we could have walked, but I'm glad Frank drove. We step inside a small reception area and register by touching symbols on a wall. Frank says, "Everything you buy can be shipped. I'll try to get you free delivery."

"No problem," Jersey says. "I can carry a fork."

Frank frowns. "I wasn't talking to you."

We stand on a descending escalator and enter a vast cavernous space.

"I can't believe I've never been here," I say seeing rows of glassware, plates, silverware, and cooking utensils on shelves, hanging from the ceiling, crammed into every corner. A yellow sign points to an elevator that says to Level Two: heavy equipment—ovens, pizza ovens, dishwashers, char broilers, ice machines, refrigerators, walk-in refrigerators. Level Three: discounted, out of date, and overstocked items.

"Going to the third level," Jersey says, scooting away.

A very small man in a blue jacket and white shirt sitting on a raised motorized cart drives toward us. He climbs down. He's a dwarf. Even in the twenty-fourth century, rare genetic challenges can slip through. He extends his hand upward and says, "I'm Danny, owner and manager. Frank tells me you're looking for dishes. The best are in the front because if we put them elsewhere people become too exhausted searching." He points to a table. "We just put those on the floor. The manufacturer calls them the hat dishes because they look like a brimmed hat turned upside down. You place the food in the indentation and if anything spills, it lands on the rim."

One look and I know that if they are in budget, I'm going to buy them, but I don't want to seem too anxious. I pick up a dinner plate and hold it to the light. It is clear with a design of suns in the middle. "How much a place setting?"

Danny totals the price based on one hundred settings. I smile. It's under my budget.

I look at Frank, who nods his head. "I'll take them. I can't believe I found something so fast. Let me charge it before I change my mind."

"I'll set up your account," Danny says. He taps his pinky; a floating page appears between us. Danny enters my information. But before I can complete the transaction, the page ripples and disappears. Danny makes a face. Then he taps his pinky again.

"Something wrong?" I ask.

"It's my pinky. I've had trouble with it. It's the second time it was regrown. I should have gotten a new one from the android parts store. Those android parts are much more reliable." A small glowing sign appears in front of him: "More time needed for transaction."

"I don't have more time," I say, reading it. "I'll be late for the dinner crowd."

Jersey arrives carrying a small package. "I splurged, got two forks because they were two for the price of one. Are we ready to go?"

"A delay with setting up my account," I say.

Frank says, "Put this on my account, Danny. We can settle this later."

Danny reaches into a pocket and pulls out a tablet. "This old thing may be more reliable."

He hands it to Frank, who picks up the stylus and signs.

I check the tablet to make sure it has the right information. It does. Then I see Frank's signature: Frances Carol. At first I think nothing of it, because that's his name. But then I think it's strange that he spelled Frances with the letter "e" rather than the letter "i" as most men do.

"Let's stop in the ladies' room before we go," I say to Jersey, giving her a nudge.

Jersey whispers, "Stop pushing. I don't have to go to the bathroom. Trenton got so tired of waiting for me standing in ladies' room lines that he bought me an android bladder for my birthday. Now I go once before I go to sleep. I could have gotten one that let me go once a week, but that seemed too strange. I love not waking up in the middle of the night to go to the bathroom or having to go first thing in the morning. If you had an android bladder, you wouldn't have to go."

"Forget it Jersey. Not going there. Besides, it wasn't only reason that I wanted to go to the ladies' room. I saw how Frank signed his name. He spelled Frances with an 'e,' not an 'i.'"

Jersey says, "That's the female spelling of Frances and also the way Rick Frances spelled his last name. Why don't you ask Frank about it?"

"Seems like a silly question."

"Nothing is a silly question when it comes to murder."

"So you would say that meeting Lena had some significance?"

"I'm just saying don't rule anything out."

19

I WAIT ON A LONG SERPENTINE line with my family for the space elevator to open its doors.

Lois says to Becky, "I'm so glad you picked Nirgal Palace to have your wedding."

Becky smiles.

Cortland says, "It's going to be wonderful. In fact, out of this world."

We laugh.

Then from somewhere behind I hear, "Molly, Molly."

Becky groans, "Oh no! Jersey."

Jersey gets closer. Her voice louder. "Excuse me, excuse me, I'm with those people ahead—Molly of Molly's Bistro and the hit pop singers The Lunar Tunes." Several stand aside and let her pass, those who don't get a not-so-gentle push. One kicks the anti-grav carry-on case that floats next to her.

"Watch it," Jersey says. "That's very valuable."

"If it's so valuable, pay extra and check it in secure storage."

Jersey glares. Draws the case closer.

Becky and Lois make faces.

Finally, Jersey stands next to us. "If Trenton and I hadn't run into you, we never would have found you."

People stare. I look down at the anti-grav case that I know

holds Trenton, his body collapsed and folded like origami so it fits into the case he designed. Now he and Jersey buy one ticket and travel two for the price of one. Jersey is almost as cheap as Trenton. She even joined Vampires Anonymous so she could get a coupon for a free pint of blood.

A green light blinks; the elevator door opens. Lois is annoyed because it's so crowded, and she and Becky can't sit together.

Cortland says, "This is a space elevator, not a prom limo."

Lois says, "Earth has four space elevators. What's taking Mars so long to build another?"

The docking station has three signs to Nirgal Palace: deluxe, standard, and economy. Jersey waves and steps on a moving walkway that heads to economy. We turn in the opposite direction and enter a deluxe tram with a clear bubble top and soft leather seats.

Cortland and I had been to Nirgal Palace twice before. First when we were young and could only afford the cheapest room on the same inner ring as Jersey and Trenton's. Nirgal Palace is shaped like a donut, and those rooms saw the gray opposite inner side.

Years later we stayed in their most extravagant accommodations on outer ring three with a wonderful view of Mars and space. But I never did get to swim in one of the swimming pools where holographs create the illusion that you're swimming among the stars. This time I don't want to miss it.

We glide into the docking station with a gentle halt. Cortland helps me to my feet. The twins are up and exiting through the door that opens directly into Nirgal Palace's lobby. They're anxious to see the hotel's main lobby that I told them about. It has the most spectacular and beautiful holographic illusion I have ever seen. We follow.

"Amazing!" they squeal together looking up and clapping their hands, as they did when they were young children, seeing the radiant artificial sun slowly rotating in the center of the ceiling. The ceiling appears to open directly into black velvet star-filled space.

"Are you sure they're only projections?" Lois almost whispers. "It looks so real."

Becky's eyes grow wide as shooting stars crisscross the seemingly endless sky. "I wish I could have my wedding right here in this lobby," she says.

The twins look at the people. They have bodies shaped by being conceived and grown in different gravities and skin, due to various types of augmented lighting on each world, in colors that rival rainbows. "I've never seen such an interplanetary crowd in one place except on holos of the United Federation of Planets conventions."

Two men approach. One wears a badge that says, "Unicycle." "Welcome to Nirgal Palace," he says. He hands bouquets of golden lilies to the twins. The other's badge says, "Juggler." He hands me a dozen silver roses. Unicycle points to a floating platform surrounded by a safety rail. We all get on.

We ride through the lobby and enter a long carpeted hallway. We go until we stop in front of the twins' suite. We face a shiny black rectangle with no latch and no doorknob. Unicycle passes his hand in front of it. The rectangle disappears.

"Ooh," Becky says. "Can I do that?"

"Won't work until I imprint your palm with a map and a code," Unicycle says. "Please go inside." They enter. A moment later, the black door appears again.

We go to our suite. Juggler swipes it open, and we enter a large living room area. A bar is tucked into a corner with a bottle of champagne chilling in a silver bucket. There are several alcoves with sliding doors. One is for dining. I take an

Asian pear from a bowl of fresh fruit. Two other areas have office dens. Bathrooms have Jacuzzis, saunas, steam rooms, and endless grooming products that I can't wait to try. There are so many pillows the suite could be used for the pillow fighters Olympics.

I point to where a far wall would be, but nothing's there. "I see the three-walled illusion that makes the bed look like its floating in space is on," I say to Juggler. "Please turn it off. I don't know if I could sleep."

"Didn't bother you last time we were here," Cortland jests.

"But we were much younger, and I was very, um...distracted."

Cortland smiles.

"We've added more features," Juggler says. "Let me demonstrate?" He points to a chair.

"Sit," he says. I sit. "Ready?" He walks near the door and touches a panel. The room disappears. The furniture remains but looks like it's floating among the stars in space.

I grab the arms of the chair, look down, and see eternity. I tap my foot and feel the floor. "Very nice," I say. "Not for me." The room reappears. "Are rooms like this popular?"

"Three year waiting list. You went to the head of the list because the twins are celebrities."

It was true the twins were pop stars. Even as children they harmonized when they sang and played the lead in every school show. They never worried about becoming popular. They were popular.

"Besides," Juggler adds, "you know Starr Bright."

"Could you deactivate it? Don't want it going off spontaneously."

Lois opens the door that connects our suites. "Mom, Dad," she calls, pushing the door wider.

"Our room is floating in space! Don't you love it?"

20

THE FIRST THING WE SEE when we enter Starr's office is a huge three-dimensional map of the hotel. Then I notice a gold bowl filled with golden flakes on his desk. I squint to read: To Sol Brody, First Prize Cereal Eating Champion. He points to some comfortable chairs and we sit.

Sol says, "I went over the forms that you sent back, and the wedding seems to be a straightforward affair. Our Garden Terrace Room is a popular choice for the dinner. But the ceremony is best performed on our Outer Space Platform. Very beautiful and very dramatic.

"The Garden Terrace Room now is now being used for a 150th wedding anniversary celebration. We're getting more and more of those. I'll show you a life-sized holo instead." He points to an area on the hotel map, taps it twice, and the walls of his office undulate until it becomes a small Garden Terrace Room.

"It's beautiful," Becky says. "I love it. What's all the stuff hanging from the trees?"

"Spanish Moss. Very plentiful in the southeastern part of the United States. Needs heat and humidity to grow, two conditions you'll never see on Mars. But here we can create most environments. Let's talk some of your options."

Cortland leans in. "The most important option is how much it will cost."

"We don't talk details until we tally the entire package. You don't want to destroy the integrity of the affair."

Cortland adds, "Is the Outer Space Platform necessary? Maybe we could have everything at the Garden Terrace Room?"

Becky and Lois moan.

"Cortland, it's your daughter's wedding!" I say.

Cortland mumbles, "First time I heard pricing fall under 'details'."

Sol says, "I'll forward this information to your room screen, and you can look it over."

The twins scoot to the malls. We go back to our room.

Cortland opens a Mars Malt, turns on the room screen, and studies what Sol sent. I lie on the bed and click hotel activities. A lot had been added since my last visit. It's easy to expand into space when no one holds real estate. There's a rollercoaster that circles the outside of the hotel that I will never, ever go on and space skiing where the slope becomes a gigantic Mobius strip. I wonder if the skiers become dizzy watching those on the opposite strip side ski upside down. An "outdoor" ice skating rink, bobsled ride, one hundred tennis courts with balls that can be adjusted to different gravities, and twenty eighteen-hole holistic golf courses.

Jersey calls. We agree to have lunch. Trenton was meeting with someone he had met years ago.

After taking several elevators and sliding runways, I find Hash Tags, a restaurant Jersey selected. It's in the discount-bargain mall. I should have known.

Jersey is up front in a booth. She wears a pink blouse and black slacks. She always wears solid colors. Being very obsessive, she abandoned wearing prints because she said that it took her hours to line up the patterns; ergo, no prints.

We sit facing each other at a table that has just been cleaned. I see that where her right pinky should have been, there's a shiny multifaceted diamond cone. "What happened to your pinky?" I ask.

"I cut it off accidentally. I was distracted chopping kelp. I was lucky Trenton was home."

"That's terrible."

"It was terrible then, but now it's a blessing in disguise."

I look closer and say, "I'm not crazy about disguised blessings."

"Trenton cauterized the pinky stump, reconfigured my engagement ring, added some new materials that he refuses to tell me what they are because he says it's beyond my powers of comprehension—and fashioned it." She rolls her eyes. "He always says it's beyond my powers of comprehension whenever he doesn't want to talk about something.

"At first I was annoyed because he ruined my engagement ring. But when we went out and people saw the diamond cone, they thought it looked fantastic and wanted to know where to get one. We were very surprised by the reaction. Now Trenton has so many orders for diamond pinkies he could almost retire from Mars Yard."

"Let me look at it again." Jersey holds out her hand. "Don't think I'm ready to be a customer."

"Well, with that expensive blue ice sapphire ring that you're wearing that Cortland bought you, I can understand. Unless…"

"Unless what?"

"You want Trenton to make you a blue ice sapphire pinky?"

"Not my thing."

Jersey leans in. "Have you read about the demonstrations protesting the rise in the android population? We've got more supporters than protesters, but the protesters are becoming more virulent."

I think of my future in-laws, Elvis and Lulu Ernie, and say nothing.

Jersey picks up her napkin and refolds it.

"What are you going to order?" I ask.

"Order? I thought we just came here to meet. I took an egg salad supplement pill before I came. Couldn't eat another bite."

21

THE NEXT DAY WE GO BACK to Starr's office. I see Avery and Lena leaving.

"Avery, Lena, what are you doing here?" I ask, trying to hide my surprise. "We seem to be bumping into each other in unexpected places."

"Not so unexpected Molly. We're here to explore the possibility of opening a Virtual Vittles at Nirgal Palace," she says. "Starr thought it a brilliant idea."

"Can't miss out on the action," Avery adds. "And if we don't do it soon, someone else will."

Lena says, "You really should have stayed for that pie eating contest in Baguette."

"It's not my thing, Lena."

"I bet you could have won. Rumor has it that you were once very overweight."

I knit my eyebrows and frown.

Starr comes out of his office and says, "I see no introductions are necessary."

Cortland and I shake our heads. Becky and Lois lower their eyes and smile.

"I'll be in touch," Starr says to Lena and Avery who have started to walk away. He turns to us. "Ready to see the Garden

Terrace Room?"

We follow him to an area called the Atrium. We see a glass wall ahead and behind it a dense forest. Starr clicks a remote, and a door slides open. A fragrant breeze filled with the smell of rain, mowed grass, and exotic flowers engulfs us.

Becky says, "Was this lush foliage copied from a garden on Venus?"

"Nope. Copied it from the garden on Earth called Tara. It is long gone with the wind during the American Civil War."

Becky says, "We studied the Civil War at King Tut U. Was that North America or South America?"

Lois, wide-eyed, looks at her sister, rolls her eyes, puts a hand on a hip, and says, "Had to be South America because it took place in the south."

Cortland turns to Sol. "So how much is the Garden Terrace room?"

Sol smiles. "Details, details, details again; depends on the entire integrity of the affair."

Cortland starts to say something. Suddenly, there is a booming announcement: "Attention, Nirgal Palace guests, the space elevator that dispatched the latest visitors reports that there was one unauthorized person on board. We are in the process of checking our records and comparing them to our registration list. Chief detective Lamont Blackberry and his partner Sid Seedless are on their way to help with the investigation. We don't want to alarm anyone, but a serial killer could be headed here. Please return to your room and remain there for the next hour. This should, in no way, spoil anyone's vacation."

We go back to our room. The adjoining door is open to the twins' suite. We hear crying.

Lois points to Becky, who is on her bed, head in a pillow, sobbing. "I can't believe this is happening," she cries. "I was looking forward to a beautiful week of planning my wedding. Now this."

I sit quietly on the edge of her bed and put my hand on her back. "At least this is not the actual week of the wedding. He could be caught soon. Besides, I heard that he never stays in one place for long. So if he's here, and they don't catch him, he's likely to leave long before the wedding."

Lois says in a forced cheery voice, "Mom's right, Becky."

Becky wipes her eyes and heads for the bathroom.

I go to our room and leave the adjoining door ajar. The house phone signals a message from Lamont and Sid. The message says that Lamont wants to meet and talk. I click "available now." I call to the twins through the open door. "If you girls don't need me, I'm closing this door."

Becky, who is now out of the bathroom and more composed, calls, "Why?"

I walk to the door, put my hand on the knob to close it. "Lamont and Sid are here."

"Really, Mom! First Jersey and Trenton and now Lamont and Sid!" Becky cries. She turns and goes back to the bathroom.

Cortland puts his arm around me. I sigh and lean into his shoulder. "I'll be in the den," he says in a soothing voice. "Gotta make some calls. But let me know if I can help."

As soon as he leaves, a light above our door signals that Lamont and Sid have arrived and are waiting in the hallway. I take a deep breath and activate the door to disappear.

Lamont and Sid stand before me.

"Hey, neat trick," Lamont says, looking at the space where the door used to be. He steps through the opening.

"Hey, neat trick," Sid says.

"Said that," Lamont snarls. He glances around the room. "I saw holos of these deluxe rooms, but I've never been in one. The images I saw showed these rooms having three sides. I always wondered about that. This one has four."

"They all have four sides," I say. I pick up a remote and activate the illusion. "You must mean this." I release the lock on the illusion switch, and the room disappears around us.

"Wow! That's the picture of what I saw."

"Unnerving, isn't it? That's why I turned it off."

"Love it," Sid says.

Lamont continues, "Nirgal Palace has more gadgets than Houdini XXIII used when he escaped from the fifth dimension. Mars Yard could use this. Might get some suspects to talk."

I push reset and the room appears. "I thought finding out who killed Rick Frances was top priority," I say. "Any progress? And how did you and Sid get assigned here?"

Sid says, "We won a raffle at Mars Yard for an all expenses trip to Nirgal Palace and..."

"Shut up," Lamont orders. "She was talking to me. No real progress as to who murdered Rick Frances, and we still can't figure out why there was one extra woman and one less man on the list of people at your restaurant. So while we're waiting for results, we came to see if we could discover who the extra person on the space elevator was. Rick's murder is not our only case."

"But it's the only case that concerns me. Restaurant patrons can be fickle. It doesn't take much for people to go elsewhere. What else are you working on?"

"Getting a raise," Sid says.

Lamont looks at Sid, shakes his head. Then he slowly unwraps a piece of gum and pops it in his mouth. Chomps down hard. "Two cases head the list, Molly: who stole the tax shelter and what is the meaning of the universe? Mars Yard is divided as to which is harder. And don't tell me that the answer to the second is 42. Even though it is the perfect score on the International Mathematical Olympiad and number of dots on the pair of dice that Irving Einstein said God wouldn't play with."

"Wasn't Einstein's first name Albert?"

"It's all relative, Molly. Depends on where you're coming from."

"Made your point, Lamont. You're overworked and underpaid. Can I offer you something from the food replicator?"

"Thought you would never ask."

I go over and choose raspberry cream cheese pastries and double espressos.

"We don't plan to be here long," Lamont says, putting down his cup. "Hotel security is handling most of the space elevator case."

"Did I tell you that I had lunch with Vanna and Nirgal Palace's banquet manager Starr Bright a day after the murder? His real name is the same as the serial killer: Sol Brody."

"You told us. We questioned him. His alibis checked out."

"He's Rick Frances' brother-in-law. His sister Carol married Rick Frances and ran a restaurant in Chryse Planitia, but they were separated. After that, she disappeared."

Lamont's brow wrinkles. "A missing person?"

"No. Not exactly. She left voluntarily. In fact, Rick Frances wanted to find her so they could finalize the divorce. But neither her brother Sol nor Rick know where she is."

"Strange," Lamont says. "But not a crime."

We walk to the door. It had automatically reverted to a solid black rectangle after they'd entered. Lamont studies it closely. "I don't remember you closing the door when we came in. How does it work?"

"The hotel imprints the palms of all the guests with maps of the hotel and codes for activating the door to their room. I'll show you." I slide my hand over the door and it disappears.

"That's almost as good as the bed in space," Sid says.

Lamont continues, "So if the serial killer is here, he would need to be imprinted with a code in order to open most of the doors. He wouldn't need it for public spaces where he could hide in plain sight." Lamont thinks for a moment. "I think Sid and I should check out that roller coaster that circles the hotel. Maybe the killer is on it. And then we should check out the ski slope where you can adjust the gravity and speeds. I always wanted to go up a hill fast and down a hill slowly."

"What's the thrill?" I ask.

"The thrill is I don't fall down, and I get to wear a cool skiing outfit."

Sid adds, "The serial killer could also be playing golf or tennis. Want to join us?"

"No, thanks. I want to go for a swim. Starr mentioned that there was a convention in one of the pool areas. I think he said 'Buddhist convention' but I'm not sure at which pool. Catch up with you later."

Lamont and Sid step through the doorway.

"You're sure going on all these activities is police business?" I call after them.

Lamont turns and waves. "Leave no stone unturned, Molly. Leave no stone unturned."

22

No one wants to join me for a swim. I change into a sweat suit, pack a tote, and palm hotel information to find the nearest pool. I see that if I walk quickly, I can be there in less than ten minutes. A group of people walk toward me from the opposite direction. They are among the heaviest, shortest, most made-up, and most overdressed of the guests I have yet seen. I interrupt their conversation, which I can hear is about where they should have dinner.

"Are you from Earth?" I ask a woman whose elaborate dangling earrings and ten-inch wide teased red hair frames her face. She shakes her bracelet heavy arm.

"How did you know?"

"I guessed, but I was also born there. I haven't been back in many years and haven't seen too many native born Earthlings currently living on Earth."

"Where do you live now?" she asks, giving me her once over that I don't think I've passed.

"Mars."

She lowers her eyes and turns her head to the side. "Oh there. It's so much smaller than Earth," she titters. The others nod.

"New Chicago, Mars. It's very nice."

"If you say so," she says walking away with her friends. I restrain myself from making a finger gesture. I see that so many on Earth still think they are the center of the universe. When I arrive at the pool, a sign reads "Convention." I assume it is the Buddhist convention. I think, *I'm just too tired to go to another pool, so I'll ask if I can join them.*

A man in a tie-dyed shirt and colorful bandana behind a reception desk says, "Our pleasure. Our organization encourages new members."

Of course, I think. *Buddhists would be friendly.* "Is the illusion of swimming in space turned on or off?" I ask.

"Definitely on. Does that bother you? Some people become disoriented and don't like it."

"No," I answer. "It's something I wanted to try. I guess as a Buddhist you feel closer to God swimming that way." He looks puzzled but releases the lock to the women's locker room.

A cheery, well-exercised looking attendant greets me and says, "Welcome. New member?" She hands me a locker key and a towel. I open the locker, disrobe, and put on my bathing suit.

She looks at me and frowns. "You're only allowed to bring the towel into the pool. You'll have to remove the bathing suit."

"Remove the bathing suit? I just bought it," I laugh. "Don't Buddhists wear bathing suits?"

"Buddhists? This is a Nudist convention."

"Oops!"

I dress and hurry away. The man at the reception desk yells, "Hey, take our card? We have other events."

I decide to go to the lobby. I check my palm map. The lobby is farther away than I thought. I scroll alternative routes. Two pass through ballrooms that are holding events. Don't want to go there. Another scroll shows an emergency service exit nearby that cuts time and distance.

The door is easy to find. A sign that says "Service Route for

Authorized Personnel Only" makes me think, *Maybe I shouldn't do this. But it saves so much time.* The door is heavy and opens with a struggle. I try to peer down the long deserted dim hallway, and the door slips: Click—lock. I yank the door. It doesn't budge. I try again. I bang on it until I'm exhausted. No one comes. I try to call Cortland on my palm, but a message says: "out of range." There is nothing to do but follow the passage. It shouldn't take long to find another door, but I wish the lighting were better.

At first, the hall slopes downward, making the walk easy. I pick up my pace. But after a while, the incline slopes upward. With more effort, I trudge on and on. Suddenly, I hear footsteps behind. "Hello," I call. "Anyone there? Hello?"

The footsteps stop. I listen for a door opening, or a vent rattling, but all I hear is silence. I think of the serial killer and wonder if he was the extra person on the space elevator. Footsteps start again. They get louder. Their pace is picking up. I strain to run faster. Perspiration rolls down my body. It's hard to catch my breath. They're closing in. I want to turn to see who is there, but that would slow me down. My mind flashes scenes of violence and murder. This doesn't help. The lights dim. I can barely see. I reach out to touch one wall to steady myself. This slows me down further, but I don't want to fall because that would be worse. The hall incline becomes steeper. Am I imagining that the steps behind sound closer? Not a time for any analysis. Just move it, Molly. Move it! Then moments before I feel like I am about to collapse from exhaustion, I see a sign with bright yellow letters: EXIT. Almost there. Almost there. I pull the door, straining with all my might. It doesn't budge. I hear a ripping sound, and then something crashes on my head. My vision clouds. I see dancing stars that I know are not part of any galaxy but my own blinking everywhere. I stumble and topple sideways. My right hand extends to break my fall. Then the dark swallows me whole.

23

WHEN I OPEN MY EYES, I can hardly move, have a terrible headache, and feel no weight, no gravity. I'm encased in one of the hotel's fluorescent green protective emergency suits that are in every room and hallway. I try to get my bearings, but everywhere is up and everywhere is down. When I move my arms and legs, I spin. I see the hotel not far off in space. A voice booms through the suit's intercom.

"Do you know where you are and what happened, Molly?"

"I see I'm floating outside the hotel in a protective suit, but I don't know what happened or how I got here."

"Do you remember walking in one of our inner passageways?"

"Yes. That's the last thing I remember. I remember hearing footsteps behind me, but the person didn't answer when I called."

"That's because he was wearing earphones so he could be in constant communication with the hotel's central control. There was an emergency."

"Emergency? What kind of emergency?"

"The hotel was in the path of a tiny meteoroid. We had just enough time to alert everyone to put on a protective suit."

"Like the one I'm in now."

"Yes. But when we did a head count, we couldn't find you. When we scanned the ship, we found you in one of the alternative service routes."

"What hit me?"

"You were not far from where the meteoroid punctured the wall. Its impact loosened a beam that fell on your head. Had you been a few feet farther, the meteoroid might have killed you. The engineer that we sent into the passage to find you carried a protective suit and found you unconscious on the floor. A few moments after he put you in the suit, the hole widened and you and he were sucked into space."

I see a man floating not far away. He waves. I wave back.

The intercom voice says, "We'll have both of you inside in a jiffy. All expenses for the rest of your stay and that of your family are on the house."

I lie on the bed in our room and turn on the hotel news. The first story is about the meteoroid. The next is about my rescue and the fact that the hotel will be picking up all expenses.

Jersey calls. "Are you alright?"

"You know I'm alright, Jersey. It was on the news."

"Well, can Trenton and I buy you a drink or treat you to dinner?"

"Nirgal Palace is picking up all of our expenses. It was on the news."

"Just remember I offered."

The next day there is an announcement that there is to be a costume ball, and costumes can be rented on level four in the props room next to the ballroom.

"Let's do it," the twins squeal.

"Not really my thing," I say.

"Dad, make her change her mind," Lois says. "It will be fun. Besides it might take her mind off Rick Frances and the restaurant stuff."

"What restaurant stuff?" I say.

"Oh just stuff," Lois says twirling a strand of long blonde hair.

Cortland says, "She has a point, Molly. Could be fun."

We go to the props room, which is lined with costumes of superheroes, historic figures, political figures, media stars, and cartoon figures.

Suddenly Becky stops and points. "Look, Lois, there's a costume of us, The Lunar Tunes! Let's take it. No one will know it's really us."

"Great idea," Lois says. "Then we can find out what people think of us."

An attendant wearing a David Bowie costume, the mask hanging around his neck, approaches and says, "And for you, madam and sir, may I suggest King Charles and his wife Camilla, both historic English figures."

We frown.

"Or the American historic figures, Bill and Hillary Clinton."

We frown more.

"Something more realistic then. How about Hans Solo and Princes Lea?"

I smile.

Cortland asks, "And how many of those have you rented already?"

"Twenty-seven but each comes in different colors."

But the masked ball is great fun, and I'm glad I decided to go. We watch Becky and Lois—The Lunar Twins look-a-likes who really are Becky and Lois—pretend to be Becky and Lois and laugh. When they are asked to sing, and they get up on a stage and do, an agent from a competing music agency wants to sign them because they sound so much like The Lunar Tunes.

The song Moon Rover plays. It's a song Cortland wrote for me long ago. We head for the dance floor. As we're dancing, someone in a large black cape keeps bumping into me. When after the third bump, I turn to protest and get a better look, all I see is the hooded back of a person walking away.

Cortland says, "Don't let it get to you, Molly. The room is crowded. Besides, we're have a nice time. And I got some ideas for the twins' next concert."

"You're probably right, as usual, sweetheart," I say kissing his cheek, suddenly tired. "But I'm ready to go. Let's call it a night."

When we return the costumes, the attendant is wearing his David Bowie mask. He checks our costumes for damage and looks to see if there is anything in the pockets.

"What this?" he says pulling a message cube from the Princes Lea costume.

"I don't know what that is. It's not mine."

"Well, it was in your pocket."

"Let me see what it says," I say wearily taking it and tapping. The message floats into the air. I read, "Stop snooping about who murdered Rick Frances or you'll end up as shredded wheat."

Feeling like a cloud of atoms whose magnetic attraction is blinking on-off-on-off, I drop the cube on the floor.

24

"YOU'RE GOING TO TELL LAMONT about that note, aren't you?" Cortland says sitting on his side of the bed. "If you don't, I will." He stands.

I say nothing. I feel like it's three in the morning, but it's only nine thirty.

"What are you waiting for, Molly?"

"I thought I might figure this out," I say forcing myself to be as detached as I can.

Cortland scowls and points to his palm.

"All right. You're right." I tap my palm.

Lamont answers with a strained voice.

"Did I wake you, Lamont? Catch you at a bad time?"

Lamont clears his throat. "You wouldn't call unless it's important. What's up?"

"Someone bumped into me during the costume ball and put a message cube in my pocket that said I should stop snooping around for answers concerning who killed Rick Frances or I would be shredded wheat."

"You should have told me about this immediately."

"I did as soon as I could."

"Let's hope there's no next time."

The next day I make a reservation for dinner in the most expensive restaurant, the Constellation Room. Becky and Lois preen and twirl endlessly in front of holographs of themselves. "We did say today, not tomorrow," Cortland calls through the adjoining door. "We want to go to the Starbright Lounge for a drink before dinner."

We are shown to the best table on a raised platform near the bar so we can see everyone and they can see us. People recognize the twins and ask for their autographs. Some ask how I am. Several try to give Cortland demo tapes.

Cortland and I order large Hadron Colliders. The twins order Lunar Lights. I am about to take a sip when I see Jersey and Trenton. I can tell Trenton is scanning the room because his head is cocked. He says something to Jersey, and they make their way toward us.

"Jersey and Trenton are coming," I say to the twins. "Be nice."

Lois rolls her eyes. Becky glares.

A hotel holographer circles closer and starts blinking his eye cam, taking several shots of me and my family that he hopes to sell after he displays them on a wall in the lobby. When Jersey and Trenton reach us and I air kiss Jersey and Cortland shakes Trenton's hand, the holographer blinks more images.

"We'll buy you a drink for your anniversary," I say. "Today is the actual day. Isn't it?"

Jersey grabs Trenton's hand. "Yes, eighteen years."

They sit.

Trenton looks better than I have ever seen him. His skin is the color of coffee with cream rather than a washed out whitish pink-yellow. I touch his arm. It's softer than I remembered. "Did you go to one of those tanning salons, Trenton? You look healthier."

"Androids don't go to tanning salons. I've been working

on creating a more natural look. Now I know I've succeeded. Notice anything else?"

"New hairstyle."

Jersey leans towards Trenton, pats his hair. "His new hair grows, not stuck on like a wig. He had to get a haircut."

"I don't know if that's an improvement," Trenton says. "Now I have to pay a barber."

"It's definitely an improvement. From the distance, one couldn't tell if you were an android."

"Really?" Trenton's eyebrows curl. "Never thought that day would come."

Cortland chimes, "And I love your jacket. In fact, everything you're wearing is very stylish. I saw a shirt like that at Mars Marcus, but even on sale, it was outrageously expensive."

"Made everything with my new clothes printer. I'm trying to develop it commercially, but so far the learning curve for the average person is very great."

"Very great," Jersey repeats. "It's hopeless unless you know string theory."

"I copied the dress from one in *Vague Vogue*."

"But I won't let him print me shoes," Jersey says. "Too much fun shopping for them!"

"Unless there are no feet," Trenton quips.

We give him a strange look.

"We might not need clothes in the future. Our bodies might adapt to temperature variations without needing a cover. In fact, we might even exist in other shapes and sizes."

I say, "Until that happens, I'm off to Mars Marcus."

"Hurry, Trenton," Cortland says, "I'd love a lower credit card bill."

Becky pushes her chair back from the table, points to Jersey's pinky, and says with obvious disgust, "Ooh, what's that?"

Jersey raises her hand and waves it around so everyone can

see the diamond cone that extends from it. "My new diamond pinky. Trenton made it for me."

"Guess Jersey won't need nail polish on it," I say, trying to sound upbeat.

There is an awkward silence while we reach for our drinks and sip.

Then two women approach and look at Trenton. They extend their hands. Both have diamond pinkies.

"Didn't think we would be meeting you here, Trenton," one says. "Special occasion?"

"My anniversary," Trenton answers.

"Congratulations," the other says. "By the way, all my friends love my pinky and want one just like it. I gave them your number."

They leave. Becky puts all her attention into her drink and finishes it.

Jersey says, "We're overwhelmed with orders." She lowers her voice. "That's how we were able to afford Nirgal Palace."

No one says anything.

Cortland waves to a waiter and says, "So, what'll it be? Hadron Colliders? Plutonian Pistols? Crab Nebulas? Inner Ring of Saturn champagne?"

Jersey says, "I'll have the champagne."

"And you, Trenton?"

"A double Exxon Sour with a twist."

Becky and Lois close their eyes shake their heads.

Cortland gives the waiter the order. "We're sorry," he says, looking down at Trenton, "I assume you're the one who wants the Exxon Sour. We don't serve them in the Starbright Lounge. You'll have to go to Silicone Slings. It's on deck six."

Trenton frowns. "I know where it is. Bring me a Carburetor Tune-Up instead."

"None of those either," the waiter says.

Trenton's eyes spin. "Then bring the whole bottle of

champagne."

"House special or Inner Ring of Saturn?"

"Inner Ring of Saturn"

Jersey puts her hand on Trenton's arm. Trenton says, "Many people say they are comfortable with androids, but what they mean is that they are comfortable being near one of us, not surrounded by so many. Anyway, we are having dinner at Silicone Slings. The winner of the Star Trek Data look-alike contest is going to sing his hit, 'Binary Code'. Want to join us?"

"Not tonight," Cortland says. "But get me his demo. *Sound of the Spheres* gave it a good review."

Becky flicks her long blonde hair and pipes in a loud voice, "Well, we're going to the Constellation Room for dinner."

"Suits you," Trenton says in a flat voice. I don't know if he means it as a compliment or an insult.

Jersey leans into the table and says, "Did you hear the news?"

"What news?" I say, hoping that the conversation is veering away from androids.

"They found the extra person that arrived on the space elevator."

Lois speaks for the first time since we sat down. "Was it the Cereal Serial Killer?"

I think of the note that was found in my costume last night. But my thoughts are interrupted when a bus boy comes with an ice bucket and bottle of champagne, puts it next to Trenton, opens it, and pours a small amount in a glass for him to taste. Trenton nods that it is accepted. Then he puts some roasted pecan berry rolls on the table. Jersey takes two and says, "No, it wasn't the Cereal Serial Killer. Just some guy who wanted to surprise his girlfriend by proposing to her at a nudist convention. They caught him when the nudists reported that although his girlfriend had come with their group, when they checked their numbers, they found that he was an extra person in the pool."

"That means the killer is probably still on Mars," I say. "I'd better call Frank and tell him to be on the lookout for anyone who orders cereal. Not that it means anyone who orders it is the Cereal Serial Killer, but why take a chance? Lamont and Sid should know this."

A voice booms behind me. "Hello, Molly!"

I turn. Lamont and Sid are sitting a few tables away wearing sunglasses and Hawaiian shirts and drinking margaritas from hollowed out pineapples with swizzle sticks shaped liked satellites.

They come toward us, pointing to the swizzle sticks. Lamont says, "Latest listening device."

I frown. "Were you eavesdropping on us?"

"Eavesdropping on everyone," Sid says. "But now that we know that the serial killer isn't here, and after we've played space basketball, bought as many duty free items that we can with our police discount, gotten a weightless massage, and caught the late show at the Starburst Theater with the Clickity Clacks…"

Cortland asks, "The Clickity Clacks? Never heard of them."

Sid says, "Leading castanet symphony orchestra from Lockheed crater on Europa, alternative music's biggest sensations." He thumps his chest. "Big fan. They revived Leroy Anderson's 'Typewriter Song'. It's a big hit."

Lois wrinkles her nose. "What's a typewriter?"

Becky says, "It was a device that made secretaries so attractive to their boss that they couldn't resist having affairs with them."

"Ooh, now I remember," Lois says. "And if they knew stenography, the boss got a divorce and married them."

25

AFTER DINNER IN THE CONSTELLATION ROOM, where Cortland and I share a four-pound lobster and Becky and Lois share one lean lamb chop, we consider going to Subsix, a disco copied from an underwater disco on Earth in the Maldives. But instead of real fish swimming outside as they are on Earth, these are robotic reproductions.

My palm signals a call. "Flo," I say to Cortland.

"Answer it or she'll keep calling."

I press receive and listen to her for a moment and then say, "Yes, Flo. Very good time. Probably will book the Garden Terrace Room. Did you call for another reason?"

Flo says, "Could we have the annual Tasters and Spitters Party at Molly's?"

I answer in a voice that makes people turn. "Definitely not! That's not the kind of publicity I want or need." Click. I look at Cortland. "She wants to have the annual Tasters and Spitters party at Molly's."

Cortland laughs.

"Holos on VueTube of people tasting my food and spitting it out would ruin business."

Cortland puts his arm around me. I lean in. He says, "Want to go back to the room or go hear the Clickity Clacks?"

Then Flo calls again.

I say, "A tasting and spitting at Virtual Vittles? Well I guess they never had anyone request that. I'll be happy to call Lena and Avery." Click.

I say to Cortland, "Let's go to Silicone Slings. I'd like to see Data sing 'Binary Code.'"

We take an elevator to deck six. When we walk toward Silicone Slings, we see that the lights are on but no music is playing.

Something's wrong.

We enter. The population, as it usually is, is mostly android. Two chairs and a table are overturned, dishes are broken, glass scattered on the floor. There are several androids holding a man who is wearing a torn android costume. He has a bloody nose and a black eye.

Trenton is leaning over an android on the floor whose chest is open and head connected to his body by a few dangling circuits.

Trenton looks up. "Molly? Why are you here?"

"Decided to come and hear Data sing. What happened?"

Trenton says, "Everyone was having a good time. I was sitting with Jersey drinking a Kuwaiti Oil Spill and suddenly I hear the high pitched screeching sound of a CPU being ripped from an android body."

Trenton points to the man in the android costume, who had been moved to a chair.

Cortland asks, "Did you call hotel security?"

"Sure I called, but no one came."

"No one came?"

"I was told that Nirgal Palace was not set up to handle this sort of thing. The best that they could do was send the perpetrator home and ship the wounded android to Mars for repair or recycling, depending on the severity of the damage."

I point to the man in the android costume. "Do you think he

will be prosecuted?" I ask.

Trenton says, "Laws about androids are still being written on planets, let alone on space satellites that don't always share the jurisdiction of the planet they circle."

Cortland grumbles, "But clearly it's a violation of rights."

"We see it that way, but not everybody does. Meanwhile, the hotel tells us that they're going to put a quota on how many androids can come to Nirgal Palace. I'm told that they don't want more than one for every fifty people."

"Is that legal?" Cortland asks.

"Off planet laws are more lenient than those on Mars. Lots of kinky stuff out here."

I look at the android on the floor. "Will he be OK?"

Trenton smiles. "Oh yes. Damage looks worse than what it is. Unlike Humpty Dumpty, he can be put back together again, but not here. He'll have to be shipped back to Mars."

We head back to our room holding hands but not saying anything to each other. Once inside and the door seals, I say, "I knew the problem with the growing android population was serious, but I never realized how serious. Elvis and Lulu may be extreme, but they do have a lot of support."

"Elvis and Lulu?"

"Our new in-laws. Burton's parents." I put my finger to Cortland's forehead.

"Oh them. Right." He sighs rolling an eye in my direction.

While Cortland takes a shower, I palm Lamont and ask if anything could be done.

Lamont repeats what Trenton told us. "It's out of our jurisdiction, Molly. Laws about androids—let alone androids on space stations—are still being written. Remember keep me in your loop if you get any more threatening notes."

"I will. Achoo!"

"You should cover your palm when you sneeze. I don't want to catch a cold."

"You can't get a cold through a palm, Lamont."

"Tell that to the atoms and molecules knocking each other out in my ear. I'm going to take two aspirins and call myself in the morning."

26

MY FIRST DAY BACK AT MOLLY'S, I open the door and see that everything looks as I had left it. Frank is sitting in his usual spot near the kitchen going over menus. He looks up, smiles. "Welcome back. Saw you on the holo floating in space. Did you know 'Property of Nirgal Palace' was on the back?"

"Just happy to be alive, Frank. What's been happening?"

"Harry celebrated his fortieth birthday in the bar by making a punch that's too small to serve for a large crowd and too large to serve for a small crowd, but we had no trouble polishing it off, and Vanna and Mario had no spats."

"Then I left Molly's in good hands. This was the first time I've been away since Molly's opened. I thought I would book a virtual vacation at Club Mood, but now I can go on a real one."

Flo calls. "Of course I didn't forget about calling Virtual Vittles," I tell her. "I was about to do it."

Frank sees me roll my eyes. I whisper, "Don't ask."

I hear Flo in my palm say, "What do you mean 'don't ask'?"

"I didn't say that," I cover. "I said, 'I'll ask'."

I move to another table. Lena answers my call. "I'm calling because my husband's cousin Flo, who spits for Tasters and Spitters, has asked me if you would host their annual party. Flo has been to VV. She knows there is no actual food, but she feels it would be a unique experience."

"Let me check this with Avery," Lena says.

I wait.

Avery's voice booms through my palm. "Love to do it, Molly. It would be great publicity—shows how versatile we are. There are some combinations like Zebra tartar with okra sauce and broccoli and wild turtle ice cream that haven't been put on our menu because we never get enough volunteers to try them."

I make a face that he can't see. "Well, you definitely have the right group. I'll tell Flo."

I go to the kitchen. Mario and Vanna are talking softly. I hear Mario say, "Well, if you really think the duck could use more garlic, go ahead and add it."

"You're sure?" Vanna asks sweetly. "I was torn between garlic and shallots."

"No, definitely go with the garlic. A first choice is usually right." Mario sees me in the doorway and cries, "Molly!"

"Molly," Vanna repeats. "You have to tell me about Nirgal Palace. Did Sol show you the Garden Terrace Room?"

"Loved it. But he wouldn't quote a price. Is the Outer Space Platform worth the added expense?"

"It is, Molly. It's a place that makes everyone think they're seeing God as one of their witnesses."

"Well, if you put it that way."

Jersey and I meet at Mars Yard. It's surrounded by a concrete wall like a fortress. She hands me a guest pass that Trenton gave her. "Follow me," she says marching ahead. I hold out my hand and feel an invisible but solid surface. "Hold your pass near the blue light like I'm doing and you'll get a full body scan. Then you can pass." When I enter, a voice booms. "One complete human who has a cavity in a back left molar and should go to the dentist and one human with an expensive diamond android pinky and regulation-sized android bladder."

"Sounds like my mother yelling at me," I say.

"Not mine," Jersey says in a voice that I won't question. We enter a covered walkway that goes from the street to the main entrance. Heavy double doors part. The cavernous lobby ahead throbs with people rushing in every direction. Glowing signs with floating arrows point to various departments.

Jersey heads to the bank of elevators, steps inside one, and says, "Third platform."

When the doors open, Trenton is there. "Saw you come on the monitor," he says bending and giving Jersey a peck on the cheek. "First time here, Molly? Shouldn't you be at the dentist?"

I frown. "Does the whole world now know I need to go to the dentist?" I sputter.

Trenton doesn't reply. Then, "This job is a big upgrade. State of the art forensic lab plus free lunch from The Flying Saucer Supermarket."

"Isn't that lunch wasted on you, Trenton? You usually have food supplement pills."

"Not when it's free, Molly. Not when it's free."

"It hardly seems fair that you can eat all of our foods, but we can't eat yours."

"That's one inequality in our favor."

Lamont sees us. He rises and stretches out his arms in greeting. "Hey, Molly, bring any treats?"

"Afraid not, Lamont."

"The old Molly used to bring me Chocolate Decadence cakes and donuts."

I smile. "The old Molly weighed 287 pounds."

Lamont pouts. "Not even a granola bar?"

I open my bag, rummage around. Ah, a granola bar. I give it to Lamont.

Sid zooms over. "And me?" he says. "What happened to all those candies you used to carry? The Chocolate Moons,

Tootsie Targets, Coconut Comets, Pluto Pistachios, Venus Vanilla Hearts, Ceres Chocolate Covered Cherries, Ganymede gumballs."

"Sorry, guys. You know how it is."

"Not really," Sid snarls.

"Come, Molly," Trenton says. "I'll show you my new lab."

Trenton opens the door to his laboratory. Smells of ozone and strange chemicals breeze toward us. The ceiling is covered with fluorescent panels. It is packed floor to ceiling with computer terminals, oscilloscopes, cables, and light fiber ducts. There are files, boxes piled like gray bricks, buttons in clear containers, switches, levers, jars of every shape, color and size, plus strange objects that look alive. Trenton points to a ladder. It has a small seat that moves up and down. It slides on a rail installed around the edge of the laboratory. "Want a ride, Molly?"

"No, thanks. Can see enough from here. Besides, I can't understand what most of this stuff is even after you explain it to me." I reach for what looks like a large white soup spoon. It is soft and warm to the touch. When I try to pick it up, two eyes appear on the handle and blink. I jerk my hand away and thrust it behind me.

"It won't bite, Molly," Trenton says. "It was a gift; a pet spooner from an underground lake on Titan."

We go back to Lamont, who motions to Sid to bring chairs. He and Jersey are drinking coffee from cups that say, "Formerly owned by public enemies number one hundred through one hundred and fifty."

"Sit," he says, rubbing his hands together. He takes a sip of coffee and peers over the top of the cup. "I was thinking about the Cereal Serial Killer."

"I thought you were going to give me news about who killed Rick Frances. People ask me if there has been any progress in the case. All you told me was that the autopsy report was negative for a poison in his system. Couldn't something be absorbed quickly and leave no trace?"

Lamont says, "Yes. Possible." He pauses then adds, "But Trenton did find something."

"And that is?" I say.

"We'll get to that."

"What's the matter with now?"

"Procedure, procedure. There is big pressure on me to tackle this first. Apparently, the mayor of New Chicago is going to marry cereal heir Wheatina Kellogg, who impressed him at a breakfast convention when she had an eighteen-hour breakfast."

"So?"

"She made a big donation to his campaign."

"Thought the police were immune to politics."

"Hey! How'd you think we got this new building? Fingerprint analysis?"

I say nothing.

Lamont rocks back and forth in his chair, which makes an annoying creaking sound. "Here's my idea," he says. "Maybe we could create an environment that the Cereal Serial Killer couldn't resist."

He rocks faster. "How about staging a cereal eating contest? I remember you had a Cereal Box Character party one week after Rick Frances' murder. Right?"

"Right. But nothing turned up."

Lamont gives me one of his "ah ha" smiles and says, "Well now's another chance to see if anything does. Isn't that a great idea, Molly?"

And before I can protest, Trenton says, "Lamont, that's brilliant!"

"Totally," Sid adds.

"Sounds good to me," Jersey nods.

"Then it's settled!" Lamont says. He unwraps the granola

bar that I gave him earlier and bites half of it.

"Not so fast," I say. "I want to run this by Cortland and my staff. My restaurant is known for its gourmet food. Hosting one cereal event was like showing a funny cartoon in between two serious films. You can do it once to leaven a mood, but too many of these events can ruin our image."

Lamont plows on. "Nonsense, Molly. You're overreacting. Didn't you host two champagne and caviar tasting events?"

"You're equating champagne and caviar to a cereal eating event?"

"He's right," Jersey pipes. "Have you considered political correctness, equality, diversity, multi-culturalism?"

"This is food, Jersey. No one cares about those things when it comes to food."

"Tell that to migrant workers."

"Well, they don't eat at Molly's Bistro."

"Yeah, but I bet they would like to."

"Amen," Lamont says, cocking his head. Then in a clear strong voice like wind in autumn that makes leaves fall so I know he's not backing down, he says, "That settles it. Besides, Sid's Shredded Wheat costume is still like new. Isn't it, Sid?"

Sid, shoulders sagging, resigned to his fate, sighs and says, "This'll be the alpha and bodega of cereal eating contests."

"It's alpha and omega of cereal eating contests," I say, still frowning.

"Omega it is!" Lamont cries. "Thanks. Done deal."

I reach into my bag and pull out a box of Chocolate Moons.

"Ah ha," Lamont says. "You had more than a granola bar in that bag."

"This is my personal box, and I'm not sharing it with anyone. I only have five left."

"Perfect number," Lamont says. "One for you, one for me, one for Sid, Jersey, and Trenton."

"I'll pass," Trenton says. "I think they're overrated. Do you have an Oily Chew?"

Everyone makes a face. Sid says, "Ugh! Oily Chews taste like motor oil."

Lamont narrows his eyes. "And how would you know what Oily Chews taste like? It's a candy for androids."

"Learned the hard way. Had the runs for weeks."

Trenton crosses his arms and says, "I discovered a few new things. The first is about your waitress, Jody. She was arrested for shoplifting on Mercury. The case was dropped. But we'll investigate her background and see if there's anything else or any connections."

"But everyone loves Jody. And she's a hard worker."

"And cute." Sid smiles.

Lamont says, "First answers are often lies. It takes time to get to the truth. But it certainly widens who and where the poison was planted."

Trenton continues, "The second is what I found from analyzing Rick Frances' DNA. Turns out he had a disease called progeria. Remember, we found a prescription with Mario's name on it for Grafton, the drug that controls progeria. They may have had similar conditions. I'll run new tests.

"Third and maybe most important, remember when we analyzed the results and found that there seemed to be one extra woman and one less man?"

"Oh," I say, passing around my last Chocolate Moon. "Yes, I remember that."

"Well, my analysis of everyone's DNA who was there that day shows that your headwaiter Frank Carol has the DNA of a woman."

My jaw drops. I'm too stunned to say anything.

Lamont hands me the empty box of Chocolate Moons. My jaw drops farther.

Jersey pipes, "I remember when we were at Restaurant Works and Frank signed his name. You noticed that he used a female spelling for Frances."

I nod. "It is also the way Rick Frances spelled Frances." I think for a moment. "This might explain why he was so reluctant to talk about his past. When I questioned him after Rick's murder and asked if he had been married, he became very uncomfortable. He said that he had had relationships and could I let it go at that. So I did."

Trenton says, "He, or should I say she, had a sex change operation. I did an analysis of every chemical in his blood. Turns out that he was filled with male steroids. Never would have been able to grow that goatee without them."

"So," Lamont says, "if Frank is definitely a woman, he may have had a relationship with Rick Frances in the past."

"Well," Trenton says, "and if his name isn't Frank Carol, could it be Carol Frances? Also, I did an analysis of the note found on Rick's palm signed C."

Jersey adds, "This doesn't mean Frank killed Rick Frances, just that he was probably married to him." She puts the tip of her diamond pinky in her mouth. I wince. I hope that she won't cut her tongue. At last she removes it, blows on it, points to Lamont with it, and says, "Where there's smoke, there's fire."

27

"YOU'LL NEVER BELIEVE WHAT LAMONT wants me to do," I say to Cortland as I pour two glasses of Pinot Grigio to go with one of his favorite dishes: spaghetti in white clam sauce.

Cortland takes a sip and listens.

"He wants me to host a cereal eating contest."

He laughs so hard wine goes down the wrong way. He coughs and coughs.

I hand him a napkin. "What's so funny?"

"The idea. You finally get the restaurant of your dreams, and it's a big success, and now the police want to use it to stage a cereal eating contest better held in a high school cafeteria."

The door opens. The twins enter. "What's so funny?" Lois asks.

Cortland tells them.

"You're kidding?" Becky says. "Don't enter us. We hate cereal. We came to talk about our Sonic Boom Crater concert."

"Have some of your mother's spaghetti and then we'll talk," Cortland says.

"Too fattening," Becky says. "I just ate an M&M."

Lois says, "I'll pass."

I look at my beautiful, talented twin daughters and think, *I love them, but they're eaters from hell.*

"I've not told you all the best part," I say gauging their reaction, which is wide-eyed silence. "Frank is a woman."

"Plant us on Pluto!" they say together.

Cortland's eyes widen.

"Do you think he killed Rick Frances?" Becky asks.

"No one knows. Just one more piece of the puzzle."

I go to VV to ask Lena if knew any more about Rick Frances. Avery gives me a warm greeting. VV is empty except for a florist who had delivered flowers and is leaving.

"Where's Lena?" I ask.

"In the back. She's getting a manicure and a pedicure. She's been so busy that she hasn't given herself any down time. Her friend Polly is a professional manicurist. They go way back to high school in Chryse Planitia. They should be finished any moment. Do you want to wait? I have real coffee."

"No coffee, but I'll wait. You and Lena also go way back. You both come from Chryse Planitia."

"Yes. We met at engineering school. I thought I wanted to be a VV engineer like Lena, but it turned out the science of virtual reality was way over my head. I'm better at business and sales. Lena and I kept in touch. She said that if she ever got a foot in the door, she would recommend me as a front man—working the room, seeing to details. She was good to her word."

"Were you and Lena ever romantically involved?"

"I wanted to, but she had an on-again off-again affair with Rick Frances. When they finally hammered out a business deal, any romance they might have had cooled. Rick also had plenty of other woman friends."

Lena and Polly emerge from a back room laughing. Polly points to Lena's feet, "Great open-toed shoes. It shows off my handiwork." She sees me and stops. "Molly! What a surprise!"

"Beverly?" I say. "I didn't know you knew Lena."

"You never asked."

She looks at my feet. "No open-toed shoes?"

"You only did one foot, Beverly."

"Oh yeah, right. Come back for the other one."

Avery looks at Polly. "Beverly?" he asks.

"Beverly Hills, Polly Pox, same person," I say.

"Beverly Hills is my professional name," Beverly says, thrusting her shoulders back.

"Avery just told me you two went to high school together," I say.

"Yup. Best friends," Lena says. "But I loved science. Polly loved fashion. Of course, I didn't have Polly's great looks. Every guy was crazy about her." Beverly beams. Lena continues, "You know, Polly, I can't get used to calling you Beverly. You'll always be Polly to me."

"It's OK," Beverly says. "It's nice to hear my old name from old friends."

"I never met so many people who come from one place," I say.

"Named after the plains of the golden land of Chryse," Avery says.

"I know. Home of the Viking One lander," I say, showing that I know my history.

"So?" Lena says. "Not so unusual that people who know each other in the past stay in touch."

"No, it isn't. But your associate Rick Frances has been murdered," I say. "That's unusual."

No one says anything.

"Have you heard about Frank Carol, my head waiter?"

"Frank? Nice guy," Avery says. "What?"

"You'll hear this eventually, so I might as well tell you. Frank had a sex change operation. He's originally a woman."

Lena sits. Beverly puts her hand to her mouth. Avery's jaw drops.

"So none of you knew."

"Knew?" Beverly rolls her eyes. "I thought he was cute!"

I find Frank sitting at his usual corner table reading a tablet that lists the day's specials. He takes a butter cookie from a white dish in front of him and nibbles. When he sees me, he puts the cookie down and peers over the top of the tablet like a sharp shooter in a mask. Then he says, "Lamont called me to Mars Yard. They know my secret. So I guess you do, too."

I inch into a seat opposite him and nod.

He puts the tablet down and looks me in the eye. "Your friend Trenton figured out I'm not Frank Carol. I'm Carol Frances, Rick Frances' ex-wife." He pauses and makes a slow circle with his finger on the table. When he sees that I don't react, he continues. "I did palm the note that was found on Rick's palm. Never thought it would incriminate me in something as heinous as his murder or I wouldn't have put it there."

"And that's why you looked familiar to Rick when he was in my office."

"Yes. But I wasn't ready to meet him. Changing one's sex involves cultural changes, not only physical ones. It was more difficult than I thought."

I say nothing.

"I worked very hard to keep my marriage together."

"What happened? Was it all about sex?"

"No."

My eyebrows rise.

"Although I might not have been the best sex partner, I knew how to fake a good performance. Besides, I loved Rick. I thought that in spite of my problems, continuing the way we were was best for both of us."

"How so?"

"We jointly owned our restaurant, Cream. I loved the work. Best time of my life. When we courted, I thought Rick loved food as much as me because he wanted to open a restaurant. But I learned that it was not food that he loved. It was everything else about a restaurant that he loved: the social life, the architecture and interior design, the location, value of the real estate, working with the staff, even doing the bookkeeping. Rick could live on food supplement pills."

Frank sighs. I wait. He continues, "Well, when Rick read about virtual reality, he was fascinated. He couldn't understand why I didn't share his enthusiasm. I thought it a passing phase. But the more he learned, the more excited he became. Finally, he said that he wanted to close the restaurant and open a virtual one.

"I asked why couldn't I keep the restaurant and he do the virtual one. But we only had enough money for one place. We argued bitterly."

"Nasty," I say.

"Then Rick met Lena, who was looking for a job in virtual reality. Lena's friend was Beverly, who had left studying virtual reality in college to become a model. She was young, gorgeous, and always hanging around. When my brother Sol told me that Rick and Beverly were having an affair, I was relieved because by that that time, I knew that I wanted the sex change. I thought it a good time to make a clean break."

"Half the lawyers I consulted with said that I would get more of a settlement if I remained a woman; the others said it shouldn't stop me from going through with the operation. I might get a sympathy vote knowing how much I suffered. Plus, Rick already had admitted that he was having an affair. So I went ahead and got the operation and figured I could hammer out the divorce details later."

"What happened to the restaurant?

"Rick sold it. The new owners changed the menu and changed the name from Cream to Creamed Cheese."

I wince. "I guess Rick kept all the money from the sale."

"He did because he didn't know where to find me. It was stupid not to be in touch with him or anyone else. But the adjustment to becoming a man was much harder than I thought. I let myself drift from one thing to another. My brother Sol told me that Rick filed a missing person's report, but the police told him that because I had left voluntarily, there was little they could do. And, of course, if they did do a search, they were looking for a woman, not a man."

"Did Sol decide to get a job at Nirgal Palace after you left and the restaurant was sold?"

"Yes. He hasn't seen me since I had the operation. You might remember that he almost saw me when you and Vanna and he were in the kitchen after your lunch at VV. Every time I call him to tell him I'm alright, he says he doesn't know if it really is me because he's not used to hearing my deep male voice. And since he told me that my transformation still upsets him, I thought it best to wait."

I pluck a chocolate cookie from the dish and say, "A reunion is long overdue." I finger another cookie but put it down. "So you knew Beverly Hills and Lena Fermi way back when."

"You mean Polly and Lena. Polly was a beauty who every guy in Chryse Planitia wanted to sleep with. I met them, but didn't know either of them well."

"After Rick died, *Restaurant News* reported that Avery and Lena were the new owners of VV."

"They're lying. Not true. I still own half. In fact, now that he is dead, I own the whole thing."

I say, "Maybe Rick made a new will and left his half to Lena."

Frank shakes his head. "Until a will is produced, it's their word against mine. When we were together, everything from his estate was to go to me if he died. If he changed the beneficiary to Lena and she does own half, she might have given Avery a piece of it to keep him from opening his own place, becoming competition."

"Maybe they said that they own VV in the hopes that if you turned up, you would sell them your half, and if you didn't, they could try to claim the whole thing."

Frank nods, frowns. "Thought of that."

"Why did you palm Rick a note? Why not simply call him?"

"I wanted to call but was afraid that he would react to hearing my deep voice the same way Sol did. So I never made the call."

"Now that you've lied about knowing anything about the message on Rick's palm, the police will question you again. Why didn't you just tell the truth if you did nothing wrong?"

Frank lowers his eyes. "Didn't want to get further involved. Rick was dead. I was upset."

"But you're Rick's widow, or should I say widower, who never got anything from the sale of Cream that you jointly owned. And you're not officially divorced. We must find that will."

Frank nods.

"This should be duck soup for Mars Yard to check," I say. "Not hard for the police to go into past records."

My palm signals a call. I look and see. It's from Lulu. "I have to take this call. I assume you have everything under control for dinner."

Frank rises, leaving the two remaining cookies on the plate. He pushes his chair under the table and walks toward the kitchen. I call after him. "So what's tonight's special?"

Frank half turns and calls over his shoulder, "Lamb pulled over a rack with a light madeira mint sauce."

"And the soup?"

Frank turns fully around, laughs, raises his hands and says, "Duck."

28

EMERGENCY: MY PALM SIGNALS.

Becky is sobbing. "Mom, Burton's father was in a terrible accident."

"Slow down, sweetheart. What happened?"

"Elvis was in a parade protesting android rights, and the float he was on exploded. Seven died, and no one knows if he will live."

"Where are you now, sweetheart?"

"At the hospital."

"Which one?

"New Chicago Specific."

Becky is in the hall outside Elvis' room pacing and running her hands through her hair. Her eyes are two deep craters. We exchange worried looks. She points inside the doorway.

Lulu is leaning over a floating platform that supports Elvis. He is connected to an elaborate life support system whose monitors beep from every corner of the room. There is a sphere encased in a yellow covering that I assume is his head at the top of the platform. The fine nano-tubes extruding from it make it look like the shimmering rays of the sun. Everything else looks either like a series of red cubes or a blue pyramids. I think of Trenton's lab. Becky tells me that this is a life support room, and Elvis can't live outside of it unless major adjustments to his body are made.

Lulu looks up when we enter. She appears transformed by a tornado: delicate with worry, fragile with shock.

Lulu says, "I'm happy you're here, Molly. Just this morning before the parade, Elvis and I had installed a new virtual program that would simulate a shopping excursion to Pluto's moon, Charon. No one wanted to go there even after they offered the solar system's only Master's Degree in assembling children's toys on Christmas Eve. So after copious research, Elvis discovered that the one place women would go in spite of the threat of radiation, terrorism, being in a meteor shower, and risk breathing toxic gases was a designer shoe outlet." Sob. Sob. "You can try on all the shoes you'd like virtually." Sob. Sob. "And, for a limited time only…" sob sob, "free shipping!"

I put my arm around Lulu. "Let's sit in the waiting area? Have you eaten? Becky can get something from the cafeteria." I nod to Becky, who pivots away on a booted heel.

Lulu collapses into the first empty seat and says in a cracked voice, "The bottom line is that Elvis won't live unless he becomes an android. The doctors say synthetic biology has outpaced all other forms of medical treatment. In the long run, biological data is much more unstable."

I say nothing.

She takes a handkerchief from her pocket and blows her nose. "And you know how Elvis feels about androids!" She takes a deep breath then, "Ah…choo! The doctor also told me that the word 'android' has been replaced by 'enhanced human.' It won over the term 'transhuman' by one vote."

"Enhanced human does sound better."

Lulu sighs. "Does it matter? An android by any other name is still an android."

"Wouldn't you rather have him alive than dead and gone?"

"Yes, but can I live with him if he's going to be miserable?"

"You don't know that he'd be miserable. Shocked at first, but when he realizes the advantages..."

"What advantages? He would be an android."

"My friend Jersey has been married to one for ten years. Would you like to talk to her?"

"Married to one? Is she normal? Is she happy?"

"Yes, very normal. She met her husband Trenton in a hospital when she was getting new eye implants and he was getting a tune-up."

"Eye implants? Then she's been enhanced."

"But people have been getting artificial parts—new hips, elbows, all kind of stuff—for a long time. It's just a question of degree."

"Jersey and Trenton? Aren't they the ones who helped you solve the case of the poisoned Chocolate Moons a few years ago?"

"That's right."

"But you never said Trenton was an enhanced human."

"You didn't ask."

"It never crossed my mind to ask." Lulu pauses then says, "I don't think it would have gone over big with Elvis."

I say, "Most of Trenton's body was destroyed in a racing car accident. Trenton said the decision was easy: better to be an android that could have a relatively normal life than be a brain in a bottle or dead."

Lulu sighs. "Dr. Kaddish Kurzweil told me that there is usually a way to communicate with the patient so they understand what has happened and either agree to the procedure or not. But in Elvis' case, the links are too weak; the process might not be successful. A transformation of someone with damage as extensive as Elvis' has never been achieved. So it is up to me." Lulu shakes, disbelieving her choice to be made. My arm steadies her.

We see Becky. "Brought some hot soup," she says. "It's easy

141

to eat."

I open the container and hand it to Lulu, who takes a sip and puts it down.

"I was about to tell Lulu about Jersey and Trenton."

"Oh," Becky says, then remains silent.

I ask Lulu, "Would you like to talk to Jersey? I can call her now."

Lulu nods. "What have I got to lose?"

I palm Jersey and explain. Then Lulu taps her palm into Jersey's number and listens. I click off to give them privacy.

Then I hear Lulu say, "You mean there is no tossing and turning? He can turn himself off and on to go to sleep and awaken, no hot and cold rooms, no getting sick? Tune-ups instead of check-ups, no learning curves—he can download new information and apply it immediately?"

Then Lulu listens for a long time. After a while she says, "And sex?"

After another, longer pause Lulu says, "You mean he can program himself to fulfill every need and desire? No complaining or bad jokes about how slow women are?"

A pause then, "All night?"

Then, "Nooo, really! I always wanted to try that, but Elvis wouldn't hear of it."

Another long pause followed by, "Case closed. I'll do it!"

I wonder what Jersey said to Lulu, but this is not the time to ask.

29

LULU CALLS. ANXIOUS VOICE. Elvis' new body is ready and could Cortland, Becky, and I come and be with her and Burton when he wakes. She tells me that she sent his favorite clothes so the nurses could dress him before we arrive.

We walk through a maze of hallways to the Enhanced Human area of the hospital. We take an elevator driven by an enhanced human who wears a green uniform that says "Enhanced Human Elevator Operator" over the left breast pocket. He bends our ears telling us how lucky he is to have this job and that we should rewrite the constitution from "we the people" to "we the created."

We exit on the ninety-ninth floor.

Dr. Kaddish Kurzweil greets us with his impenetrable brown eyes. He curls his mouth upward in a half smile. When no one returns his smile, he says, "Call me Kaddish."

"Isn't that the name of the Jewish prayer for the dead?" Cortland asks.

"Yes. It really means sanctification. It's all about praising God's greatness and eternity despite the loss."

This explanation makes Lulu turn to me and sob. I put my arm around her and give Kaddish a serious frown.

"It's a family name," Kaddish pipes. "My ancestor was Ray Kurzweil, an early promoter of artificial intelligence."

Cortland says, "Thought his only contribution was the sixty-four-note polyphony."

"That too. Wish he could be here today to see Elvis awaken, but he's unveiling a great scientific breakthrough. Something on the level of man's first artificial heart."

"Really?" Cortland says.

"It's a cow that produces no-calorie, pasteurized, homogenized chocolate milk. Want to buy stock options? My brother is a broker."

"What are you talking about?" Lulu asks, feeling more composed.

"Business and pleasure," Kaddish says, opening the door.

The room is bright and sunny and looks more like a room in a luxury hotel than a hospital.

Elvis, or the body that is now Elvis' body, lies on the top of a made bed; his head is raised slightly on a pillow encased in a light blue case. He has been dressed in his clothes. And, as we have been told to expect, his face is covered in gauze with cutouts for his eyes, nose, mouth, and ears to limit the shock when he sees himself.

"We'll keep him here a few days to adjust," Kaddish says tactfully. "He is going to feel stronger, have finer vision and hearing, and learn that he can eat anything without gaining weight. When we see him relax and he fully understands what has happened to him, we remove the face covering. Some new enhanced humans want a few tweaks like being made taller or different color hair. In the end, however, everyone who has had this procedure has thanked us for saving their life."

Lulu says, "There is always a first time."

Kaddish looks at Lulu and without any expression, says, "I understand."

Lulu sighs and sighs again.

"Ready?" Kaddish asks.

Lulu nods, grabs my hand.

We wait. At first, we think nothing is happening. We wait longer. Then, when we think that nothing is going to happen, Elvis' eyes flutter and open. He raises his arms and runs his hands over his covered face. He turns his head and sees Lulu and smiles. Then he swings his legs over the side of the bed. Sits up, extends his arms, and stretches. "Feels like I just had the best sleep of my life. I feel like a trillion starbucks!" he says. "But why are my hands and face covered?" He sees the rest of us off to the side. "Why are you all here? Where am I?"

Lulu stiffens. She forces herself to step closer and says in a voice flattened to minimize trembling, "What is the last thing you remember, sweetheart?"

"I remember the protest parade. And then…"

"And then what?" Lulu prods, voice wobbling.

"A strange chemical smell. Then everything went black."

"There was a terrible explosion, sweetheart. You just woke from something like a coma."

Elvis says nothing. Then he snaps, "Coma? Coma? What kind of coma?"

"It's been almost a month since the day of the parade," Lulu says.

"A month? In something like a coma?"

Burton comes near and grabs his hand. "It's great to have you back, Dad."

Cortland takes a step closer, waves, and makes a thumbs up. Becky and I smile.

Elvis stands and stretches again. "I feel so good! In fact, if I didn't know better, I'd say I feel like I used to in my twenties." He shakes his right arm. "No creaking elbow, no arthritic shoulder." He does a deep knee bend. "Don't feel any strain in my legs or back; could do a hundred of them. When do I go home? Do I need these things on my face and hands?"

Kaddish says, "Those coverings will be on a few more days to protect the tender new skin on your face and hands. Now that you're awake, you must realize how badly you were hurt in the explosion. Adjustments had to be made or you wouldn't have survived. Some of these adjustments enhanced your bodily functions. If you don't like the settings, we can change their strength. It may take a little while to get use to all of them."

"Well, Doc, I never felt better." He points to Becky and me, who are whispering. "In fact, I can hear Molly and Becky. They're whispering that I am doing so well. Isn't that right?"

"Right," I say. "That's exactly what we said."

"I never could have heard that from this distance before. What's not to love? Doc, you're a genius!"

"Now that you know how well you can hear, while everyone is here, let me show you your vision." Kaddish removes a pair of glasses from his pocket and puts them on. "This is so I will see the same things you can see naturally, Elvis." He walks to the window, lowers the blinds, and turns off the lights.

The room instantly becomes pitch black. "Hey!" I yell, reaching for Cortland and Becky's hands.

Elvis asks, "Why do you look scared, Molly? Why did you grab their hands?"

"How does the room look to you, Elvis?" Kaddish asks.

"Pretty much the same. Slightly dimmer. No big deal."

"Well, for us it's pitch black," Cortland shouts. "Turn on the lights."

"You mean I'm seeing you in the dark?"

"All the way from infrared to ultraviolet."

No one says anything.

Kaddish raises the blinds. "We need to keep you here until you're comfortable using your new skills."

"Whatever you say, Doc. You're the boss. What happened to my friends on the float?"

"I'm afraid they didn't make it. Only you survived."

Elvis sits on the bed. "Oh God! No!"

"Molly," Cortland says, "Elvis and his family need time alone. We should go. Coming, Becky?"

Becky walks toward Burton. He puts his arm around her. "I think I'll stay," she says.

Cortland says, "Great to see you up and running, Elvis. We all missed you." He turns to me and says, "Let's go home, Molly. I want to send my new group The Bottlenecks a song I wrote."

"What's it called?" I ask.

"'The Commuter'."

30

AT MY DESK IN MY OFFICE I palm Lulu. She answers in a measured voice. "Becky must have told you how well Elvis did the next few days after you saw him."

"She did," I say. "In fact, she and Lois visited a few times. They told me that he made jokes about how the doctors made him into a superman. And, in a way, they did."

"Then?"

"Then a few days later, the doctors told me they thought he was ready to learn the truth."

"I'm braced."

"So next day, we went to the hospital. I sat and held his covered hand. When the doctors came in, they told him that the reason he feels so well is because the only way he could survive the explosion that destroyed all of his body except for a few brain cells was to remake him."

"What did he say?"

"He said he didn't understand. So they repeated it again adding that remake meant he was rebuilt cell by cell into an enhanced person. Then he asked, 'What's an enhanced person?'"

"Oh. Oh."

"When they said it meant that his consciousness had been

placed into an android body, he didn't believe them. He said that he felt just like he always did, only healthier and stronger. Then he accused them of being part of a subversive plan to convert people who protested the growth of the android population to more sympathetic views."

"Then the doctors asked him if he thought having dental fillings make a person less of a person."

"He must have said, 'Of course not'."

"Yes. That's what he said."

"Then they asked about a hip replacement. And he said that made no difference, too. Then they asked him, if a person had a stroke and a new connection in his brain using a man-made material that circumvented the damaged area and restored full function, would that matter?"

"What did he say?"

"He thought about it for a long time, but finally, he said no, it wouldn't matter. The person was still himself. Anyway, they went on and on with different parts of the brain and body and Elvis seemed to be agreeing, but he was getting increasingly agitated. Then..."

"Then?"

"Then he jumped up and shouted frantically, I know where you are going with this and I quote Matthew 16:26 'What good will it be for a man if he gains the whole world, yet forfeits his soul?' I was speechless. I didn't even know he read the Bible. We're not religious people."

"Guess he and all his friends are afraid they will lose their souls if all their organic parts are replaced by inorganic parts."

Then Kaddish said, "Book of Proverbs chapter 23 verse 7: 'As a man thinketh in his heart, so is he'."

"Then?"

"He fainted. His CPU crashed."

"The doctors wanted to revive him immediately. But I needed time to think about what had happened. So they explained the pros and cons, which I hardly understood, but in the end, I said revive him because Elvis would be able to make the decision himself."

"I would have done the same thing had it been Cortland."

"After he was revived, Kaddish asked him if he understood what had happened, and he said that he did. Then they asked him if he felt love for me, and he said yes. He loved me the same as he always did. But then he asked if they thought God would love a machine the same way he would love an organic person."

"What did Kaddish say?"

"Kaddish spent a lot of time explaining that he was not just a machine—he was far greater than the sum of his parts, the same way an organic being is not just the sum of its parts. Then Kaddish said the one thing that made him pause."

"And that was?"

"He said it was impossible to know the mind of God because currently we are not smart enough or evolved enough to know that. What was important was that we love, we empathize, and we grow."

"I could tell Elvis was skeptical, but then he said, 'Never thought of it that way.' And he wanted to mull it over and say a prayer to Hallowed."

"Hallowed?"

"Hallowed. Hallowed. That's God's name."

"I guess God has a lot of names: Jesus, Buddha, Krishna...but I never heard of Hallowed."

"Let me refresh your memory. 'Our Father who art in heaven, Hallowed be thy name.'"

Gulp!

Lulu continues, "Then Kaddish asked Elvis if they could remove his face and hand coverings, and he said OK."

"How did he react?"

"He didn't seem to mind when they removed his hand coverings. In fact, when he saw how young and smooth they looked, he flexed them and clapped. Then he rolled up his sleeves to see his new arms. But when they removed his face covering, and he saw his new face, he crashed again."

"Oh, oh!"

"So they put the covering back on his face and woke him up. When he regained his composure, he agreed to go home, but only if the doctors let him keep his face covered."

"Are you at the hospital now or at home?"

"Home. Been home a while. But Elvis refuses to remove the face covering even when he's asleep. However, he's fascinated by what he can do. He can hold his breath for three hours. Has worn out seven treadmills, five exercise bikes, curls two hundred pounds with one hand, reads three books at a time—that he likes—he learned eight new languages including Jovian slang and Saturian hip hop. He likes the media implant the doctors inserted on his right wrist and the latest iPalm on his left. But he won't go out. Some of his old friends called and want to see him. Of course, they don't know about his transformation. Elvis told them that his face was badly burned and he has to wear a protective covering on his face for an indefinite period of time."

"How did that go over?"

"They said they understood. They're happy he survived. But he pushes them off and refuses to go out."

"Tell him about Jersey and Trenton and ask him if they can come and visit. I'll come too."

"Good idea. But it must be at night because he won't want anyone seeing Trenton come into the house."

"Would it be better if Trenton came in his carrying case?"

"Carrying case?"

"Trenton found a way to collapse most of his body so it fits into a special case. I love Jersey and Trenton dearly, but truthfully, they are very cheap. Trenton did this because he realized that if he was in the case, he and Jersey could buy one ticket and travel two for the price of one."

"But if more androids did that, they might travel more."

"What's wrong with that?"

"If they had more money to spend on real vacations, they might book fewer virtual reality vacations. That would hurt our business."

"Didn't think Elvis would do business with androids."

"Even though we are protesting certain android rights and don't think they should be full citizens, we can't afford to turn away business. Money is money: lifestyle neutral."

Rather than talk about double standards and hypocrisy, which is what I want to do, I say, "Should I ask Trenton to come in his travel case?"

"Yes. I'd love to see how it works," Lulu says. She looks down for a moment then raises her eyes. "Can I ask you something else?"

"Of course. What?"

"Elvis says that just before he drifts off to sleep, he hears a voice in his head that says, 'Electric dreams presented to you by Philip K. Dick, Inc.' Isn't he the guy who wrote 'Do Androids Dream of Electric Sheep?'"

"Yes, but as to the voice, you'll have to ask Trenton. The doctors may have implanted a commercial to offset your expenses."

An hour before dinner, Vanna knocks on my office door. "Mario wasn't well and went home," she says. "He agreed to let me do tonight's dinner. I told him to go to a doctor, but he said all he needed was rest. Except for a few of the specials that Mario won't tell me how he makes like roast duck with skin as thin and crisp as a potato chip, the menu will be the same."

"Not to worry, Vanna. If I hadn't hired Mario first, I would have hired you as my number one. In fact, I'm always afraid that someone will snatch you away and make you their head chef."

"I know, Molly. But I love working here, and there are few so creatives that I can learn so much from. Mario's one of them."

31

WHEN I FINALLY GET AROUND TO telling my staff that I got roped into hosting a cereal eating contest, everyone groans. "Not cereal again," Jody sighs. "Is this considered overtime?" "This could be dangerous," Frank says. "The real Cereal Serial Killer might come." Everyone shakes their head.

Harry the bartender snaps a towel and says, "Wouldn't someplace like the asteroid Ceres be a better place to have this contest? Lots of organizations have been booking their new convention space. I was offered a job to train a team of bartenders there."

"You were?" I ask, concerned, voice rising.

"Yup. But I turned them down. Why leave a hot bistro in New Chicago with a wonderful owner for a rock in the middle of nowhere?"

"Hear! Hear!" everyone cries.

"I could call Lamont and ask. I didn't realize you all felt so strongly about this."

"We have our standards!" Mario chimes.

"Standards, standards," others repeat. Then everyone talks at once. I hear disjointed fragments. Jody says, "Of course a Yoko Ono is a sushi. It's more expensive than yellow tail."

Frank interrupts Vanna talking to Harry. "'Over the

Rainbow' was written about Venus because their thick atmosphere makes the best rainbows in the solar system."

Mario says, "The reason sports fans put mustard on hotdogs during ball games is to show their team that they have the faith of a mustard seed that they will win. That was a tie breaker question on *Spice Up Your Faith.*"

Just as the room goes operatic, Lamont calls. I wave my hands over my head and point to my palm. The room quiets.

"Hi, Lamont."

Everyone leans towards me.

"Of course we will be disappointed," I say with a big smile making a thumb up. "I'll let my staff know."

"Know what?" Frank asks.

"He said he thought about the cereal eating contest, and if the killer shows up, it would be easier and safer if we held the event at the convention center on Ceres."

Round of applause.

My office computer blinks several messages. The first is Becky. The second is Trenton, who says that an analysis using a new scope that picks up micro evaporation rates and levels of viscosity that other devices can miss found two ingredients in Rick Frances' body that if there was enough, could make a lethal poison. He's still doing tests on the dosages. One came from Ceres and another from Mercury where it was manufactured at Crystal City, a new city on top of Mercury's northern polar ice. Sid is checking to see if anyone on Mars made a recent journey there. The last message is from Holly Wood, who asks me to call.

I decide to answer in the order that they were received. I set the palm to visual so Becky and I can see each other.

After two rings, Becky's holo image shimmers, stabilizes, and projects in front of me.

"What's up, sweetheart?"

Becky says, "I was shopping on Rodeo Dive for gifts to give my bridesmaids and found a sculpture of a tiny foot. I realized that I could put a gold charm inside, and it would make an adorable gift. The store owner said he would engrave it with the date of my wedding and the words 'walking down the aisle' for free."

Immediately I remembered the little foot that I had seen in Beverly's apartment that she said Rick Frances had given her.

"Mom, Mom. Are you listening? What do you think?"

"Lovely idea, Becky. What store on Rodeo Dive had it?"

Becky thinks and says, "Fingers and Toes, between Fallen Arches and Bended Knees."

Next I palm Trenton and say, "You're sure the poison came from Crystal City on Mercury?"

"Definitely," Trenton mumbles.

"What? Are you eating something?"

"Eating a Motor Oil Moon, a new candy from Exxon; it has chocolate on the outside and motor oil on the inside."

I gag. "Sounds terrible. I can't fathom the combination."

"It's a treat for an enhanced person. Regular supermarkets won't sell these products because they're dangerous to humans. Fuels, a new supermarket chain that caters to enhanced people, just opened in my neighborhood. You have to be over eighteen to shop there. They even carry Brand X."

"No kidding, Brand X?"

"Yup. Brand X's gone legit."

"You said that Sid was checking to see who has been to Mercury in the last year. Does he know yet?"

"He's found four people. The only one he is sure about is Jody, your waitress. She definitely made a trip. Can you talk to her about it without arousing her suspicions?"

Holly Wood is the last call.

"Hi Holly, it's Molly returning your call."

Pause.

"No, I don't know if Cortland heard the tapes that you gave me, but I did give them to him. Sometimes he has an assistant listen first."

Pause.

"You have something to tell me about Beverly that I might not know, but you won't tell me until he has listened to your tapes."

Pause.

"Then I'll have to call you back."

I close my palm, rise, and go to Rodeo Dive. I find Fingers and Toes and go in.

All the tables and shelves have cute things for hands and feet. Then I spot the foot sculpture. A saleswoman zeroes in. "That's a best seller," she says. "We're trying to get customers to buy two, but everyone wants only one. Give you a discount if you take a second."

"How long have you had these?"

"Oh, a few months. Let me think. I believe they came in about four months ago."

"You're sure. Not before that...say a year ago?"

"Definitely not a year ago." She picks one up, turns it over, and points to a date near a copyright mark. "Look," she says showing me, "only made five months ago."

Rick Frances was murdered about three months ago, meaning he must have bought the foot and visited Beverly soon after the foot sculptures arrived in the store, I think.

"A friend of mine bought one of these and then he died," I say. "Any chance you could tell me exactly when he bought it?"

"I will if you buy two."

"OK, I'll buy two. His name was Rick Frances."

"Sounds familiar. Hey, he wasn't that guy who was murdered at Molly's Bistro?"

"Yes, him."

"I remember. He came with a woman who said she gave

pedicures, Beverly something. I saved her card. Just a sec. And I'll get you the exact date."

When I get back to my office, Flo calls and in a high speed, animated voice says, "Don't know if you heard, but our Tasting and Spitting event at VV was a sensation. Lena and Avery were wonderful. We signed a contract to do it again next year. We also want to do more specialized things like breakfasts and pizza events. In fact, we just got a new member—a cereal specialist. I think he said that his name was Sol."

Mental note: *Tell Lamont.*

Then I ask Cortland if he has listened to Holly's music. He tells me that it was not unique, but better than he expected. If it helped, he could book her into a backup chorus.

Holly buzzes me into her apartment. I tell her what Cortland said, and she's thrilled. She says that Beverly, Rick, and Lena knew each other in Chryse Planitia. I say that I already knew that because I went to VV and Lena and Beverly were there and were obviously good friends.

"But is that all you know?" Holly blurts, voice all serious business.

"You mean there's more?"

"Beverly and Rick had an affair."

"Know that too."

"But did you know that Beverly had a child with Rick, a little girl who lives at Far Horizons in Utopia Planitia, a community for people with autism? Rick sent money, but he never visited the child. That upset her. Upset her a lot."

"I wonder why she said that the last time she last saw Rick it was over a year ago, and the truth was that it was shortly before he was murdered. Maybe it was to distance herself from the whole thing. Maybe to protect her child."

Then I add, "Oh, I know Roger Orbit who runs Far

Horizons. I could ask him if he knows anything more about Beverly or Rick."

"Is he single? Sounds like a catch."

"Too late, married a former Miss Asteroid Belt."

"Maybe he has a friend."

32

"CRYSTAL CITY, MERCURY, no pun intended, is a very hot place," Cortland says. "I want to book the twins and another group in their new Metadrum. Come with me. Mercury's temperatures reach 800 degrees. Better than going to Neptune where it's minus 370. You hate the cold."

"I'd like to go. It will give me a chance to ask some questions."

Cortland's eyes narrow. "I don't like you doing detective work. It's dangerous."

"Rick Frances was murdered at my restaurant. I feel an obligation to find out more."

Cortland huffs.

Lamont calls. I answer and listen. "No kidding, thanks for the info. Bye."

"So?" Cortland asks.

"He said Lena, Avery, and Beverly went to Mercury months before Rick was murdered. The surprise is that Jody went also."

"Jody? Your cute, sexy waitress."

"One and the same."

"So you'll come."

I kiss him on the cheek. "Sure. Murder, mystery, and music. Great combo."

160

"Two out of three, Molly. Two out of three."

Later, I call Jersey. When she answers, her voice is muffled and unintelligible. "What's that sound? Can't hear you. What are you doing?"

"Making a month's worth of Trenton's silicone milkshakes. What's up?"

"Cortland's booking a concert on Mercury. Avery, Lena, Beverly, and Jody traveled there before Rick Frances was murdered."

"If Trenton and I join you, he could write this off as part of the murder investigation. This way I won't have to twist myself into a Feynman equation to get him to agree to go—he can be so cheap."

"I know," I sigh, thinking Jersey is not much better. "What happened when you visited Lulu and Elvis?"

"Trenton gave Elvis a box of Motor Oil Moons. When Elvis had one, he said they were far better than Chocolate Moons. Elvis has all the latest updates. Between you and me, and off the record, Elvis is better looking."

"So Elvis took off his face mask?"

"Yes. He did with us. Maybe if he and Lulu took a trip to where no one knows them, he could adjust faster."

"That's it, Jersey! You're a genius!"

"Besides that obvious fact, what do you mean?"

"Let's go to Mercury with Lulu and Elvis when the twins have their concert at the Mercury Metadrum. It'll be fun. Trenton can make Elvis a carrying case."

"Great. Done deal."

I go to Molly's a half hour before we open for dinner as I usually do. Jody is seated at the bar tasting Harry's new drink.

"What do you call this, Harry?" Jody says licking her lips. "It's delicious."

"A Pumpkin Bellini. I think it will be a Halloween hit."

"Sorry to interrupt," I say. "Can I have a word, Jody?"

She puts her glass down. "Sure."

We walk from the bar. "Did you ever go to Crystal City, Mercury?" I ask.

Jody frowns and lowers her voice. "How did you know about that?"

I think quickly because I don't want her to suspect that Lamont told me or that I suspect that the poison that killed Rick Frances came from Mercury. So I ignore her question and say, "Cortland wants to book the astrodome on Mercury for a Lunar Tunes concert, and I plan to go with him. So have you ever been there?"

Jody relaxes. "Yes, once. Didn't have time to see much. It's the newest city in the solar system. So modern."

"Why did you go?"

She pauses then says, "Oh, I went to visit my brother. He lives there."

"Anything else?"

"No. Don't think so."

That evening when Cortland comes home, sits on the sofa, removes his shoes, and hands them to the service bot to polish, he says, "Mind if I go on to Mercury a day ahead of you, Molly? I have so many meetings and people to see that I need extra time there."

"No problem. I'll go with Jersey and Lulu. They're bringing their husbands in traveling cases."

"Then I'm glad I'm going early."

33

LULU, JERSEY, AND I WAIT to board the Mars-Mercury transport. The conductor sees three people because Trenton and Elvis are in carrying cases.

Jersey says, "Lulu told me it was easy to convince Elvis to have Trenton make him a carrying case. Isn't that right, Lulu?"

Lulu says, "What husband doesn't like to save money? When Elvis heard that Jersey and Trenton travel two for the price of one, his eyes spun."

"As long as they're spinning to the right, then it's a positive sign," Jersey pipes. "If Trenton doesn't like something, they spin to the left. But here's a tip: if they pulsate and blink, meaning he's confused, spray him with WD forty million and they'll stop. All that silicone might even make him feel sexy."

I follow directions to my room on the transport. It is very small. There is a tiny porthole, like an architect's afterthought, where I can see a black velvet sky with sharp, unblinking stars. I unpack a few toiletries, get undressed, and go into an efficient bathroom. It has a sterilizing mist cubicle instead of a shower to save water, and hot air blowers to save towels. I set the mist for fresh mowed grass and step inside. It is not as good as a shower, but it does the job. Then I slide into bed, unroll and tap my soft screen, and read about Mercury.

Mercury has almost no atmosphere because it is too small and too hot to hold what little there is for very long. Much goes into space, but with the help from solar winds, it is replenished. Anything that's in a shadow, like the bottom of a crater, never gets sunlight and is freezing. The poles never get direct sunlight, and that makes them look like they are in perpetual twilight, ergo an ideal place for a city. The North Pole is covered with water ice two and a half miles deep, and it is where most of the people live, that is until they finish building Crystal City South at the other pole, which has similar conditions and water. Crystal City was built mostly by robots, each of which cost millions of starbucks. On a human scale, Mercury is almost like a small town, with everyone who lives and works there knowing everyone else.

I try to read more but doze off. The next thing I know, a voice says, "Good morning, Mercury! Transport hopes you had a good night's sleep. If you need another hour of rest, press one. Ready for breakfast, press two." I press them both and the automated voice says, "Techno-deficient individual now registered—we will assign a room for the handicapped when you make your return trip. Have a good day."

At Mercury's spaceport, Jersey, Lulu, and I find the tram that will take us to Crystal City. It travels within a clear, enclosed monorail. We slide into comfortable seats next to tinted windows that cut light and radiation. Jersey points to a sign below the window and reads aloud, "Day temperature on Mercury can reach 427 degrees Celsius or 801 degrees Fahrenheit. The window is made from an amalgam of fifteen ultra-high ceramic materials and can withstand up to 2000 degrees Celsius."

"Let's hope that's right," I say. "We don't want to learn that it should have been made from an amalgam of sixteen ceramic materials not fifteen."

Lulu shakes her head. Jersey rolls her eyes.

I peer at the black sky dotted with stars. "I thought I might see some color in the sky, but I guess with so little atmosphere, the sunlight isn't scattered at all," I say.

Lulu says, "I think I see deep purple."

"That's as good as black," Jersey says. "But the sun is huge. Maybe three times the size we are used to seeing."

"Spectacular," Lulu squints and says while removing a pair of sunglasses from her bag and sliding them over her eyes. "Worth the trip."

For a half an hour the tram winds through rocky, empty miles filled with deep craters.

"Boy, this makes the most desolate parts of Mars look like the Disney Planet," Jersey says. "No wonder scientists call a lot of the surface 'weird terrain'. Mercury is so much smaller than I realized. The numbers meant nothing to me until I saw how much closer the horizon looks." She peers out the window. "Yup, really close." She takes a brochure from a pocket in the armrest of her seat, scans some highlights, and says, "Would you believe that Mercury is not the hottest planet because of its almost nonexistent atmosphere. The hottest planet is Venus. All the saunas are free there."

"Anyone thirsty?" I ask, bored with the subject of Mercury's deficiencies as a planet. Jersey and Lulu nod. I push a button and hail a porter.

A dark skinned porter wearing a blue and gold uniform with an embroidered sun over the right pocket approaches almost immediately. "What'll it be ladies?" he asks.

Then, suddenly before we can order, in the distance there is the massive presence of a multifaceted crystal dome that encloses Crystal City. The porter leans over, points, and says, "Kind of sneaks up on you, doesn't it?"

Jersey breathes, "Beats the Emerald City of Oz."

"Bring us three Mercury malts. No ice," I say. Jersey and

Lulu nod again.

Suddenly, the tram stops. A voice sounding neither male nor female says, "Tram stopped because of debris on the tracks. There is no problem unless we don't move within one hour."

"I wonder what happens after an hour," Lulu asks.

"I really don't want to know," I say.

The porter returns with our drinks and says, "Brief delay."

"We hope," Jersey mumbles.

We sit in silence, sipping our malts. Then there is a lurch forward and the tram moves. We watch the crystal dome grow larger and larger until all we can see is a wall of crystal. Finally, the tram stops. The same voice says, "You have arrived at Crystal City's first air lock. Please remain seated." A door at the front of the monorail slides open. The tram moves forward until the outer door closes behind. Then a door opens in front again, and the tram moves slowly into the second air lock; then into a third and a forth before we are allowed to disembark.

We stand on a sliding transparent walkway that winds through several subsurface tunnels until we emerge into the lobby of the Heartbreak Hotel.

Years ago, the Four Seasons Hotel chain sold to the Heartbreak Hotel chain. They were very anxious to sell because as man colonized the solar system, most worlds never had any seasons, let alone four seasons, and they were losing a lot of money.

Heartbreak Mercury, which is the newest, got a superstitious crowd: people who wouldn't leave their house without knocking on wood filler, wore St. Galileo medals, and (saying it wasn't a pet, but everyone knows better) carried a rabbit by its feet.

We are shown to our rooms. Mine is luxurious. I undress and jump into a real shower. Then I lie on an emperor-sized bed. I pick up a tablet on the night table that tells me about the hotel. After an hour, Lulu calls me and tells me that Elvis and

Trenton have emerged from their cases.

"How did Elvis feel?" I ask.

"Wonderful. Like he was sleeping and is now well rested. He and Trenton went out to explore the hotel. But I'm exhausted."

Cortland makes a reservation for dinner in the hotel's main dining room. The owners could have been more creative by calling it something other than the Sun Room, but it is lovely, covered in a shimmering gold metallic material. Everything else—plates, glasses, even the waiters' uniforms—is also in gold, but with soft lighting like the afterglow from a sunset. The ceiling is looped with gigantic soft screens that project images of the sun pulsating with plasma and electromagnetism. Every now and then we see sunspots erupt and spew immense explosions of high frequency radiation into space.

Our table is in the center of the room. We order two crystal cocktails while we wait for the others to arrive. Cortland is in a great mood because the Mercury astrodome is even better than he thought, and the hotel, anxious to book The Lunar Tunes, gave him a terrific deal.

"You know, Cortland. I thought my idea was unique—that of having Lulu and Elvis come to Mercury where no one knows them to get used to their new life together—but look. Have you ever seen so many mixed couples—humans with enhanced humans before?"

"Just thinking the same thing. At least half the room has either mixed couples or enhanced human couples."

Then he spots Trenton, who has just entered with Elvis and their wives. They see us and wave. Trenton and Elvis are having an animated conversation.

"Looks like you're having a wonderful time," I say to Elvis.

"Sure," Elvis says. "I love this place."

"What'll you have?" Cortland asks.

"Going to try my first carburetor tune-up." He turns to

Trenton. "You said it took some getting used to. But I think I'm ready."

"You're doing better than me when I first had the transformation," Trenton says. "Every year there are upgrades and improvements."

A waiter approaches with drinks and puts them on the table.

Elvis is looking over Trenton's shoulder, and he lowers his head and says, "Oh no!" He turns his face away.

"What's the matter?" Lulu asks.

"It's Boris Loffcar, the leader of the protesters against the rise of the android population. It doesn't look like he's with his wife, Mary Shelley."

Elvis grabs a menu and puts it in front of his face. "I don't want him to see me. On the other hand, he may not recognize me. I hardly recognize me. What's he doing now, Cortland?"

"He and the woman are getting up. He's draping a shawl over her shoulders. They're talking to someone. Wait, she's turning around. You won't believe this."

"What won't I believe?"

"She's an enhanced human."

34

"I can't believe Boris' wife is an enhanced human," Lulu bellows.

Before I can say anything, Frank calls, and Cortland mumbles, "Let it go to voicemail."

"Too late, I already clicked."

Everyone hears me say to Frank, "What do you mean Jody quit? Did she leave a forwarding address?" Pause. "No? Thanks for telling me, Frank." I click off. "Sorry, guys. Excuse me. I have to call Lamont immediately. This is smoke beneath a door."

Cortland, who has finished his drink, raises his hand, catches a waiter's eye, and says, "Bring me a large Sun Stroke."

"Make that two," Elvis chimes.

Lulu adds, "A Hadron Collider."

The waiter looks at Jersey and Trenton. "And for you?"

Jersey picks up the drink menu. From past experience, her serious look signals that she intends to go through the entire menu quizzing the waiter if the ingredients are fresh or frozen, organic or inorganic, how many calories, how many vitamins, and on and on. But Trenton yanks it away and says to the waiter, who feared what was coming and now smiles, knowing he has been saved from getting the third degree, "Two

Tarantula Nebulas."

Jersey whines, "I was going to order that."

"Now you did," Trenton says.

Lamont picks up on the first ring. "Did you know…?" I ask.

"We're on it," he says.

"On it? How did you know what I was going to say?"

"Jody booked a transport to Mercury. Showed up on Travel Trix. I'm sending Sid to follow her. By the way, we checked, and Jody has no brother on Mercury."

"What do you mean, no brother? She said she had one."

"Well, she doesn't," Lamont says.

"You don't have to send Sid. I'm already here at Crystal City with Cortland, my new in-laws, Lulu and Elvis, and Jersey and Trenton. I could find her and question her."

"Look, Molly, I don't want to spoil your holiday and then have Cortland bang bongos in my ear. Sid can handle this. How hard is it to follow one pretty waitress?"

"Unless she's not just one pretty waitress."

"Sid's already on the Mercury transport."

"Just one more call, guys," I beg. "Bear with me. I want to call Sid."

Sid answers. I say, "Only want you to know that I'm offering to help. I'm staying at the Heartbreak in Crystal City. Where will you be staying?"

"The Hellsgate. It's also in Crystal City but on the lowest level, inner circle ten."

"Keep me posted? I liked Jody."

"Finished?" Cortland asks. "Would you like another drink?"

In my sweetest voice, I say, "I'll just have a sip of yours, Cortland."

"No way. Not sharing. Your sip could be half the drink." Cortland raises his hand, catches the waiter's eye, and orders another Sun Stroke. Then he turns to Elvis. "So what are you going to do? Go over and introduce yourself or sneak out the side exit with a bag over your head?"

Elvis says nothing.

"Well, decide now because they're headed this way," Cortland urges.

Suddenly, the lights flicker.

Jersey blinks several times. "What was that?"

A siren wails.

A voice over the hotel's intercom booms, "Attention! Attention! We have just been alerted that in the next two hours Mercury will experience a Carrington Effect."

Jersey smirks. "Bet that's something named after someone named Carrington."

"Shh, this is important. I want to hear this," I say.

The announcer continues, "This is a coronal mass ejection from the sun, named for Richard Carrington, the British scientist who discovered it."

"Told you so," Jersey mumbles.

The announcer says, "Although the sun is always hurling spiral washes of plasma like those from a rotating sprinkler system, every now and then one that is larger than most is flung in our direction."

Lulu grabs Elvis' hand. "Doesn't sound good."

The announcer continues, "When this happens, gusts of the solar wind may penetrate Mercury's magnetic field and can erode some surface material. Ionized sodium will escape from weak parts in Mercury's magnetosphere. As a precaution, we want everyone to proceed to our lower level that is insulated with a thick layer of leadadye immediately. Communication with the surface will be suspended during this time."

Lulu adds, "Maybe it's a drill."

The announcer booms, "This is not a drill, Lulu Ernie."

Lulu jumps. "How did they know it was me?"

"On the hotel questionnaire, you checked that you failed a fire drill in the seventh grade."

The crowd chants, "Failed the drill, failed the drill."

The announcer roars. "Move it, people!"

Everyone moves toward a bank of descending escalators. Mercury's national anthem "Mercury O Mercury, the Planet with Wings on its Heels" plays. When we reach the bottom, I turn to find Boris Loffcar and the woman, but they are lost in the crowd.

Cortland says, "The hotel never told us that that sun blasts could disrupt holidays because it would scare off business. But they're well prepared. Look: there's a food court, several bars, a theater, a game room, and more."

Trenton says, "We might have a good time."

Our ears perk when we hear, "The talent show that was to be held upstairs later this evening will be held in the theater on this level. Those interested, please sign up outside the theater."

Lulu brightens. "It's been a long time since we sang together, Elvis. Let's do it."

"I didn't know you and Elvis sang," I say.

"Elvis is named after a famous American singer of the twentieth century," Lulu says. "Can't remember his last name. I think it began with the letter P."

"Elvis Polansky," Cortland chimes. "He played a kazoo made from an elephant tusk. It's used during Jewish New Year services."

"Are you sure?" I say.

"I'm accessing Bible Music 101 in my data bank," Trenton says. "It says that he also played the chauffer and got the rabbi's wife pregnant."

"We haven't sung since college. But I guess this is as good a time as any to try out my new voice."

"I would love to hear you," Jersey says. "I wish Trenton would sing."

"Not in my program files," Trenton says.

"But they could be added so easily, sweetheart."

Trenton smirks and says nothing.

Then there is a loud gong and sharp whistle. Everyone stops what they are doing.

Holographic red arrows appear and float in front of us and point to another escalator at the far end. "Attention guests! Please follow the red arrows and proceed to the lower, lower level. We have been alerted there will be a sun blast larger than we first thought. Have a nice day."

Then there is a cracking sound followed by several more cracking sounds, and I'm pushed and shoved from every side. I grab the railing with two hands and don't let go until I reach the bottom. This space looks like an industrial bunker. We are jammed together. Fluorescent lights make everyone glow green, which only pleases those from Ganymede whose skin has a greenish cast and who have begun haggling over the price of the lights.

Lights flicker in various colors then go out. The management makes an announcement that the lights are still on but only the black lights work. This is followed by a lot of moaning and screaming. I reach for Cortland's hand.

"Is that you, Cortland?" I ask.

"No," a voice says. "But it's nice to hold your hand. My name is Randy. I sell life insurance."

I drop my hand. "Cortland? Are you there?"

"I thought I was holding your hand, Molly."

"Who are you?" a female voice says. "No funny business."

Trenton and Elvis begin to laugh. Soon there is a lot of laughter.

"What's everyone laughing about?" I say.

I recognize Trenton's voice. "Not everyone is laughing, Molly. Only the enhanced humans are laughing. We all see in the dark. Jersey has eye implants and can see. Right, Jersey?"

"Right," I hear Jersey say. "No problem. Just activated my high beams."

"Well, take my hand, Jersey, and lead me to Cortland. I can't see a thing."

She takes my hand and places it in another hand. "Are you sure that is Cortland?" I say.

Cortland says, "It's not me, Molly."

"What?" I yank my hand away.

"Only kidding. It was too good to resist."

Eye roll in a jet black room.

There is a loud boom. We scream. A sign glows on the ceiling. We read. "Crack in the outer hull. Please remain calm." Then the sign changes, "Estimate time to repair: twenty minutes."

"Twenty minutes is not so long to wait," Lulu titters.

"It is if someone is stepping on your toe," I say. "Jersey, please see who is doing this."

The ceiling sign glows brighter. "New estimate repair time: thirty-three minutes."

"Oops," Jersey says. "Sorry, Molly. It's me. Thought I just broke a heel."

The ceiling sign blinks: "New time estimate…" and that's all we get.

"So how much longer?" Lulu asks.

"How would we know?" says an angry voice in the crowd. "This was my wedding night."

"Attention hotel guests, we are experiencing technical difficulties."

Several shout, "What kind of technical difficulties?"

"Our technician is in the bathroom. He says the toilet won't flush and he's embarrassed to come out."

"Isn't there someone else?" another voice shouts.

"It's his day off."

Then we hear a roar.

"An attack from the sun?" a voice shouts.

"No, he flushed. Be patient, people."

Trenton shouts, "Patient like in Pluto time or Mercury time?"

Just as things are about to escalate, the lights come on.

"Attention hotel guests. The crack has been repaired enough for you to return to the first sheltered area. You must remain there until the sun storm passes, which we estimate to be in two hours. Free drinks will be served in the bar." Everyone cheers. "If you were planning to sign up for our talent show, this is a good time."

After our free drink, Elvis and Lulu sign up for the talent show. They sing "Amazing Grace." Elvis makes ethereal electronic sounds that complement Lulu's harmony so beautifully that everyone joins in and demands an encore. I clap so hard my hands hurt.

Cortland says, "I'm overwhelmed! Make me a demo recording? I think I could market it into a hit."

Elvis and Lulu laugh. Elvis says, "Really? We could call ourselves The Virtuals."

Out of the corner of my eye, I see Boris Loffcar and the enhanced woman push through the crowd and head in our direction. Boris calls, "Lulu? Lulu? I thought I recognized you. What are you doing on Mercury? Who are you with?"

"I could ask the same thing myself, Boris? Who are you with?"

"I asked first," Boris answers.

Elvis says, "Have I changed that much, Boris?"

"Elvis? You sound like Elvis."

"Yup. It's me."

"Thought you were badly burned and were recuperating."

"I was. But it was more involved." Elvis looks at the woman and studies her closely, then says cautiously, "Boris, that's Mary Shelly, your wife. What happened?"

Mary says, "Bad rover accident. Guess we've had a similar experience."

"And chose to cross over to the dark side," Lulu quips. Mary forces a smile. "Not hard when the options are live or die."

"Hey," Boris says, peering at Trenton closely. "You're famous. Aren't you the first human android?"

I look at Trenton who takes a deep breath and pauses. I can tell there's something rattling in his mind. Then Trenton nods and says, "I really like that new term 'enhanced human'."

Boris narrows his eyes. "Well, the terminology doesn't change much but the terminology. But I have to admit that I never realized until Mary had her procedure that a few of you were different, not, mind you, like the majority. I'm sorry, Trenton, for putting that sign outside your house that said 'Go back to Oz, Tin Man'. You're not like the others. Neither are you, Elvis. The others have strange habits and can be so pushy. Go where they're not wanted. Sometimes I think I can even detect a different smell." He sniffs. "No. No smell." He sniffs again. "In fact, is that Hermes aftershave?"

"Yes. My favorite," Trenton says. "Jersey bought it for me as a New Year's present. But it's so expensive."

"My favorite too," Elvis says. "I bought my own."

Trenton is about to speak, but Elvis puts his hand on Trenton's arm stopping him as he thinks he should leave well enough alone for now and saying more would accomplish nothing. Plus, seeing a lucrative opportunity to make a sale to Boris, whose mood has softened, moves and closes a deal with him to the top ten most expensive virtual vacations with all the extras.

I am no sooner back in my room than my palm signals. It's Lamont. "Forensics discovered that a product called Contam can become a poison; it needs to be added to another ingredient—in other words, it's harmless by itself. Contam is mostly used to make dishes shine. Half of what's imported to Mars comes from Mercury. And anyone can buy it. See if you can check this out while you are still there. I'm sending you their address and palm number. Tell them you're a restaurant owner and heard that it makes dishes shine. That way they won't be suspicious that the call came from Mars Yard. Besides, it's true—you do own a restaurant and need shiny dishes."

The plant is located in a domed crater named Ailey too far from the hotel, and Cortland would never let me go, so I call. They confirm Lamont's information. They warn me that if mixed with a product called Inate, it becomes a poison. Sort of the reverse of how salt is made. Salt is a product of two poisons: sodium and chloride. Together it's harmless. Here each ingredient is harmless, but together they're lethal.

Sid calls and says, "I couldn't find Jody. I was locked in the Hellsgate Hotel because of the sun storm."

"Didn't you have to go to a lower level for extra protection?"

"Nope. We just stayed in our rooms. We're already on the lowest level."

35

HOME, RELAXED, FRESH FROM A SHOWER, I'm deciding what to eat when Lamont calls and says, "Sid was stuck in his hotel room during a sun storm. The lock on his door jammed, and he was the last one out."

"I know that, Lamont. I spoke to him."

"But bet you didn't know that he was able to find out that Jody left Mercury and went to Nirgal Palace because he just called."

"No, I didn't know that. I wonder why she went."

"Well, you're already talking to the banquet manager, so maybe you could get some information."

"No problem," I say. "Was forensics able to find out more about Inate?"

"We've learned that it's fatal to certain bacteria. It can make a person sick, but most people don't die from it. It's used in a lot of common products—foot powder, adhesives…"

"Where does it come from?"

"Mostly from Ceres."

"Ah, not from Mercury, like Contam. Any idea who imports it?"

"Restaurant Works in Baguette."

"I was just there with Frank."

"Well, don't tell Frank, but maybe you could call Restaurant Works and see what you can find out."

So I call Restaurant Works and put Danny in a good mood by telling him how much I love my new dishes—which is the truth. Then, sounding like an afterthought, I ask if he has ever heard of a product called Contam. And he says, of course, and if I really want to get dishes to shine, there is nothing like it. He says he didn't mention it when I was there because it is very expensive, and since restaurants use so much, he didn't know if it was practical for me to spend all that money when a little extra soap and water was sufficient.

Then he says, "Didn't Frank tell you that he bought a box of Contam when you were here? In fact, I sold him one the last time he came, about six months ago. He came with a bartender who works for you and a pretty young lady who said she was a waitress."

"Harry is my bartender and Jody one of my waitresses. Did either of them buy a box of Contam?"

"Let me check." A moment later. "Yup, here it is, six months ago, I sold two boxes of Contam. One to Frank and one to Harry. Harry also bought some Inate and a small espresso machine. Jody bought nothing."

"Did Harry say why he bought these products?"

"I just sell things. Can't be too nosy or my business might dry up. I also sell a lot to Nirgal Palace. Records show that Sol Brody also ordered those products several months ago."

I make a note about Sol Brody. "I never saw Frank buy the Contam. When did he buy it?"

"He came an hour before you. We wanted to catch up on old times. Bought it before you came in with your friend Jonsey."

"Her name is Jersey."

"Blocked it out. Boy, can she bargain. Warn me if you come with her again, and I'll let an old robot handle her."

36

SOL CALLS. "GUESS WHO'S LOOKING for a job?" he says.

"Jody from my restaurant."

"How did you know?"

"Long story. Did you hire her?"

"No. We don't need anyone, but Roses Heaven, that spa for overweight people who love to eat in low or no gravity in space, always needs waitresses. Their clientele is the most demanding in the solar system. They want everything immediately, and they always want more. Their staff has an enormous turnover. Jody said that she didn't care and needed a new job. She might already be there."

I call Lamont. And when I tell him what Sol said, he says, "Well, if you really want to help, you can go to Roses Heaven and find her. I don't have anyone that can go now. Besides, you were once were there and know the place."

"Yes, but…that was years ago. I'm no longer fat. I no longer weigh 287 Earth pounds. And I fear that being in a place that has an endless twenty-four hour buffet the size of a football field could be my undoing. I still dream about it. I'm not sure I can do the job. Jody is tall and thin. How can they hire her?"

"Lots of thin people work at Roses."

"I never saw any."

"Those less than 250 Earth pounds wear a fat suit."

"Jersey wished she could see what Roses was like, but she's so thin. Now she can come."

So before you can smell the chocolate rising from a double rich chocolate mascarpone cheesecake, Jersey and I are on the shuttle line going to Roses Heaven.

"Sorry I'm late," Jersey says. "I had to take the cat to the vet."

"Didn't know you had a cat."

"Got her at the robo-cat shelter. Turns out that she barked instead of mewed. Trenton won't fix it because he says he is allergic. It was so cute that I didn't want to return it. I named it Dog."

"I didn't know one could be allergic to a robotic cat."

"You could be if you were an android."

All the heavy people waiting in line give us dirty looks because we are thin. Jersey tells them we're scientists and will be adjusting a new ice cream machine so it triples production.

"Well, we certainly need that!" several say.

When we arrive, regular clients step to the right into a hallway that smells of waffles and melted butter. The smell is so seductive that Jersey grabs me hard to stop me from following them. Roses has so little gravity that as soon as they enter, their fat no longer hangs on them in folds but balloons up around them like a ring of Saturn. On Mars, they would have had a hard time walking. In Earth's heavier gravity, they would have sat and been wheeled. But here they move and bounce easily—faces and bodies like smooth soap bubbles.

The hallway to the left smells of an industrial cleanser; an arrow and in tiny letters says "employees." We walk down a long passage until we reach a very heavy woman behind a large desk wearing a loose blue smock. Her mouth is wide and expansive, her eyes penetrating. Her nametag says, "My Name is Mammoth." She doesn't smile. She hands us lots of forms to fill out. When we finish, she checks them for a long time. Finally, she extends a fleshy hand and says, "OK, fat suits are in the red closet near the back of the room. You'll both need the ones with extra padding."

Jersey and I struggle to pull on the fat suits. We look at each other's full moon face, heavy-lidded eyes, and round, puffed cheeks. I look in a mirror. "I can't believe I looked this way once," I sigh.

Jersey looks and says, "And you were still able to get a nice guy to marry you."

"I did. Didn't I?"

We wobble toward the desk. Mammoth says, "I'm starting you both off replacing empty platters at the endless buffet. It is not as easy as it looks. Some of them have been licked so clean you would think that they had been washed. If you are not sure, use this." She hands us a stick that looks like a thermometer. "It checks for bacteria."

It is not hard to find the endless buffet. Like old Rome, all hallways lead to it.

"Ah," I say, watching the door of the buffet peel back. "Looks as I remember it—maybe better."

As far as my eye can see, there are rows and rows of standing rib roasts, racks of lamb, shell steaks, filet mignons. Platters of lobsters, clams, shrimps, scallops, and enough fish to fill a sea, bowls of artfully shaped pastas that could stuff Italy, potatoes that would cover Ireland, fields of green vegetables, and a wall with spigots that pump every kind of sauce. When the smell from newly baked bread—from brioche to matzos—makes me swoon, Jersey holds out her arms and catches me. "Knew that was coming," she says.

Best of all, branching to one side is a sign with circling lights like the marquee of a theater that says, "Paradise Found—Desserts." One wall has frozen treats, another has cakes, another for pies, and one for cookies. At the far end is a golden sign that says Room of Chocolate Dreams. I tell Jersey that she better work in that room because if I enter, I will never come out.

After checking our emergency signals to see we never lose contact with each other, we join other workers who are clearing meat platters.

Soon Jersey says, "This is boring. Maybe we should do vegetables." We walk to the vegetable area. I pause in front of a table filled with eggplant parmesan and hesitate next to a mountain of French fries. Jersey grabs my arm and pulls me away. "Walk faster," she says.

"Look," I point. "Doesn't that look like Jody?"

"It's hard to tell because either that person is really so fat or she's wearing a fat suit like us."

"Her eyes and nose look just like Jody's. I think it's her. She's headed toward that tower of mashed potatoes."

We walk closer. "Maybe you just wanted to get closer to the mashed potatoes. I didn't see anyone."

I reach for a sample. Lick my fingers. "Delicious."

Jersey tries a small mouthful. "Too much butter."

I frown. "Potatoes can never have too much butter." I take more. Jersey rolls her eyes. "Look," I say, licking my fingers and pointing, "Over there beyond the white mashed potatoes, there is a tower of sweet potatoes. Look to the right side of it."

37

JODY SEES US AND STOPS. We waddle closer. Jersey loses her balance and grabs the side of a table to steady herself. Unlike me, she was rail thin her entire life and is having trouble walking as a fat person. I, on the other hand, move easily. Like swimming and riding a bike, it's a skill that once learned becomes yours forever.

"Are you two following me?" Jody calls, her voice wobbling with tension. She comes closer and peers at us. "Molly? Jersey?"

"That's us," I say.

"Why are you here? Why are you wearing fat suits? Are you working here?"

"Not exactly. We came to find you. You left so suddenly," I say. "You said that you were visiting a brother on Mercury. But Lamont found out that you have no brother on Mercury. Isn't that right?"

She lowers her head and nods yes, and her fat suit's double chin shakes.

"When the police realized that you had lied about your reasons for going to Mercury, they became suspicious because the poison that killed Rick was from Mercury. They thought those things might be linked. They wanted to bring you to Mars Yard for questioning. We thought it best to get to you first and hear your explanation."

"I'm so sorry for leaving you in the lurch. I loved working at your bistro. It was the best job I ever had. But when I heard that the police were investigating everyone again and that they were interested in those who had gone to Mercury, I panicked. Truth is my past is something I'm not proud of. I was an exotic dancer and escort at The Hot Spot, Mercury's wildest club. I was also arrested for shoplifting. My boyfriend dared me to snitch some of those no-see-it-no-feel-it condoms. So stupid. Mercury police put it on my permanent record. As soon as I saved some money, I left and started over. I didn't want this coming out again. I found that people say they understand, but then they avoid me."

Jersey says, "Come back to New Chicago, and we'll help you clear this up. I don't think this is as big a deal as you think." She reaches for Jody's arm. Suddenly, a hole in the suit makes a loud pop, followed by louder pops. "Ouch!" Jody yells, rubbing her arms as the fat suit collapses around her.

"Hey," yells a very fat person. "You're not one of us. What are you doing here? We don't want spies."

"Run," I yell. "Before more see us." And we do. All the way home.

Mario and Vanna throw Jody a welcome home party. I have nothing to wear because during my brief my time at Roses Heaven, I gained ten pounds.

The following week, after eating nothing but black coffee, low-calorie gazpacho, a rice cracker, and one stalk of celery that has minus five calories—five calories in the celery, minus ten for chewing and digesting—Lamont calls me at my office.

"We've done extensive background checks on Beverly Hills. We spoke to the staff at Far Horizons and found information about the child she had with Rick was accurate but couldn't find any motivation for her to kill him. Although Rick didn't visit the child, he always sent money for support. So it would not be in the best interests of either Beverly or the child if she murdered him."

"What about an insurance policy?"

"We found no insurance policy."

"And Holly? Anything on her?"

"Can't find any motivation or opportunity in the time for the poison to work."

Three days after that and two pounds lighter, Trenton calls me and invites me to go to Silicone Slings to celebrate his android birthday—that is the day he was transformed from human to android. I'm neither surprised nor disappointed that Cortland can't make it because it gives me time with Jersey and Trenton, whose quirks Cortland frequently has no patience for.

When I enter, I have to cover my ears. "Mechanical Man," Becky and Lois' latest hit is being blasted from their sound system. Androids can adjust the receptive volume in their ears, but I can't. I find Jersey and Trenton who, like everyone else, are joining in on the chorus, "I'm gonna live forever." We do the air kiss thing. I order a regular Margaretta and sip. Suddenly, I see a man who looks like Avery from VV come in and go to the bar. I poke Jersey. "Could that be Avery?" I ask.

Jersey, who is wearing a shocking pink day-glow t-shirt that says, "Android Birthdays Are Real Birthdays," turns and looks. "Could be," she says popping several almonds into her mouth and crunching.

"I'm going to find out," I say. I walk to the bar and hear the person I think is Avery order a Mobile Malt. I see him nibble a few Chocolate Oil Moons from a dish near his right hand.

"Avery?" I say. "Avery? Is that you?"

He turns away pretending not to hear.

I repeat, "Avery, is that you?"

He looks at me, eyebrows rising. "What are you doing here, Molly?"

"Celebrating my friend's android birthday."

The bartender places the drink, which I know is a Mobile Malt because it's served in a glass shaped like a red horse with wings. "I didn't know you could drink one of these," I say. "Won't it make you sick? Human digestion can't process that very well."

Avery rolls up his sleeve, shows me his arm, opens the wrist panel, and says, "Fooled you too!"

I gasp. "You did. You certainly did. But you don't look like an android."

Avery smirks. "That's like saying someone doesn't look Jewish. No one checks for a circumcision, or in our case, checks to see if we have a navel or toenails—the real giveaways."

"Do you mind if I call my friends over to meet you? One of them is an android, the old-fashioned kind. In fact, the first one. It's his birthday that I'm celebrating."

"Only if he can keep a secret. I'm not ready, as they say, to come out."

"Does Lena know?"

"Not yet. She teases me about wearing long-sleeved shirts, but it probably wouldn't matter if I told her. Not a prejudiced atom in her body. Her favorite cousin just had the procedure."

Trenton and Jersey approach. I introduce them. Avery says that because of a very serious, but not life threatening, health issue he volunteered for a new procedure that kept his original head intact. But androids didn't accept him as one of their own because he didn't look like an android. So it was easier to pass as human if he covered his body—which he did. When there were further advances using better looking materials, he was one of the first to have the procedure done to his head. He thought androids would then accept him. But they still didn't.

The new materials used to make the new android head worked so well that although he looked different from his original self, he still looked human.

"Most don't know what to make of me," he sighs. "Neither fish—nor artificial fish."

I reach out to touch his hair, hair that looks so real. Ordinary hair on top of an ordinary average-looking head. Yet wasn't. Not even close. Avery, walking evolution. I wonder when and where it will end.

As quickly as I had reached to touch Avery's hair, I retract my hand.

"It's OK, Molly. My hair feels just like yours." And it does.

Trenton says, "It can be lonely being the first of anything."

Avery nods. "But you found Jersey to love you."

"She's not the only one out there," Trenton says. "Besides, it can't be long before there are more of you."

Avery gulps half his drink. "I wish I didn't feel like a fraud. But keeping a low profile protects me from extremists like my late boss, Rick Frances, who hated androids."

"I didn't know Rick felt that way," I say. "I thought he was a nice guy."

"Why shouldn't he be nice to you, Molly? You're not an android."

Trenton says, "I read about the new procedures but was too busy to follow the new advances. Now I see how successful they are."

"I love you the way you are," Jersey pipes sensing that Trenton might be considering the new procedure. Then appealing to his cheap side, a ploy that always worked, adds, "No need to spend money on an upgrade, sweetheart."

Trenton says, "Point well taken."

Avery watches the bartender struggle to remove difficult spots on the glasses. "Why don't you use Contam?" he asks. "It's the best thing for getting dishes clean and shiny."

"Is it a new product?" the bartender answers. "Never heard of it."

"Not really that new, but it can be dangerous. Poisonous, in fact, if it is mixed with a product called Inate."

"How do you know that, Avery?" I ask.

He reaches for his glass, drains the last drops, and says, "Don't know. Just know."

Back at my office desk, I open a drawer to retrieve some notes about the wedding and my correspondence with Sol. I hear a knock on the door. "Come in," I say. "It's open."

Mario enters and asks, "Do you have a moment, Molly?"

I close the drawer. "Sure," I say pointing to a chair. "Sit."

"Not necessary. Just one question. Who's making the cake for the wedding?"

"The chefs at Nirgal Palace. As a matter of fact, I was going to review some possibilities from holos they sent me. Maybe you could help me select one."

Mario frowns. "That's not what I had in mind. I wondered if I could make the wedding cake."

"That is a very nice idea, but I'll have to clear it with the caterers. I'll talk to Sol Brody."

"The one who calls himself Starr Bright?"

I nod. "We're getting a package deal—meals, rooms, flowers..."

"I wouldn't charge for my time, only for the ingredients. I've never had the opportunity to make a wedding cake, and I feel it would be a capstone to my career."

"I was going to invite you and the rest of the staff as guests."

"Then let's make it my gift to Becky."

38

CORTLAND SAYS, "THE TWO MOST EXPENSIVE words in the English language are 'I do'."

We decide money's worth spending to have the ceremony on the Outer Space Platform and dinner in the Garden Terrace Room. Details concerning menus, bridesmaids' dresses, whom to invite, flowers, the morning after breakfast, in short—everything—are overwhelming.

Flo, who never lets anyone forget that she is the bride's aunt, tells me that she would be delighted to do a tasting and spitting for free. When I say that I don't consider that a wedding present, her face drops, and she says I don't appreciate her talents.

Jersey and Trenton once gave a cat as a wedding present to Jersey's cousin. Jersey apologized because she wanted to give them a Schrödinger's box with a live cat inside, as they had two cats and two Schrödinger's boxes. But Trenton wouldn't part with one because he said he loved to bring both boxes to Silicone Slings, place them on the bar, and have his friends bet on the odds of two cats emerging dead or alive at the same time. Besides, he said that he couldn't part with one of the boxes because one could never be too rich, too thin, or have too many Schrödinger's boxes. Jersey asks if getting a cat from the pound is a suitable compromise. And I say no. So she asks, "How about a dog?"

Some questions are best left unanswered.

In Molly's Bistro, the floors are being polished. Mario and Vanna are working quietly in the kitchen. I won't disturb the tranquility. Harry is standing behind the bar moving a white rag in little circles over it. I enter and say, "The bar looks great, Harry. Are you using something new to get that shine?"

"I am," he says holding a bottle up. "It's called Contam. Went to Restaurant Works and bought some months ago. This is the first time I'm trying it because I gave the one I bought to a friend and she hasn't given it back. This is Frank's bottle. He says he uses it to polish his rover, it and does a better job than cholesterol."

"I went to Restaurant Works with Frank. That's where I bought the new dishes. Did you go to Restaurant Works alone?"

"No, I went with Frank and Jody."

"Do you think that they sell anything that might be useful but hard to get?"

"Hundreds of products fall into that category."

"Ever hear of Inate?"

"Oh yeah, Inate. Kills bacteria. I bought some of that too."

"Do you have any?"

"No, gave all of the Contam and all of the Inate to my friend."

"Do you know what happens when you mix Contam and Inate together?"

"I'll venture a stupid guess because you're asking, and you have a reputation for being good at murder investigations. It becomes a poison? Right? But it can't be called Contaminate. That's too obvious a name for a poison."

"Think so? What better than hiding in plain sight? Now, tell me who your friend is."

Harry hesitates.

"Come on, Harry. It's me, Molly. You can tell me."

"It's Lena," Harry blurts. "Surprised?"

When I say nothing, he adds, "I went to VV because I wanted to try virtual food. When I met Lena, I asked her questions about the kitchen. Afterwards she invited me back to see it. I thought she was very attractive, so I asked her out."

"How long have you been seeing each other?"

"A few months."

"So Lena has the Contam and the Inate."

"Yes, I told you. She said she wanted to shine something and needed the Inate to kill bacteria. Isn't that what everyone uses those products for?"

"Can you think of anything else?"

"Jody actually brought it to her. She asked me because she had never been inside VV and wanted to get a peek. We could have gone together, but our schedules were different."

Back in my office, I call Lamont, who says, "I'll send Sid to VV to check and see if Lena has any Contam and Inate, although having it is circumstantial. Lots of people have both products."

"Danny at Restaurant Works told me that Sol Brody had both products shipped to him at Nirgal Palace. I told you that he was Rick Frances' brother-in-law. Could be a connection."

Lamont says, "Could be."

Later, when I call Cortland and tell him what I know, he says, "I thought Sol was a crook when he added a time capsule with holographs of the wedding to be sent to three galaxies. I don't remember ordering it. And five thousand starbucks for pink rose petals with magnetic charges to fly around the Outer Space Platform after the ceremony. He said it brought good luck. But for whom?"

"For him," I sigh.

Later, I palm Lulu. "Are you busy, Lulu?"

"Elvis and I are exploring ways to get more business. We're thinking of adding a frequent flyer miles bonus to Club Mood's trips."

"But no one really goes anywhere on your trips. Everything is virtual."

Lulu says, "Travel is in the mind of the beholder."

"Isn't it 'beauty is in the eye of the beholder'?"

"Picky, picky, Molly—as a man thinketh so is he, she, or it."

"I don't think virtual travel miles can be applied to real trips."

"That's OK. They can be donated to a political candidate of their choice. They take anything."

"Are you as excited as I am about the wedding?"

"Of course. And I should've asked sooner. Anything I can do to help?"

"Could you go over the holographers' résumés? We want someone whose images show lots of feeling."

"Happy to do it. In fact, before I was working on the virtual miles bonus, I organized my personal holograms. I found a few that Elvis and I took the night of Rick Frances' murder. Some were blurry. Thought I would delete them."

"Don't delete them!" I cry. "They could be evidence! There may be something important in the background."

"You're amazing, Molly. I never thought of that. You think like a real Shylock."

"Sherlock not Shylock."

"Whatever. So you think some of my holos may have something important on them?"

"You never know. I never put security cameras in the restaurant. I thought it would be bad for business. Who wants to know that they're being watched, especially when they're enjoying a wonderful meal?"

Lulu says, "Especially if they're with someone they don't want others to know about. We don't have any security cameras at Club Mood for the same reason."

"Since you have holos of that evening, maybe others do also. I'll ask Lamont. I remember that you were seated by yourselves near the kitchen. How come you were seated there?"

"We weren't sure how serious Burton and Becky were, so we set the invitation aside. Then when we did get around to responding, the only table left in the main dining room was that one near the kitchen."

Then I call Lamont, who says he is too busy to talk. So I call Trenton, who says, "What's up, Molly? You must come to dinner again. This time bring Cortland. I've made lots of improvements on my food replicator. My pizza tastes like it was baked in a Mercury sun oven—it's the Beethoven Tenth of pies! What's that you say? I thought we collected holograms from everyone who was at the restaurant that night. We found nothing."

"Well, you missed Lulu."

When I tell Lulu what Trenton said, she tells me that she never heard any announcement about submitting holograms because those seats near the kitchen are as noisy as the music at twenty-first century weddings, whose brides and grooms, if they reached their tenth anniversary, gave each other hearing aids as gifts.

39

I BRING LULU'S HOLOS to Jersey and Trenton's home rather than Mars Yard because I want to go Silicone Slings one block away. Sol Brody sent me Silicone Slings' new menu from their outpost in Nirgal Palace, but I didn't like many of the selections like sea shells retrieved from oil spills and drinks made from refrigerator coolant that Trenton tells me taste like mint.

Trenton's home lab has many duplicates from his lab in Mars Yard but not all. Things dangerous, expensive, or big like Lion Scans can be accessed remotely from Mars Yard. I was also anxious to visit them again because Trenton said he would make his special pizza. I hoped that by eating it I could head him off about inviting Cortland, who refuses to budge about eating in their home.

Jersey greets me with a glass of sparkling pomegranate water and a dish of poton chips. I take a handful of chips and crunch. They have just the right balance of onion and potato flavors. Then I take the water. We go into the living room. She places the poton chips on the silver and glass coffee table in front of the sofa. "Those chips are delicious. Did Trenton make them?"

"No. The chef at Silicone Slings called and said that you would be coming after you saw us, and he sent them over.

He thought you'd have fewer preconceived ideas if you tasted them in someone's home. It's made to appeal to both the human and android palate."

I take more. "I'll order some for my bar. Maybe even serve some at the wedding." I wrinkle my nose. "Smells good. Pizza must be ready."

Trenton's pizza is delicious. After we finish, Jersey brings coffee and cookies dotted with orange and lemon bits and puts then on the table.

"Don't tell me. These are not really orange or lemon bits, and androids and humans love them."

"Right," Jersey says. "They passed a test run with both groups. The Flying Saucer Supermarket is going to sell them."

I give Trenton Lulu's holograms, and he slides them into a scanner. Before he presses view, he says, "Humans and androids are growing more alike. But there is a long way to go from cookies and chips to humans loving flat tire filets, something we prefer rather than pate de foie gras and caviar."

I make a face.

"See," he says, pointing at me, "that's what I mean." He presses view.

The first series of images are of Sandy Andreas seated at his table talking and everyone listening except his wife Solaria, who seems to be adjusting her bra.

"Nothing there," Jersey says. "Do you think her boobs are real?" Before I can answer, she says, "Next."

The following yield nothing, unless you count one of the owners of Ruby's Spa trying to switch her large dessert with her neighbor's small dessert because it has fewer calories.

Finally, I point and say, "Stop there." We peer at an image of Jody that looks like she is dropping something into a glass of water. This is followed by her offering it to Rick, whose outstretched hand circles it. Then there is one of Rick drinking it.

Trenton enlarges the first image and clicks slow motion forward. He splits the screen to compare the images looking for any inconsistencies. Then he copies the file and sends it to Mars Yard.

There are more innocent-looking images, like ten of Becky and Burton kissing, until we see one that makes us all yell, "Stop!"

Sol and Rick are standing together holding glasses of white wine, followed by a shot of both of them placing their glasses on a table, then another of Sol switching his glass with Rick's and each drinking the other's wine. "Best to forward these to Mars Yard," Trenton says. "Easier to see greater details on their projector."

I thank Jersey and Trenton for the pizza. I tell them that is was so delicious that it tasted like it was made in the south of France rather than in a replicator. Trenton asks if that is supposed to be a compliment or an insult. I roll my eyes and say if he doesn't know, then androids need more work. Jersey and Trenton shakes their heads, mystified.

I leave, cross the street, and enter Silicone Slings.

Silicone Slings looks empty except for electricians standing on a ladder installing a new light fixture. There are buzzing sounds from the kitchen, and a bartender is arranging bottles and glasses. The bartended is different from the one I met when I was last here. I introduce myself and say I had called earlier because I wanted to ask what he recommends I serve at my daughter's wedding, as many enhanced humans would be there.

He walks to the side of the bar, removes a menu from a drawer, and brings it over. "We have had more cross-cultural affairs lately," he says.

"Cross-cultural? Is that the new politically correct term?"

"Yup. We just had a party for seventy-five individuals. And notice I said the word 'individuals' not humans, androids, or enhanced humans."

"So?"

"One recipient worked for the APCP, Association for Politically Correct Politics, and saw that his invitation said androids and humans instead of cross-cultural and individuals. He wouldn't come unless we did the invitations over."

"I'll have to tell my staff."

He takes out a stylus. "Here, I'll highlight items on the menu that we served that were hits. Avoid anything with fiberglass—it can scratch and perforate a human's internal organs."

I listen carefully.

"If it weren't for one drunken guy, it would have been a perfect party. I didn't think he was an android until he rolled up his sleeve and showed me. I thought I had seen everything. One customer, who is a teacher, had an eye put in the back of his head. But this guy looked so human. I'll be honest, he threw me. His name was..." He pauses and taps his forehead several times. "Running through my data base...had something to do with birds...one moment...one moment...ah, got it: Avery. He's been in before and always drinks too much. Prefers the lighter motorcycle oils rather than the double diesels or heavy crude. I think his system is not used to it because he's clearly high after one."

"Does he work at Virtual Vittles?"

"How did you know?"

"My restaurant, Molly's Bistro, is next door. In fact, I was in here with friends and bumped into him. He seems like a nice guy. I've never seen him drunk."

He peers at me more closely. "You must have been here on my day off. I usually remember everyone who comes in here, and I'm sure I would have remembered you. Avery sometimes says strange things like 'Death is so final. I should have...could have...'"

"Are you sure you heard correctly?"

"Definitely and I can prove it. I've installed a recording device near my throat because bartenders can be accused of a million things. I always turn it on when I'm working."

"Can you make me a copy of those conversations? It may be helpful in solving a crime."

"Sure. Just a sec." He leaves the bar and goes in the back and brings out a small clear plastic card. He holds it to his throat. I watch his Adam's apple rise and fall as he swallows. Then he hands me the card. "Here, no problem." He looks off in the distance as though thinking of something to add. Then he says, "Are you really Molly of Molly's Bistro?"

"I am."

"Molly of Molly's Bistro who solved that Chocolate Moons crime a few years ago?"

"One and the same."

"It's a pleasure to meet you. I've always wanted to go to your bistro, but either I have no time or no money. Maybe for my birthday next year."

I smile and say, "Tell you what, next time Avery comes in and says something, make a copy and send it to me. I'll make sure your name is added to our complimentary list."

When I return to Molly's, Jody is standing in the middle of a circle surrounded by the staff. She's tugging at her hair and crying. Everyone steps back to let me get closer.

"What happened?" I ask.

Jody sobs, "I've been called to Mars Yard for more questioning. They found a holo of me putting something in Rick Frances' drink the night of the murder."

I ask, "Did you put something in his drink that night?"

"Yes. Rick asked me to."

"What was it?

"He took some kind of supplement, a vitamin, maybe a

medication—I don't know what it was. Frank told me that he took a call from Lena, who said that when she saw it lying on a counter, she realized that Rick didn't take his daily dose and said Avery could drop them at the back entrance because she knew how much was going on in the restaurant."

"Frank told me that after it arrived he asked me to give it to Rick. I said, 'Of course'. When I told Rick, he said, 'Add it to my drink'."

"That's all?"

"That's all. He drank it and seemed fine until…"

I put my arm around her shoulder. "Then you have nothing to worry about. Just tell Lamont what you just told me. I'm sure Lena will corroborate your story. If it will make you feel better, I'll go to Mars Yard with you."

Jody and I sit in Lamont's office. Her hands fidget so much you would think she was playing the pianolyn. She repeats her story. Lamont nods a lot. Says little.

Finally, his eyebrows knit and his voice shifts. "I have to call Lena to corroborate your story. I'll put her on the speaker. Don't interrupt." Then he looks around to the rest of us but focuses on Sid and says louder, "Don't interrupt!"

After a few opening words from Lamont, we hear Lena gasp then cry, "I don't know what you are talking about, Lamont. And I don't remember seeing anything of the sort, nor do I remember calling Molly's Bistro. Frankly, I was so overwhelmed with the party, all my energy went into making sure that each table was programmed correctly."

Lamont disconnects the call. He turns to Jody. "You heard what she said. Do you want to change your story?"

Jody is shaking. She's whiter than an igloo on a polar ice cap. "That's what Frank told me," she says. Then with tears in her eyes, she looks at me and repeats it. "That's what Frank told me."

40

THE WEDDING DATE IS SET.

I fear some neglected detail in the wedding plans will start a disastrous butterfly effect followed by a disastrous domino effect that ruins everything the butterfly effect missed. Jersey gives me a rabbit's foot, scarabs, four leaf clovers, horseshoes, and wishbones and says stay away from butterflies and dominos.

I sit in my den, recently painted a color called No Longer Politically Correct Skin. My books are back on the shelves, desk in place, and pictures rehung. I kick off my slippers, breathe the aroma of hot cinnamon coffee, and sip.

I wonder how people in the past did so much when their days were filled with mundane chores. Robotic Services cleans and sanitizes my home daily. The refrigerator has a panel that lists what needs replenishing and a keypad to reorder. My life-sized 3D avatar shops and tries on virtual clothes while I watch and choose the ones to be shipped home.

Lamont calls. I drain my cup and put it down. I never thought that a call from him would be a welcome diversion from planning the wedding, but it is. He says, "Thought you would like to know that Sol Brody will be arriving on the space elevator this afternoon. We want to question him about why he and Rick Frances switched glasses."

"Ring me when the interview is over. I need to ask Sol if we have to go back to Nirgal Palace to arrange more for the wedding. Cortland is taking Becky and Lois to the Metadrum on Mercury for a concert. It leaves me to finalize the wedding arrangements."

"Anything else?" Lamont asks.

"I sent you a recording a bartender at Silicone Slings gave me. Let me know what you think."

Jersey calls and asks if she can bring her cousin to the wedding because she has never been to Nirgal Palace. I say no because we are over the limit for the Garden Terrace Room.

It had been difficult dealing with Sol, who quoted prices in an intimidating and confusing way. For example, if we asked how much extra for the bridal party to walk down a floating aisle, he would quote the price by saying one number, as in: "It costs five." Then we would have to ask if five meant five starbucks, five hundred, or five thousand. Usually it was five thousand. I asked if the floating platforms for the ceremony could be suspended with colorful balloons instead of the gravity changer, but Sol said, as though personally insulted, that if I was looking for a bargain affair I should book one on Deimos or Phobos.

Fifteen minutes later, Trenton calls. "The recording the bartender at Silicone Slings made arrived at Mars Yard. I analyzed it…"

"You analyzed it?" I say. "So fast. Are you sure you are not missing something?"

"I know what I'm doing, Molly. This is robotic child's play."

"OK…so…"

"Unfortunately, there's nothing to pin Avery to the murder. He did something he is sorry about, but nothing indicates murder. Lamont's having him come in tomorrow. Maybe we will find out more."

I barely catch my breath when there is a call from Sol. "You wanted to talk to me, Molly?"

"Well, yes…no."

"Which is it?"

I ask, "Will we have to make another visit to Nirgal Palace before the wedding?"

"No. Everything's on schedule. Oh, one thing you should know."

"And that is?

"Elvis called. Because so many of his new friends are androids, many of his old friends and family didn't want to sit at a table with them. Some said that they barely tolerated Elvis after his transformation, but family was thicker than computer parts and they loved Burton. Plus, they wanted to see Burton's rock star fiancée Becky and her twin sister Lois whose Lunar Tunes albums they love and want them to sign. Plus, the opportunity to go to Nirgal Palace at a discounted wedding rate was too much to pass up."

"What'll you do?"

"We're putting all the androids except Elvis in a separate area. We call it separate but equal."

"There is no such thing as separate but equal. There's always discrepancies. Cortland and I are paying, and it is going to be a cross-cultural affair or we'll cancel the whole thing."

When I tell Cortland, who is feeling all powerful and is on his way back from Mercury after a sold out concert that got rave reviews about the band's new polyrhythmic cadences and percussive thumps (already being sold on Carbon Copies Media outlets), his voice drops into his most serious sounding notch. "Let me handle this."

Two hours later, Cortland reports that he spoke to Elvis and Lulu. He tells me that with a lot of arm twisting and crying from Lulu, who says she is losing most of her family and everyone is calling her a very bad name, they agreed to let everyone sit where they wanted. What changed their minds was that Elvis would buy them a block of seats to the twins' next concert.

Later I call Lamont. "Anything I should be concerned about regarding Sol Brody? The wedding is only two weeks away."

"On the contrary, Molly. Sol was happy to explain everything about switching glasses with Rick Frances. He said that when he used to work at Rick and Carol's restaurant, he and Rick created a ritual of switching glasses for good luck before dinner guests arrived. That evening when he was with Rick, they did it again for old times' sake."

"How do you know he's telling the truth?"

"He told me that some of the staff from Cream now work at Creamed Cheese. And although Creamed Cheese didn't have the panache of Cream, it had its merits, especially when served with bagels. Everyone I questioned said that they remembered Sol and Rick doing the switched glass ritual."

41

I INVITE JERSEY FOR A SWIM. I take the stairs instead of the elevator to the pool two floors below. It's in a high-ceilinged room with expansive glass windows. As soon as I enter, the green tile floor begins to warm. The robotic lifeguard, sensing my presence, activates. I ask it to adjust the water to the last time I swam, as Cortland likes it much colder. Then I sit and wait for Jersey.

Every time I see the bony unclothed bodies of native Martians, I'm amazed. They are much taller and thinner than those Earth born because the light gravity causes fetuses to elongate. Becky and Lois were conceived and born on Earth's moon and tower over me at six foot eight. Jersey is also six foot eight and weighs 158 pounds.

Jersey arrives, waves, disrobes, and dives into the pool and crawls for several laps. Then she climbs out. "You have no idea how much I needed that," she says. "Thanks for inviting me." She takes two fluffy pink towels, wraps herself in one, and carries the other to a turquoise chaise. Her skin is tanned and healthy. I know she has not been in the sun, so it's from one of the supplements that she takes. She plops down and adjusts the angle of the chair and says, "So Lamont has no new leads—nothing that would suggest premeditation and intent."

"That's right. So far everyone who we thought guilty has a good alibi."

Her eyes narrow. "Including Holly Wood and Beverly Hills?"

"Not enough on either of them. Rick sent Beverly money for child support. So it's not likely she would murder her child's meal ticket. Nothing to link Holly to the murder either. For now they're just two old jilted girlfriends."

Jersey leans forward, wet hair dripping into her eyes. She pushes it away with the back of her hand. "Did Lena ever confirm Jody's story about her calling and sending over Rick's medicine?"

"She finally did. She called Lamont and apologized to Jody for causing her so much trouble and gave her a gift certificate for VV. She said that she was so overwhelmed with the party that she forgot she made the call."

"Did Lena know what the medicine was for?"

I reach for a moisturizer and rub some on my legs. Then I hand it to Jersey, who does the same. "Rick had told her that he had progeria but, as she could see, it was not life threatening."

Jersey says, "We knew when the autopsy on Rick was done that he had progeria, and I remember that when the police did a sweep of your restaurant, a prescription for Grafton, the medicine that controls it, was found with Mario's name on it. Think progeria is catching?"

"Call Trenton; he'll update us."

I lean in and try to hear what Trenton is saying, but I can't, so I lean closer. But all I hear is Jersey saying, "No. Well that's good news." Pause. "Really, Trenton? Hmmm." Pause. "You don't say. No kidding!" Pause. "Wow! Amazing." Pause. "OK love you too. Bye."

I lean back. "So what did he say?"

"He was able to access Mario and Rick's records and found that they were born in different places but born the same year."

"That describes millions of people."

"But luckily we were not conceived or born that year or were pregnant. That year wheat crops were being destroyed by a strange new virus. After a year, scientists reported that they made a chemical that kills it. It was tested and deemed safe and effective. So they added it to the irrigation water. When they thought the virus eliminated, they discontinued it."

"But it wasn't safe. Right?"

"For thirteen years, there were no problems. Then some children started to age more quickly than their peers. But luckily, before you could say walker and wheel chair, a vaccine was developed and the problem contained. But those already infected had to take a medication for the rest of their lives or they would start to age rapidly again."

"And Mario and Rick were two of those children."

"Yes. They were."

"That's why they both took the same medication."

"Right again."

Jersey reaches for a third towel and rubs her hair. "Hey, these towels are nice. Can I take one and have Trenton try it?"

"Keep it. I have plenty. But I'm sure they're more expensive than what you buy."

"Oh, we wouldn't *buy* one. What makes you think we would *buy* one? Trenton would make it in his replicator. He could tweak a few minor features so we weren't infringing on anyone's copyrights."

I sigh and say nothing.

Jersey asks, "What about your bartender, Harry? Anything on him?"

I shake my head. "Nothing to directly link him."

"And Sol?"

"Although Cortland jokes that he's a crook because of what he's charging us for the wedding, we have no hard evidence. Same for Frank."

Jersey gets up and walks to the stairs leading into the pool. She puts one hand on the railing and says, "I never would have believed Frank was once a woman. I think he's a great guy. He even has sex appeal."

Before I say anything, she disappears under the water. I watch her lap the pool again and admire how gracefully she swims. I adjust my chaise back and look at the ceiling. I'm so glad Cortland spent the extra money to have it vaulted and painted with stars. I close my eyes and relax. Then, like a rumpled moth exiting its chrysalis, I slowly make a connection. "Come out, Jersey." I call. No response. I walk to the side of the pool. "Come out, Jersey," I repeat.

"Why?" she looks up and calls back. "Just getting started." She swims to a side that has a small ladder that extends into the pool and ascends. She grabs several more towels, comes over, and plops into her chaise.

"Whatever you tell me, I'm going back in to finish my laps," she says, water pooling at her feet. "We're both so busy and it's such a treat to have time here." She drapes a towel over her shoulders and rubs her body.

"Deal," I say. "You know all you have to do is call and I'll arrange for you to use the pool."

"I know. It's not the access. It's the time. I need to edit my life."

"We all do."

Jersey rubs herself harder and leans closer.

I say, "The night Rick died, we had trouble with the dessert. Most of them had slid off the serving trolley and fallen on the floor. We had to stall for time. Frank and Vanna went into the basement to see if we had enough Saturns—those balls of pistachio mousse surrounded by pink meringue rings that we served before the regular dessert—and we did. Frank and Vanna had access to the Saturns. Frank, as he had been Rick's former wife, Carol, had to know that Rick had progeria.

Vanna might have known that Mario had progeria also, as they worked closely together, and Mario may have declined tasting certain things. Lamont told me that Grafton, normally a harmless food coloring product and easy to get, could be deadly in the right proportions for those with progeria. It would be easy to put some in one of the Saturns downstairs when the other was not looking—it was dark, and with a little slip of the hand—there you go."

Jersey's eyes widen. "The killer may have been carrying it for a long time waiting for the right opportunity. And then there it was."

"So?"

"So...that puts both Frank and Vanna back in the picture. Didn't you tell me that Vanna came from a family of scientists?"

I pick up a towel that had fallen to the floor and place it on my chaise. "That's right. Her mother is a chemist and her father a biologist. Although not a scientist herself, she might know a lot more about chemical interactions than the average person."

Jersey nods and says, "But you told me that Vanna held the spoon to Mario, not Rick."

"But Mario refused to take it. He said he couldn't judge the quality of the dessert if he was rushed and under pressure, so I offered to taste it, but Rick grabbed it first and ate it."

"And died," Jersey adds.

"And died," I repeat. We look at each other and don't speak. Then I say, "Are you thinking what I am thinking?"

"You first," Jersey says. "What are you thinking?"

"I'm thinking that it was meant for Mario, not Rick. Vanna and Mario seem to have a truce, but there is always tension. She's more than capable of being a head chef."

"Molly, you might have eaten it. You reached first," Jersey says, distressed.

"Yes. But nothing would have happened. I don't have progeria."

42

WHEN I TELL LAMONT THAT I think that the wrong person might have been poisoned, he quips, "Nice work, Sherlock. But it's speculative. Just bread crumbs. But we'll increase our surveillance on both Frank and Vanna. We should have a plainclothes man at the wedding.

As the wedding grows closer, I become more nervous.

Mario has made several trial wedding cakes. Becky favors a pink strawberry concoction, Burton wants something with chocolate, Elvis and Lulu want anything they can recreate for those who want a virtual wedding, and Cortland and I both love the Grand Marnier butter cream.

Then Mario makes an announcement that he has made two cakes in a tradition attributed to the American South: having a bride's cake decorated in a light textured color and a darker groom's cake that incorporated chocolate and fruit. He rolls out a serving trolley with two four-tiered masterpieces, one in antique white and another in rich brown chocolate. Both have vertical lines in fondant frosting that have edible flowers and fruits cascading down one side. We all swoon.

One problem down, 999 more to go.

The next day I call Lulu. After several rings, she answers.

"Did I interrupt you, Lulu? You usually pick up on two rings."

"Sorry, I was so engrossed. I'm reading a study that said children who ate alphabet soup had higher IQ's than children who didn't."

"Who did the study?" I ask.

"The company that made the soup."

"Do you think that's reliable?"

"As reliable as the candy company that makes Milky Ways and said that it comes from the Milky Way."

"I read that since forming, our Milky Way Galaxy has rotated sixty times. You would have thought that enough time to bring down the price."

I say, "I bought the most beautiful dress for the wedding."

"Me too," Lulu says. "I was going to surprise you."

"Mine is light blue overlaid with white lace."

"So is mine."

"Does it have a sash in white silk?"

"Yup."

"Did you get it at One of a Kind on Rodeo Drive?"

"Right again."

Turns out we bought the same dress. When I call the store, they tell me that one of a kind means one of a kind of people, not clothes, but clones can order discounted copies. Since Lulu and I can't agree on who is to keep their dress, we decide to wear them and announce that the same dress is a symbol of family unity.

Sol arranges for us to send everything except the wedding cake to Nirgal Palace three days before the wedding. His staff will unpack the clothes, press them, and hang them in our closets.

After a totally emotional day filled with arguing, crying, laughing, hugging and kissing, Becky, Lois, and I greet the UPS (United Planetary Service) attendants. The team loads the luggage onto their truck where they will deliver it to the space elevator. I thought I gave a generous tip, but they just stand there with long faces even after I add a few more starbucks. Then I call Lulu to find out if her things were picked up, and they were.

That evening we have a quiet family dinner at home.

An hour later, Lois and Becky, who went into our den to watch the news, are screaming.

Cortland and I, relaxing after the exhausting day and enjoying an after-dinner decaf, stop and put down our cups. We go into the den and look.

"Oh no!" I yell.

Becky's wedding gown, Cortland's tuxedo, my dress, undergarments, makeup... in short, everything we sent UPS, is floating in orbit around Nirgal Palace. A voiceover says, "No one knows how the lock on the cargo bay opened, and no one knows why the containers were not secured, but it seems that this is a delivery destined for a wedding at Nirgal Palace. A crowd is gathering on their observation deck. In one moment, we will have video contact. Please wait while we clear technical problems."

"Mommeeeeeee!" Becky wails. Then a moment later, Click. Buzz. Hiss. Buzz. Hiss. And in a booming voice, we hear...

"Reporting from Nirgal Palace's observation deck is one of our reporters who is here with his wife..."

Static interruption.

"Sorry about that folks, correction, one of our reporters who is here with a friend of his wife."

My palm rings, first with Cortland's cousins Billings and Flo asking what we're going to do, followed by Lulu, whose garbled voice is hysterical, and Elvis who wants film rights so he can use the footage to produce a virtual Psycho Honeymoon. Meanwhile, Becky on her palm with Burton says, "Let's elope." And Cortland, who I can see from his expression, is calculating how much this is either going to cost him and/or how much is he going to get if he sues.

"Turn up the sound, Lois," I say. "What's the reporter saying?"

Then we all hear, "Don't worry folks, Nirgal Palace just called 1-800 Space Vacuum."

Cortland says, "Why is it always 1-800? Who uses all the other numbers through 799?"

Sol calls Cortland. Cortland moves to a corner so he can hear better.

"What did he say?" I ask, closing in.

"Sol says he has everything under control."

"It doesn't look like things are under control," I say.

"He also said looks can be deceiving."

Two hours later, Sol calls Cortland again and tells him that it looks like nothing major was harmed and everything made it through the detox radiation chamber and/or would be replaced.

"What did he mean and/or?" I ask.

Cortland shakes his head.

Could this have been a deliberate act of sabotage? Was it meant to unnerve me so I would be overwhelmed with wedding problems and less focused on Rick Frances' murder or finding clues about the Cereal Serial Killer? If so, they almost succeeded.

The next morning, two days before the wedding, Mario and Vanna go to Nirgal Palace. They bring ingredients that Nirgal Palace might not have and cake decorations that they have premade for the wedding cakes. Both are in good spirits.

Later that afternoon, Becky and Burton go to Nirgal Palace. I think they just want to get away from Lulu and me who, after doing most of the work, are told that we are taking the fun out of their wedding and ruining their lives.

Lamont calls and says that he found a technical glitch that gives him a reason to get search warrants for Frank and Vanna.

43

THE DAY BEFORE THE WEDDING, I travel with Lulu and Jersey, who bring their husbands in their carry-on cases. Cortland, who is busy with last minute music arrangements, will travel with Lois. Becky and Burton are already there.

We enter an enormous enclosed circular ring that surrounds the base of the space elevator used for arrivals and departures. The high-ceilinged space is filled with glowing boards displaying connecting flights, information about the docking station, taxies, hotels, rover rentals, duty-free shopping, restaurants, bathrooms, and showers. Floating holos advertise Disney Uranus, Neptune, and Pluto. Announcements blare louder than bands at space ball halftime.

We circle round a long line, go through a security check, hand an attendant our tickets, and finally, finally, check in. We have an hour and a half before we can board the space elevator. A blinking arrow ahead points to duty free shopping.

"Do you think they planned the delay so we could shop?" Lulu asks.

Jersey rolls her eyes and says, "Do we need water to live?"

"You don't have to be sarcastic," Lulu says.

"Let's get one of those carts chained up next to the wall," I say. "We can cover more ground if we put Trenton and Elvis in it."

A woman passes and booms, "You've given your suitcases names? What planet do you come from?" Others nearby stare.

Jersey and Lulu scowl. We go and select two carts. A squinty-eyed redheaded attendant unlocks them and says, "That'll be twenty starbucks."

"My treat, Jersey," Lulu says. "You've helped me so much."

"It's twenty starbucks per cart," the attendant says.

"Oh," Lulu says, pausing, hoping Jersey will volunteer to pay for her cart, but I know there's no chance. Then, when Lulu sees she's stuck, she shakes her head, makes a face that Jersey ignores, and says that they'll take one cart because both cases can fit in it.

Lulu and Jersey take turns pushing the cart down a wide aisle trying to resist going into the shops. But when we see "Solar System Shoes—for feet that have had too little or too much gravity," we stop. "I'm tempted," Lulu says.

A man carrying a very full shopping bag approaches. He's scowling. The closer he comes, the more he scowls and the more familiar he looks.

"You're Molly Crocker," he says. "I never forget a face. I'm Greg Heinz from the pie eating contest in Baguette. Remember me?"

"I told you my name is Molly Marbles, not Molly Crocker."

"Whatever you call yourself, I haven't forgotten that you ruined the contest." He shakes his arm so hard that a box falls out of his shopping bag. Jersey picks it up. It's a box of Shredded Wheat.

He grabs it from Jersey's hand and snarls, "Oh that," and stuffs it back in his bag.

A couple approaches whose faces are familiar. "Molly," the woman says. "Nice to see you away from your bistro." She points to her husband. "You remember my husband, Andy? Are you going to Nirgal Palace?"

Then, relieved that out of context I remember so quickly, I say, "Ann and Andy Andromeda—you always have frozen asteroids for dessert. Yes. Going for my daughter's wedding." Before Ann can say congratulations, I add, "Ann, would you please tell this gentleman that my name is Molly Marbles Summers, not Molly Crocker?"

She looks at me. "Of course." She peers closer. "I see the resemblance, but I can vouch that you're not her."

I turn to Greg Heinz. "See," I say.

The Andromedas smile and walk away.

Greg Heinz snarls and leaves.

I say to Jersey, "Might Greg Heinz *be* the Cereal Serial Killer? I should tell Lamont my suspicions and what happened."

Jersey says, "A box of Shredded Wheat falling out of a bag is no big deal. On the other hand, who travels with a box of Shredded Wheat?"

But before I can call, I reach for the cart. No cart! I turn in every direction. No cart!

"Where's the cart?" Jersey screams.

"Where's the cart?" Lulu screams louder.

"It was just here," I say, voice shaking. "We all saw it here!"

"How could we have let ourselves get so distracted?" Lulu cries. "Shopping carts with carry on cases all look the same. Someone must have mistaken it for theirs."

We look around. Off to the side there's an unattended carrying case. "Looks like someone left this and probably took ours."

"They couldn't have gone far," Jersey says. "Trenton gave me a remote that will send a signal to his case if it was lost."

"But what about Elvis?" Lulu sobs.

Jersey says, "They're probably still in the cart." She pushes the remote. Immediately we hear a blaring recording of Becky and Lois singing "Like a Floating Stone."

"It's coming from the left," Jersey says.

We run.

A woman stands with the cart.

"Excuse me," Jersey says. "You've taken the wrong cart."

"Did I?" she says sweetly. "I'm sure it's mine."

"You did. I'm the one who activated the music coming from this case." She points to her case.

The woman's eyes glaze over like a seven-year-old at church. "Oh, I hadn't noticed. I love that song."

Jersey puts the remote in front of the woman's face, clicks it off, and says, "You had better go back and get your cart. It was unattended."

"I don't want the cart," she wails. "I want a new husband."

"How did you know that the cases in the cart contained someone?"

"You both had the look of a concerned mother watching a child. Hard to miss."

"Well, you can't have ours," Lulu says, pushing the cart away.

I check the time. The elevator leaves in ten minutes. We run. Faster. Faster. A red light is blinking above the elevator doorway. We leap through as it closes, panting and sweating as we throw ourselves into the first empty seats. Jersey and Lulu refuse to put their cases in the overhead bin and keep them by their sides.

Our blue and green striped seats are large and comfortable. I remember reading that the builders chose the colors because Mars had been successfully terraformed: green for Green Mars and its new vegetation, and blue for Blue Mars, whose dusty pink sky now with more oxygen became blue. One could still see old red Mars in places preserved by preservationists who think Mars should have more red rocks and fewer malls.

The elevator rises. The trip to the space station's docking station used to take over twenty-four hours. Now it's done in seven. Jersey comments that she wishes it could go faster but quips that we might get the bends. They nod off. But I call Lamont and tell him what happened with Greg Heinz.

"You interrupted me while the coroner and I were discussing the autopsy results from the brain tissue of an animal rights activist who was murdered at a nature preserve. A bullet entered his hippocampus while visiting the Hippo Campus in an impact crater in Amazonis Planita."

"Hippo Campus. Nice place. Went there when..."

"How can I help you, Molly?"

I tell him about Greg Heinz.

"He may have a record. His name might be an alias. I'll check and call you back."

I doze off. When I wake, the space elevator has risen significantly. The sky is black and filled with the unblinking stars of space. Every time I see them, I'm reminded of how shocked and transfixed I was seeing them for the first time on my way to my freshman year at Armstrong University on Earth's moon. I look behind. Mars fills the window. Jersey and Lulu are standing and stretching. An attendant passes out food, but from past experience, I know space elevator food is not worth the calories. So I brought salmon pesto sandwiches on crunchy French baguettes, Brie cheese, fresh fruit, and chocolate chip cookies. Hungry eyes watch us eat. I hand them my card.

Lamont calls and tells me that he's still checking on Greg Heinz but results of a new sweep of Molly's Bistro came back. Unlike the last forensic sweep after Rick Frances was murdered, when a tiny amount of Contaminate was detected—later deemed not enough to kill—more than the usual amount of Grafton was found in the dining room.

"How could that be missed?"

"We're good, Molly. Not perfect. In hindsight, we should have gone over the room several more times, but we didn't. When we get a negative sweep, we repeat the process three more times. That's usually plenty, or we would never move on."

I say to Lamont, "We've been running around looking for Contaminate, and now you tell me that Grafton might have been used to kill him. I thought Grafton was the medicine used to control progeria. I thought it was a good thing. But now I know the wrong dose can be poisonous."

Jersey says, "I remember Trenton telling me that Grafton was one of the products that is absorbed very quickly—it could leave no trace. The time Rick was lying unconscious in the back of Molly's without anyone helping him was probably enough time for it to disappear from his system."

"We're all concentrating on Rick Frances. Might it have been meant for someone else?"

"Or someone else as well," Jersey adds.

44

CORTLAND AND LOIS, BECKY AND BURTON are waiting for us in Nirgal Palace's bridal suite. The bright main room is used as a private dining and meeting room. A spectacular radiating "sun" chandelier, a smaller version of the gigantic one in the hotel's lobby, is suspended from the ceiling. The sofas and club chairs, set in a semicircle, are a wash of yellows. The soft light makes everything glow.

A pale peach hallway to the left leads to a bride's wing; a cerulean blue hallway to the right leads to the groom's wing. In front and back are floor to ceiling windows that view space. Lulu sets Elvis' case down with the relief of one whose journey has ended. She turns to Jersey and assures her that she can handle Elvis' emergence from the case by herself; if not, she'll call.

Burton kisses Becky good-bye, takes Elvis' case, and walks with Lulu to the groom's suite.

My family and I go to the bride's wing. The space has rose-colored furniture, three media walls, a kitchen alcove with a deluxe food replicator, and a well-stocked bar. Leading from it like the spokes of a wheel are six bedrooms and six bathrooms. I sink into one of the deep sofas and kick off my shoes. Cortland slides next to me, and Becky and Lois sit opposite.

For what seems like a long time, we look at each other in silence. Then I say wistfully, "This is one of the last times we'll all be together like this." Becky's eyes are tearing up. Lois' eyes are tearing up. A moment later, we are all tearing up. I manage to say, "Tears of happiness, right girls?"

They nod. We laugh. "How about a nap before the rehearsal dinner?" I say. We do a family group hug. And another. And another. Then Becky and Lois, arms around each other, go to one of the bedrooms like when they were children and shared a room.

I toss and turn and finally poke Cortland to tell him that I'm taking a walk. He pulls the sheet over his head and groans because I woke him.

I stop at a café and order a cup of tea. It comes with a chocolate cookie that I eat and think of Jersey and Flo who I know wouldn't touch it. When I reach for a napkin from the other side of the table, I see that someone left a memo. It says "Things to Do." Most items are ordinary like get new towels, make reservation for space elevator. Then I stop. The last item says, "buy poison for M."

I'm unnerved. I signal a waitress. "Do you know who sat at this table before me?" I ask.

"There are lots of people who sit here, madam."

"Well, one of them left this memo."

She takes the memo and reads it with no expression, no reaction, then says, "Sorry, can't help you."

I rise and decide to take the memo with me. As I'm walking back to my room, a woman who is out of breath catches up with me. "The waitress said I might catch you. I just realized I left my memo on the table. Do you have it?"

I hand her the memo and say nothing.

"Thanks so much," she says turning away.

"Wait," I say. "May ask what does 'buy poison for M' mean?"

"Buy poison for mice. Do you think I'm going to poison

someone?" She laughs. "Mice have been a big problem. There's a shop called "Solutions" on deck three that sells tax free products not easily available on Mars. Anything else?"

"Sorry. I should have left it on the table. I have a lot on my mind."

In the early evening, a large round table is set in the joint space between the groom's wing and the bride's wing for the rehearsal dinner. The ceiling chandelier has been dimmed to show a darker sky with stars. Hotel staff pour Jovian champagne from 2336, the year Becky and Lois were born. Everyone is having a wonderful time. I laugh and cry watching old holos that capture highlights of Becky and Burton growing up. There's smoked salmon, rack of lamb, potato croquettes with truffles, and vegetable custards.

Elvis and Lulu are happy and animated, as Lulu didn't have to call on Jersey to help her with Elvis and his case. Elvis says that being in the case is like taking a deep nap and nothing ever happens. Lulu and I exchange glances.

Elvis says, "We're sending the kids on a virtual honeymoon to Xbox, the new planet that was just discovered in the Horsehead nebula. We just got images from the faster than light loop." He reaches into his pocket. He puts a small yellow cube on the table and clicks. The room fills with images of high rises on a beach, a promenade, shops, outdoor cafes, and palm trees.

"Are you sure that's it?" I say. "Why send them so far when it looks exactly like New Miami Beach? What about that hotel complex on Io that's built into the phosphorus caves that glow, or The Arms, the spa in Venus' blue rain forest, or the executive suits on Disney's rock candy asteroid, or a skiing excursion through Saturn's rings?"

"Have you no imagination, Molly? It's the Horsehead nebula! Don't be such a nit-pick stick-in-the-mud!"

"It'll be good for business," Lulu says flatly. "And Burton will inherit the business."

"If he wants it," pipes Becky, kissing Burton's cheek.

Awkward silence. Then the dessert arrives. It looks like a half of a large hardboiled egg—but is a white chocolate shell exposing a lemon curd yolk sitting in the middle of white meringue. It's called the Michel Richard after the chef who invented it. It gets more oohs and ahhs than the new blue ice sapphire necklace Cortland bought for me.

Then my palm signals a call from Vanna. I listen but say little. I click off, look at everyone, and tell them Vanna said that as soon as Mario finished making the wedding cake, he got sick. She also said that she'd call New Chicago Specific Hospital and have them examine Mario. And not to worry because she will bring the cake.

While everyone is talking about this, I go to another room and call Lamont. "Send a forensic to Molly's Bistro immediately. Vanna says Mario is ill and is resting in my restaurant's staff lounge. When you get there, have Mario tested for Grafton poisoning. If it's not done immediately, it may dissolve and leave no trace. Also, check and see if Vanna did call New Chicago Specific Hospital. If she's just saying that she did but didn't...well, not a good sign."

45

ON THE DAY OF THE WEDDING, Lulu calls and says, "Ready?"

"Except for being exhausted from meeting each other at the refrigerator at all hours during the night, we're ready."

My palm signals a voicemail. I click. The voice sounds artificially deep, camouflaged. "Stop finding out what happened to Rick Frances or you and this wedding will be ruined."

Do I tell Cortland? I don't want to spoil this day.

I call Lamont.

"Can't trace that call, Molly," Lamont says. "When you are off planet, the privacy codes are almost impossible to crack. Mars Yard calls them Turing's Torture. Could have come from within the hotel or could have come from Sedna, 2012 VP113, or another object beyond Pluto in the Oort cloud. On the other hand, I could come to the wedding."

"No, I don't think that's necessary."

"Are you sure? I heard that a new race track that circles the hotel has been completed. Greyhounds are scheduled to race in one third Mars' gravity. You know, not only people like to do things in gravity lighter than they are used to. Animals love it, too. Say the word. My tuxedo is packed."

"Thanks again, but no."

"Sid could go, but he only has a Shredded Wheat costume."

"No."

"Final answer?"

"Bye, Lamont."

Room service beeps signaling that a complimentary breakfast is waiting outside the suite. I put on a robe and open the door to the living room that adjoins the suites and call Lulu. Four people in grass green t-shirts that say "Congratulations" in gold wheel in three dollies with large silver trays. They are laden with breakfast treats that would shut down the Diet Network: blueberry, peach, and plum melons that have an official stamp showing that they came from Mercury's underground melon farms; pink rose petal juice from Venus; giant eggs from giant chickens from the free range crater on Ganymede, prepared boiled, scrambled, fried, poached and sauced; as well as quail eggs from the quail crater placed on artichoke hearts topped with salmon roe. Added to this are breads from Calisto whose recipes are as secret and protected as that of Coca Cola. Popovers, pancakes, waffles, Jupiter-style stuffed French toast that looks like gigantic challah breads, and that's only on the first dolly.

"Looks like it was catered by Roses Heaven," I whisper to one of the waiters.

"It was, madam. We have a standing order with them for special occasions. Our chefs are too refined to tackle the breakfast needs of wedding parties. But between you and me, it's our biggest hit."

Everyone overeats.

Elvis and Lulu holograph everything and say they will make its virtual equivalent. I doubt they will succeed. Nothing tastes like real cholesterol!

We waddle back to the bride's wing, and the Ernies go to the groom's wing to rest and recover.

Two hours later, masseuses, manicurists, make-up artists,

hairdressers, dressmakers, and others trained to make the homeliest person look beautiful arrive. We start by jumping into hot showers.

Then the lights flicker and dim.

I make a quick exit from the shower and wrap myself in one of the luxurious terry robes embroidered with our names that we can take home. Becky, Lois, and Cortland, looking like people evicted from their homes in a storm, come out of their showers.

We go to the common area to see if the power works better there and meet the Ernies who look the same.

An announcement blares: "Due to technical difficulties, Nirgal Palace will be operating on auxiliary power."

"Technical difficulties!" Becky cries, towel in hand rubbing the wet hair dripping over her face. "What does that mean?"

"Nothing works," Burton laughs. "Maybe we'll do everything in the dark."

Becky glares. "Not funny, Burton."

"We'll get through this," Lulu says. "Everyone relax their minds and think of obscure spare parts. Be positive."

I think, *Lulu can be positive—all she's thinking about is this wedding. But I've gotten threats. Is this a diversion related to the Cereal Serial Killer giving him more time to evade capture?*

Suddenly, the room brightens.

"See," Lulu says. "It worked."

An announcer says, "Sorry, folks. Who would recognize the modern world without technical difficulty? Especially if you are in a hotel on a space station whose life depends 100% on artificial constructions?" Then, in a lighter tone, "And as long as I have everyone's ear, today we're celebrating the wedding of Becky Summers and Burton Ernie.

"The ceremony will be held on our Outer Space Platform and the reception in the Garden Terrace Room. Becky, with her twin sister Lois, are the hit singing team The Lunar Tunes. You can hear their music all day in the Starbright Lounge."

Everyone relaxes.

I answer a call from the grooming staff who asks if we are ready to get dressed. Everyone says yes.

It's a soothing, coddling process where each step makes us all look better, and Cortland and I younger. Cortland looks at me and says, "Molly, you look so beautiful. I would marry you again if I could."

He comes to give me a kiss, but I pull back and say, "You'll spoil my makeup."

He laughs. "You never would have said that when we got married."

Suddenly we hear sobbing coming from Becky's room. I think, *What now?* Becky emerges crying and says, "Mom, am I doing the right thing?"

She is only half dressed. Crying has ruined her makeup. A stylist removes a veil and steams away the wrinkles.

Cortland and I say reassuring things. She calms down. Then Lois says, "You can always get a divorce, Becky."

This sends her sobbing harder back into the bathroom. Click. Door locked.

"Becky, sweetheart," I call, tapping gently on the door. "Let me talk to you."

"Leave me alone!" she wails. Louder sobs, running water, many toilet flushes. We all wait. Finally, head down and totally disheveled, she emerges.

One of the stylists asks if she may continue. Becky breathes like one about to start a swim race and nods yes.

Finally arm by arm, layer by layer, zipper by zipper, button by button, she is helped into her gown. She fidgets and examines herself in the holos as the moments tick by, and after a scrutiny of details only a bride can see, she finally blossoms with joy and glows.

46

TWO WEDDING WHISPERERS IN WHITE TUXEDOS and high white hats stand next to a gold and silver chariot covered in a pink veil. It is pulled by ten miniature white horses. As soon as they see us, they bow. One tells us that the groom and his family have gone ahead.

Cortland puts out his hand to stroke one of the horses. "Are these horses real?" he asks.

"As real as robotics can make them," the other whisperer answers.

Cortland lowers his hand.

The whisperer pulls the veil from the chariot and helps us climb aboard.

We wind our way through the hotel, stopping in the central lounge. Our holograms are beamed throughout the hotel and out to the media.

"This is something Sol forgot to mention," Cortland says, smiling his professional smile through tight jaw muscles. "We should get a discount for the free publicity that we never asked for."

But Becky is beaming and enjoying the attention. She leans from the coach, gracefully waving like a princess to her admirers. Flower petals rain over the coach.

Finally, we reach an area outside the Outer Space Platform and exit the coach. Our makeup and clothing are checked. Becky is sprayed with Venus Number Five. She is handed a bouquet of pink peonies and peach roses.

Lois, the maid of honor, is escorted ahead and joins the bridesmaids and ushers. Soft music plays, and we know that they are walking down the aisle and waiting in their places.

One whisperer whispers, "It's time."

Becky beams like there had never been any problems. Cortland and I stand on either side of her. My palms are sweating. My heart is beating so loudly I can hardly hear the first notes of "Here Comes the Bride." A door opens. Except for the smoky, silvery-white aisle ahead, there is nothing but luminescent pearl-like stars above and below creating the illusion that we are suspended in space even though our feet tell us that the aisle is solid and we are not going to fall or fly away. The guests sit to the sides on tiered floating iridescent gold cushions watching. The music grows louder. No one moves.

"Don't look down," one whisperer says as he places his hand on my back, giving a little push. I feel like I'm walking a gangplank. I squeeze Becky's elbow tightly and walk toward the podium where Burton, looking like he's floating on a white cloud, stands and smiles nervously. When he takes Becky's hand and brings her toward him, they rise on the cloud that stops at the podium. Cortland and I move to seats in the front of the audience opposite Elvis and Lulu.

Everything is a blur until I hear the words, "You may kiss the bride."

Curtains of light descend. Gauzy layers of color radiate. The sky spins. Becky and Burton, shivering with excitement, turn and are lifted into the air on an invisible anti-gravity platform and are swept to the exit as the recessional music of Widor's Toccata from his fifth organ symphony plays. Gold and silver flakes sparkle in the light and dissolve on the floor leaving no trace.

Everyone moves into the foyer of the Garden Terrace Room for the reception.

The room shines as though from a million fireflies. A waiter passing a tray of juicy shrimp balls tells me that the light comes from plants that have luciferin proteins inserted in their DNA as they mature, causing the glow. I nod and smile, masking ignorance.

Becky and Burton stand in the middle of a reception line greeting well-wishers. The Oxygen Orchestra plays soft music that I wish would go on all evening. But I know as people eat and drink more, it will escalate into the ear-piercing sounds that the young people love.

Time feels like it is passing more swiftly than a flash snowstorm in spring. Fortunately, holographers are recording the wedding, complete with smells and taste, and will give me a life-sized walk though playback.

My palm signals a call. It's Vanna. Cortland watches me tense my back. The connection is poor. "I delivered the wedding cake to the Nirgal Palace kitchen staff. I stayed while they added the finishing touches. It looks as wonderful as Mario would have wanted," she says.

"Where is Mario now?" I ask

"Can't hear, Molly. So much noise."

"Where is Mario now?" I repeat.

"Can't hear. Congratulations!" Click. Disconnect.

Jersey and Trenton push through the crowd. Jersey is wearing a violet and gray one-shoulder dress in an abstract print that seems to defy gravity. I've never seen her dressed this way, and she looks lovely.

"Beautiful abstract print on your dress," I say.

"It's not abstract. It's the answer to one of the Saturian quadruple reverse calculus problems. Trenton designed it."

"Well, he did a very good job. It's very flattering."

Jersey beams and winks at Trenton. "See, sweetheart. You shouldn't have worried. It's totally appropriate for a wedding."

Trenton swirls his drink and winks. "I have to thank the bartender at Oils for recommending you serve these Bloody Exxon Sours." He smacks his lips. "Delicious! That anti-freeze pushes the envelope. Now everyone at Nirgal Palace will want one."

"Not everyone, Trenton. It will never replace..." I'm about to say champagne when he and Jersey catch someone's eye and scoot off. A tray of crunchy spring rolls appears at one elbow and a tray of foie gras balls coated in chopped cashews at the other. I take one of each. Lulu and Elvis wave like pennants at halftime and do a thumbs up.

The lights dim, followed by a trumpet fanfare. Everyone turns. The back wall has been transformed into a massive waterfall. A voiceover booms: "Please move from the reception area to the dining room through the waterfall."

"I'm not going through that!" a woman cries. "Not after all the money I spent to look this good."

"It's a holo, madam," a waiter says. She hurries through.

There is an exquisite smell of fresh young foliage that covers the walls. Stars peek through trees. Pale blue linen and Wedgewood-inspired china cover the tables. Tall silver candelabras surrounded by fresh flowers sit in the middle. Bands take turns playing from a carousel that slowly circles the room.

We find our table. A waiter with one white-gloved hand behind his back hands us menus. Cortland and I order the stem cell grown herb crusted prime rib with a horseradish cream, garlic mashed potatoes, broccoli custards and green onion-parmesan popovers. Lulu and Elvis share a six-pound grilled lobster from Enceladus whose underground sea farms grow the best seafood in the solar system.

Everyone is so engrossed in their meal and conversations

that we hardly realize that the walls are undulating and slowly shifting.

47

THE LIGHT BRIGHTENS. Loud peppy music gives everyone a jolt. The dining room has been transformed into a circus tent. A ringmaster in a top hat and tails stands in the center. He tips his hat and booms, "Ladies and Gentlemen, welcome to the Big Top at Nirgal Palace."

Green clowns descend from the ceiling and pass thornless roses. Blue clowns spin plates on sticks. Gymnasts hurtle through high hoops. Lions dance with tigers, zebras prance, and jugglers send torches into the air. Dolphins sing from water tanks that rise from the floor then shatter into pixels that dissolve in the air. It's supersensory overload.

My palm vibrates a message. I refuse to look.

The ring master calls, "Please welcome your hosts, Mr. and Mrs. Burton Ernie." Everyone applauds. He points to a carpet in front of him and motions for Becky and Burton to sit. Burton climbs on first. Becky wraps her arms around him and holds on. The carpet rises and flies through the room. Becky blows everyone kisses.

When they return to their seats, the room undulates again and shifts to the way it looked when we arrived, but now a dance floor is in the center.

Cortland leans into me and says, "I have never seen such

wonderful stage technology. I must find out who created this."

Drum roll.

Music picks up.

Ginger Snaps, the band leader, puts two fingers to his eyes and points one finger at Becky and Burton and says, "Time for that first dance." They move to the floor. When I hear the soft soothing sounds of "A Squared Plus B squared Equals Love," it's the last time I don't need earplugs.

A wheel of fortune descends from the ceiling. "Gravity Mix!" Ginger shouts, giving it a spin. The word *Charon* lights and blinks. "It's the gravity of Pluto's moon, Charon. Anyone not steady on their feet, please, please sit this one out." He pauses looks around and shouts, "And a one and a two and a three..."

"We can still do this," Cortland says, grabbing my hand and yanking me to the floor before I can protest. Over my shoulder, I see Elvis doing the same to Lulu. Jersey needs no prodding, already twisting and sailing with Trenton.

Then Ginger calls, "Gravity shift for a medley: On your mark, get set..."

First it's the Horah, which segues into the Neptunian Neurosis, the Misalu, the Venus Fly Trap, the Virginia Reel, the Plutonian Pickle Virus, the Alzheimer's Confusion, the Foot and the Fiddle, the Cupid Shuffle, the Electric Slide, the Bicycle Pump, the Kleenex Box, the Chicken Dance, the Achy Breaky, the Macarena, the Cotton Eye Joe, the Cha Cha, the Fringe, the Conga, the Satori, the Speed of Light, the Mercury Sundial and the Hoedown Throwdown.

I dance one dance with Trenton. Cortland dances two with Jersey—so you know he's had plenty to drink and feeling no pain.

The music slows and stops. Lights dim. Then brighten. My palm vibrates again. I ignore it again.

"Find your seats," Ginger says. "Will the bride and groom

come to the podium for the cutting of the wedding cakes?"

A tall porter approaches me. "Message came to the hotel for you, madam. Shall we palm it or should I send it to your mailbox in your room?" Cortland sees me move to the side with him.

"Why was it sent to the hotel? Why wasn't it sent directly to me?" I ask remembering that two attempts were made, but I ignored them.

"Sometimes guests like us to answer all their calls to show the sender that they are registered. Some people say that they are staying with us but are really at Motel Six. Other like to receive the personal touch to show others how important they think they are."

We touch palms. His fingers are long and strong and warm. When he backs away, I read, "Stop snooping. I mean it."

Cortland asks, "What was all that about?"

"Tell you later."

Two chefs dressed in white kitchen uniforms and high chef's hats—*neither of whom really made the wedding cakes*, I think—guide an anti-grav platform with the bride's cake and place it on a table in the center of the room. This is followed by two more chefs guiding another anti-grav platform with the groom's cake, which is placed next to the bride's.

Ginger calls Becky and Burton to cut the cake. Music rises. First they kiss. Everyone cheers. Then one of the chefs hands Burton a knife. Becky puts her hand on top of his as he cuts a slice from the groom's cake. Then Burton places a piece of his cake into her mouth. Louder cheers. Becky repeats the procedure with the bride's cake. The crowd goes crazy.

Plates are passed. Cake is eaten. I hear the words remarkable, wonderful, best party ever. Coffee and after dinner drinks are served and sipped. Soft music plays. Dancing is slower. Take home treats are given to the guests. I am as happy as I have been since my own wedding.

Then it's over. All those months of planning reduced to a period at the end of a sentence.

48

THE FIRST DAY I'M HOME, Mario calls.

"And you're all right?" I ask.

"Yes, of course I'm all right. Vanna called New Chicago Specific Hospital and made sure I got the correct medication. Didn't she tell you she was going to do that?"

"Well, yes, she did, but with everything happening, I wasn't sure that…"

"She was wonderful, Molly. Stood by me like a trooper."

"So your squabbles are at an end?"

"Yes. In fact, we have something we want to share, but we're still organizing the details."

"And that is?"

"I said still organizing the details."

I say nothing.

I view some of the holographs for the wedding album. I see two holos of Cortland dancing with Jersey. When I ask him if he wants them included, he said that there had to be some mistake because he never would have danced with Jersey.

Yeah, right!

Later, I call Sol at Nirgal Palace. "Just want to say that the wedding was as wonderful as I had hoped it would be. I'm still coming down from a cloud."

"Just keep us in mind when her twin sister wants to tie the knot. We could have done two for the price of one. You would have saved a bundle."

"But Lois doesn't have a steady boyfriend."

"You could do the wedding and she can find someone later."

"Don't think it works that way, Sol."

"Just showing flexibility."

"To change the subject, Sol, do you think that the Cereal Serial Killer is on Nirgal Palace?"

"You really have been consumed by the wedding. Haven't you heard? Mars Yard caught the guy inside the base of the space elevator. His name is Greg Heinz. Someone in a Shredded Wheat costume, who said because of popular demand he was making a documentary about serial killers who loved Shredded Wheat, helped elevator security link him to a shipment of Shredded Wheat going to a storage facility on Calisto."

"Calisto?"

"Jupiter's moon, Calisto. See you weren't even sure where it was, were you?"

"Well, if you give me a moment to think."

"No thinking, Molly. Missing the point. Let's free associate. If I say Calisto, what's the first words that come to mind?"

"Inferiority complex."

"Right. Not moon of Jupiter. Inferiority complex. That's what everyone says, but they don't know why. Calisto's inferiority complex was caused because although it is about the same age as Jupiter—4.5 billion years—it looks older because it is the most heavily cratered object in the solar system."

"Who knew? Not even moons want to look old."

"It wanted to distinguish itself, do something noteworthy, get people's minds off its craters that resembled adolescent acne. So when the Shredded Wheat archives looked for a home, Calisto's government said, 'Dump it here. We'll undercut the price of any planet or moon!' So today when one says Calisto, one no longer says inferiority complex; one says Shredded Wheat."

"Calisto Shredded Wheat," I say softly rolling the words off my tongue, trying out the combination.

"That's the sprit, Molly. It's poetry!"

I sigh.

Sol continues, "Heinz protested that he was an innocent businessman, only a middleman, and didn't know what the shipment contained and that they should find Molly Crocker because she was the one responsible. But by that time, an analysis of his fingerprints matched the ones for the killer on file at the Yard. The guy making the documentary did five takes from different angles plus a selfie with Greg Heinz holding a box of Shredded Wheat."

I say nothing.

"Are you there, Molly? Mars media found a picture of Molly Crocker and just released it. I'm embarrassed to say, but you look like her."

"So I've been told."

"Any idea who the guy in the Shredded Wheat costume might be?"

"No idea."

But I do have a good idea and so does Lamont, who I call.

"Can't let good disguises go to waste Molly," Lamont sighs. "Taxpayers wouldn't like it."

Molly's is packed with regulars. Jersey and Trenton are dining with Elvis and Lulu. I'm sure Trenton has found some way for Elvis to pick up the check. Frank is wheeling a cart of live lobsters that arrived from Enceladus this morning toward Sandy and Solaria Andreas who are sipping Sunspots. An orange bubble hits Solaria's nose. She sneezes and dabs her nose with a napkin. They see Frank with the lobsters and wave him over. Frank rolls the cart closer. He starts describing various preparations when Sandy sees me and interrupts him. Sandy rises and turns to Solaria. "Order what you want; I need to talk to Molly." He walks toward me and says, "Can we speak confidentially?"

He follows me to my office smiling and waving to other diners like a politician running for office. We enter my office. He doesn't sit.

"What's this all about, Sandy?"

"Solaria and I have been so busy we haven't had time to take a vacation. My new organic farm on Venus flooded. Don't know why I let myself get talked into investing in a planet that's all humidity. It should have been named Arthritis, not Venus. Solaria has been so busy at the Culinary Institute…"

"She must love being the director. She is so well qualified and…"

Sandy, annoyed with my interruption, quells me with a look.

"As I was saying, Solaria has been so busy planning the Beef Jerky Eaters World Cup gala that she said, 'Let's book a virtual vacation at Club Mood instead of a real one.' So we did."

I say nothing and let Sandy continue, fearing that if I don't, he'll start again from the beginning. "Lulu and Elvis made us feel comfortable immediately. They're your in-laws, aren't they?"

"Our daughter Becky married their son Burton at Nirgal Palace."

Sandy nods and says, "Love that place. I told Lulu and Elvis that our first virtual experience was the night Rick Frances was killed during that joint dinner you had with Virtual Vittles. Then Lulu mentioned that she had found a holo that she thought had a clue concerning your waitress Jody, but it turned out to be a dead end. That made me wonder if something could have been missed from those I had, so when I went to my office, I asked my secretary to go through holos of that evening again and she found one that might interest you.

"My holo is not too different from Lulu's, but instead of showing your waitress, it shows your head waiter Frank putting something in a drink that he hands to Rick Frances."

Sandy reaches into his pocket removes a holo chip. "Here," he says, handing it to me. "Take it to Mars Yard."

"Why don't you bring it to Mars Yard yourself?"

"Want to be anonymous. Don't want the publicity of being involved. You, on the other hand, are already involved."

"Lamont Cranshaw can be discreet."

Sandy gives me a look meant to intimidate, but not seeing an enthusiastic response, he leans toward me and says, "Thanks, Molly. Knew you would do it. In fact, this could be just the information needed. This case could become more famous than the parting of the Dead Sea."

"Wasn't it the Red Sea that parted?"

"Yeah, but we're on Mars. They're all red."

"I'll see that Lamont gets it," I sigh.

The next day I decide to share the holo Sandy gave me with Jersey, who had come to take out Mario's unsweetened lemon mousse with sea trout and roe that many thought tart enough to clean copper pots because Trenton wanted to see if he could duplicate it in his replicator.

"Sure looks suspicious," Jersey says, brows knitting. "Better call Lamont. Trenton's too busy to take a peek now. Orders for diamond digits are overwhelming ever since he did the big toe of that new singer Big Foot. This is his first project that has ever made money. We're still recovering from the time the gold he wove turned into flax."

When I call Lamont, he says, "You're just the person I want. Mars Yard has put me in charge of the Police Benevolent

Association fundraiser. I could use some advice."

"You know, Lamont, I run a catering business, and I charge by the hour for advice."

"OK then, just give me your opinion."

I take a deep breath and say, "To change the subject, an anonymous source gave me a holo of Frank adding something to Rick Frances' drink."

"I thought we cleared Frank," Lamont says.

"You did, but this is new information."

"Might you tell me who this person is?"

"He wanted to remain anonymous."

"Sandy Andreas, right?"

Becky and Burton come to my home glowing from their honeymoon.

"What was the best part?" I ask.

"Oh," Becky says, "the virtual one that Lulu and Elvis sent us on."

"Really? I thought that place looked like New Miami Beach. What was so special?"

"We went to so many exotic places and ran around till we were exhausted. We wanted a familiar looking place with a lot of pampering. This was it."

"You could have found many places a lot closer."

Burton winks. "But not one that would bring Mom and Dad new business."

No sooner do Becky and Burton leave and I am about to take a shower, Frank calls. His tone is tense. "Did you know that Lamont wants to question me again, Molly?"

"Yes. We spoke."

Later that afternoon Frank returns from Mars Yard.

"How did it go?" I ask.

"Lamont showed me a holo of me putting something into

Rick's drink. The holo didn't show that right before that image, Rick handed me the substance himself. I remembered how sensitive his system could be and asked if it was safe. He looked at me for a moment with that same look of recognition that he had in your office and asked why I asked that. I said too many club drugs were getting into the wrong hands and one couldn't be too careful.

"Lamont got a holo enhancer to see if any shadow imprints could be recovered of the time before I added the substance to the drink."

"And?"

"Sure enough, there was an image of Rick handing me the substance. It never crossed my mind an hour later when Avery sent over Rick's medicine, the medicine I gave to Jody to give him, that the combination might cause an overdose. Rick must have been so excited and distracted that he forgot he had taken something earlier."

My eyes narrow. "Or he knew he had taken vitamins earlier and thought the combination safe. Maybe it wasn't just medicine that Avery sent. Or the wrong dose."

Frank says, "You're some detective, Molly. I never would have thought of that. Ever think of becoming a pro?"

"Once or twice. The twins even bought me a Sherlock Holmes hat, but I love the food business more." I pause. Then as an afterthought as though talking to myself, I say, "Could it be Avery? If so, more evidence is needed."

Frank blinks in surprise and taps my forehead.

49

I'M HOME WITH CORTLAND, swooning over seafood pasta with a shocking amount of garlic smell rising into the room. Cortland breathes in the aroma, raises his glass, swirls his Pinot Grigio, and asks, "If Frank was guilty, would he have gone to a men's or women's prison?"

"Men's, I think." Then after a delay, I say, "Yes, definitely men's. He wanted to be a man and has lived as one for years. So he should be treated as a man."

Cortland nods. When he adds, "Does Lamont have evidence to nail Avery?" my palm signals a call.

"Guess who?" I say.

Cortland silently mouths, "Lamont." He leans closer to listen.

I say. "Um, that's interesting, Lamont. Hmm, wow, really. No, not taking a table, but put us down for two tickets. Bye."

"Two tickets? To what?" Cortland asks, eyebrows curling.

"The Police Benevolent Association dinner."

"You know I hate to go to those things."

"I know, sweetheart," I say, patting his hand. "I'll give the tickets to Elvis and Lulu. They'd love to go. Some of their best clients are policemen and firemen who can't get away and need to de-stress." I point to my empty glass. Cortland refills it.

A service bot clears the table and goes back to the kitchen. Another brings chocolate chip studded cannolis that I'd bought earlier at Half Foods. They are made with artificial low calorie ingredients. Ingredients Mario and Vanna would never use, as they consider them laboratory products, not food products. They have a point. Cortland crunches his last crumbs and signals the bot for another, but the bot doesn't respond. "I only bought two," I say.

"Why did you buy only two? You know I love these."

"Sold out."

Cortland frowns. "Weren't they just sold out of Red Rocks Pie? Seems that Earth created Whole Foods. Earth's moon created Half Foods. Looks like Mars is creating Quarter Foods."

I've not finished my cannoli, so I give him the rest of mine. Cortland's eyes light up. Among other things, a good marriage is not made in heaven but on a plate.

I decide to go to VV under the guise of planning another joint dinner. After all, it was a good idea and successful. That is if Rick Frances hadn't been murdered. I palm their code.

Avery answers, "Sorry Molly, we're painting the dining room and Lena is upgrading the kitchen. Would you like to come to my apartment for tea at four o'clock to discuss it? I make the best scones and have clotted cream and wonderful strawberry jam."

I leap at the chance to go to Avery's apartment and have tea. When served correctly, it's a treat I usually skip. As a former overweight person, I still feel guilty when I do enjoy its calories. But fortunately today I had skipped lunch, so I feel vindicated.

Avery says, "I live in a new building on San Francisco Place." He gives me the address.

I go to my rover parked in a lot that several businesses share. There is a note tucked into the windshield. It says, "Leave well enough alone." I look around to see who is near, but there are only three people in the lot—teenage girls walking in different directions. Not likely suspects. When I tap my palm to release the door lock, an automated voice says, "Lock released earlier." I turn the handle. It's open. Strange. I thought I had locked it, but I've been distracted and rushing, so maybe I didn't. I walk to the other side of the rover to see if anything else is amiss and spot a puddle underneath. Could it have been there before I parked and not noticed it?

In ten minutes, I'm at the top of San Francisco Place. Like its namesake on Earth, it is winding and steep. The address Avery gave me is near the bottom. I turn in from Tharsis Street and begin my descent. At the end of the first block, my speed accelerates. I'm sitting in a ton of plasteel that I'm not controlling going faster and faster. Brake! Brake! Nothing. Repeat. Repeat. Nothing. I signal the emergency that deactivates the rover. Airbags inflate. The rover slows and finally stops, facing sideways. I'm stunned and feel like a cloud of atoms whose magnetic attraction to each other is blinking on-off-on-off.

A passerby asks if I need help. "You're lucky," she says. "This is a dangerous street."

"Let me see if I can restart the car and park it."

She waits and watches as the motor turns over, and I slowly roll to the curb. I cut the motor and turn the wheels in backwards toward the curb so it doesn't roll. I get out just in time because smoke pours from the motor, but the engine doesn't ignite. Then the smoke stops. I call rover service, tell them what happened, and give them the address.

Avery greets me with no expression. I tell him about my rover. He sympathizes and says he is glad I'm not hurt. He lives on the ground floor of a new building in a bright one bedroom flat painted light grass green. There is a small enclosed garden in back. Lots of photos of friends and what he told me were pictures of his former self are on bookshelves in the front hall.

"Ever miss what you used to look like?" I ask peering at the old photos.

"Never. Why should I? I'm better looking now. And if I don't like a part, I can redo it." He touches his nose. "Third nose."

"Mind if I use the bathroom before we get started?"

"Sure. Down the hall, second door on the right."

I open the medicine cabinet and quickly look at what's inside. There is an empty space—which could have held anything—but outside of that, nothing looks very suspicious. I take one of the absorbent cloths I brought from home and rub it along each shelf and put it into a secure pouch in my bag. Then I take another and rub other surfaces and add it to the others. Then without using the toilet, I flush it.

Avery has brought the tea to his dining table that is set with pretty gold and white china. He sits opposite me. I take a small, artfully cut watercress and goat cheese sandwich and put it on my plate. "My favorite," I say. I add a scone. When I load the cream on my spoon, I deliberately jiggle it, and spoon and cream drop on the floor. "How clumsy. I'm so sorry," I say.

Avery gets up. "No problem. It's a reason I don't put rugs under a dining table. I'll clean it and get you another spoon."

As soon as he leaves, I wipe as many surfaces as I can and put the cloth in my bag.

The tea is as delicious as it looks. Avery gives me some scones and strawberry jam made from strawberries he grew in his garden to give to Cortland.

"This may never reach Cortland's lips," I say.

Avery smiles.

50

I CALL LAMONT WHEN I GET HOME. He sends Sid to pick up the absorbent cloths and get a sample from the spot that was under my car.

When Sid arrives, he sees the scones and says that he would love one but can't ask Avery or he will know we've been in touch.

"I'm sure I could get the recipe to give to you," I say.

"No matter what some believe, Molly, you can't really eat a hologram." His face droops.

I give him a scone. Bright smile. Generosity has nothing to do with it, just a way to augment will-power and save calories.

The results on the cloths showed traces of Grafton enhanced triple strength. One dose would be poisonous to Rick or anyone else who had the same condition. The spot under my car matched brake fluid from my rover. The garage that is fixing my car said there was a hole in the brake lining.

Lamont and Sid go to VV to pick Avery up for questioning.

Lena says, "You just missed him. He just left for Pluto to open a branch of VV at Disney City. But you might be early enough to catch him at the spaceport. Don't know why he was in so much of a hurry. But he said no time like the present, palmed a reservation, and left.

"Opening a branch on other worlds was not a new idea. We had discussed it in the past, especially after we saw how successful VV was on Nirgal Palace. So although I thought his departure abrupt, I understood. The virtual business is evolving. Newer places have started to undercut our prices and some selling virtual fast foods have opened although why one would want to go beats me. Avery said that Pluto was very cheap, their laws the most lenient in the solar system, and if we didn't do it, others would beat us to market. But then…this is silly, probably not important."

"What?" Lamont asks. "What?"

"He mentioned that Pluto's extradition policies favor those hiding from the police." She pauses. "I wonder why that should concern him."

Lamont says, "Pluto is desperate to attract new businesses. They want more colonists. They've had good results with criminals. Many become model citizens because if they don't become model citizens, they spend their last days working on a satellite circling Pluto."

Lamont calls Mars Yard for backup. Two plain clothes men go to the spaceport and yank Avery off the space elevator and arrest him.

Lamont calls. I turn from Frank, with whom I'm discussing adding a cheese course to our menu.

"We've brought Avery in for questioning. Got him off the space elevator. Ten minutes later he would have left and risen beyond our jurisdiction."

"I'd like to come in and hear what Avery has to say."

"Done."

I go in the kitchen and ask Mario for a great dessert he can pack quickly. I'm sure eating something delicious will strengthen those working on this case. Mario packs two Chocolate Decadence Cakes and gets a bus boy to help me put them in my rover and carry them into Mars Yard. It feels like old times because this is the first cake I ever brought Lamont years ago, and he never forgot.

Security in the lobby stops us.

My eyes narrow. "Don't you dare ruin these cakes with your scanner. I'm not hiding razor blades and knives. They're for Lamont Cranshaw and his staff. Nothing inside but whipped cream, vanilla toffee cake, and five types of chocolate."

"All the more reason to do a taste test," the head guard argues.

I call Lamont and tell him the reason for my delay. Finally, the guard says I can go, but to expedite things, a slice of cake would help. So I give him one.

He says, "You could make it larger," instead of thank you very much.

Once upstairs Trenton opens his door and waves. The bus boy puts the cake boxes on Lamont's desk and leaves. "Looks like old times, Molly," Lamont says, eyes bright.

"Thinking the same thing, Lamont."

Lamont points and says, "I think it best if you wait behind the one-way mirror over there during the questioning."

I go. I watch and hear Lamont say to Avery, "We found Grafton enhanced to triple strength in your apartment. Can you explain this?"

Avery doesn't answer.

Lamont repeats the question.

"Guess you must know everything if you found that," Avery says.

"No, not everything."

Lamont waits. He leans in and peers at Avery. Avery doesn't blink. Lamont leans closer.

Finally, still not blinking because he can control his eyelids, Avery says, "I sent it to Frank, who I hoped would get it to Rick. And with Jody's help, he did."

"Do you think Jody or Frank knew it was lethal?"

"Of course not. What makes you think they're involved?"

Lamont says nothing for a long time hoping Avery will volunteer more information. When he sees that he's not going to say more unless asked a direct question, he says, "Why did you do it?"

Avery says, "Can I first ask a question?"

"Of course."

"Do you think I'm an android?"

"I never thought about it. Why? Is it important?"

"Well, I am. I'm the latest model." Avery rolls up his sleeve. "See?"

Many in the office gasp and gather round.

"Back, people," Lamont growls. "Give us space." They retreat.

Then turning to Avery, he asks, "What does that have to do with the fact that you just admitted to killing Rick Frances? If you killed someone, you are guilty of a crime and need to be put on trial. Actually, we had some information that you were an android when you were one of the earlier suspects. It came from someone who patronized Silicone Slings. But that information wasn't evidence nor made you a criminal."

Avery nods.

"So why did you do it?" Lamont repeats.

"I was frustrated and very angry." His voice rises. "Very angry," he repeats. "Rick established a fund to lobby congress to restrict and reverse the rights of enhanced humans. I was tired of having to hide my true identity to a boss that was so prejudiced or lose my job."

Avery becomes more agitated, but he continues. "Besides Rick wanted everyone on his staff to sign a petition restricting the growth of the enhanced human population and give a week's salary to the cause."

Avery stands and waves his arms. "I can't stand it," he

shouts, turning his hands into fists and looking like he would attack anyone who came near. "I can't stand it!"

With that outburst, Lamont signals two officers to restrain him. Then he points to Sid who jabs Avery with a syringe filled with silicone sedatives. Avery slides into a chair, head down, eyes closed.

Lamont signals that I should join them. "I'll let you ask Avery about the threatening notes, the hole in your brake lining and message cube in your Princes Lea costume at Nirgal Palace's costume ball. I know you want to. Besides you're good at it."

Avery's eyes flutter open. "What are you doing here, Molly?" He rubs them, sits up straight. "Can I have some water?" he asks.

An officer brings water in a cup that says "Rescued from Recycled Recyclables." Avery chugs about half.

"You tried to kill me in my rover," I say.

"Never! Never! I only wanted to scare you. I knew the make and model of your rover and knew that it had the latest safety features and that you wouldn't crash but roll to a stop."

"Well, you succeeded. But I didn't know I could stop until I stopped."

Avery studies the floor as though its cracks held a clue as to how he could get out of this.

"And what about those notes and threatening calls?"

"I only meant to scare you and stop you from pursuing the case. I heard that you had experience being a private eye in a case about Chocolate Moons, and I wanted to throw your investigation off track. I'm sorry. Really, I'm sorry. I like you."

I roll my eyes. "Who said keep your friends close but your enemies closer?"

"One military fact I happen to know," Lamont pipes. "Suntzu, a Chinese general and military strategist in 400 BC."

Sid says, "And all this time I thought it was Batman. But BC does mean Before Chocolate, right?"

"Right," Lamont says, cutting his first large slice of Chocolate Decadence Cake. "Everyone knows that."

The next day I call Lena.

"This must be very upsetting," I say. "Can I ask you some questions?"

"Sure, Molly."

"Did you know that Avery was an android?"

"No, I had no idea."

"Did you know he was unhappy?"

"No again. He seemed happy."

"Did Rick ever mention his will?"

"Yes. Rick was acutely aware of his medical condition and knew if he didn't get his medicine, he would age rapidly. He also said he was tired of looking for Carol, who might never show up. He wanted to change his will, making me his beneficiary. I told Avery and said since we made a great team, if and when the time came and I inherited VV or at least half, if Carol ever materialized, I would make him a partner."

"So you would have thought he would just stick it out."

"Yes. But he must have been suffering too much and was afraid Rick's ideas would snowball into a full-fledged movement."

"Did Avery know about Carol?"

"There was no reason he would know."

"What if I told you I know where Carol is?"

51

"I'M NOT CHANGING BACK to a woman because I'm meeting Lena," Frank says.

"I never said you had to. I'll give her a heads up so she doesn't faint when I tell her who you are."

"What do you think I should wear, Molly?"

"Now you're acting like a woman. A man wouldn't ask."

The meeting between Lena and Frank is a big success. Now that everyone knows that Frank is Carol, hiring a good lawyer to go over the wills is easy. Frank has no interest in VV and Lena is happy to buy his half.

And before I can catch my breath, Mario and Vanna come into my office glowing with excitement, hand in hand, and announce that they are getting married and want to have the wedding at Molly's.

Two weeks later, Frank visits his brother Sol at Nirgal Palace. He calls me and says that he wants to start over and will be leaving Molly's, but he will help find a replacement. He is taking the money that he got from selling his half of VV and investing it with Sol in Out of This World, the space shuttle business that would bring gourmet treats to those working on space stations.

Frank tells me that they had been searching for a theme song for the shuttle. They both agree that Beethoven is the right composer, but since there were nine composers named Beethoven, they couldn't decide which one. So they flipped a coin. "Ode to Roy" from Morris Beethoven's Bar Mitzvah classics won. Cortland offered to write them a new theme song, but they said with all due respect, nothing beats Beethoven.

Burton opens a branch of Club Mood in New Yellowstone, an hour away if you take the six hundred mile an hour tram. Becky and Lois continue to make hits. Cortland signs a new group called the Andromeda Strain, whose lead singer dates Lois. Stay tuned.

Avery's sentence is that he is sent to Pluto—where he wanted to go anyway. He is the first enhanced human on Pluto and becomes a celebrity.

Sol sends me a new head waiter from Nirgal Palace. We have just reviewed the menu. Page one includes salmon tartare spring rolls, artichoke and baby spinach salad with duck prosciutto, consommé with foie gras, swordfish with lobster sauce seasoned with lemon grass, Greek moussaka, sushi arranged like a flower, rack of lamb with a toasted almond crust, Peking duck, handmade spaghetti with clams, pancetta and emerald broth, roasted chicken with sautéed chanterelles and potons, double veal chop with fiddlehead ferns, bison tacos with red and green guacamole, and porterhouse steak with roasted pepper couscous.

Tonight's special desserts, in addition to those on our regular menu, are a rhubarb napoleon with sweet wild sumac and ginger ice cream and a warm chocolate cake with hazelnuts and double espresso ice cream.

White chocolate covered strawberries and butter cookies come gratis with the bill.

I check the time. It's getting late, time for dinner. No reservation? No problem. Come as my guest. How many in your party? I'll make sure you get a great table.

Jackie Kingon has published two articles in the New York Times: A feature piece about her experiences teaching in an inner city school called 'A Year in the Trenches' and 'Beautiful Music', about her son diagnosed with autism who is currently a pianist for the Alvin Ailey Ballet Company and school. Other non fiction articles have appeared in journals for autism and learning disabilities.

Her first book, *Chocolate Chocolate Moons*, also about Molly Marbles, was called "delightful" by Kirkus Review and "hard to resist," by the San Francisco Book Review. Short stories have been published in Flying Island Press-Pieces of Eight, The Fringe Magazine and Static Movement Magazine.

She has a Masters degree from Columbia University Teachers College in New York City; a Bachelor of Arts from Lesley University in Cambridge, Mass and a Bachelor of Fine Arts from The School of Visual Arts in New York City where she won the outstanding student award.

She has been a member of the board of the Empire State Plaza Art Commission in Albany, NY and on the board of the Friends of Vassar College Art Museum.

Jackie Kingon lives with her husband in New York City.

CPSIA information can be obtained
at www.ICGtesting.com
Printed in the USA
LVOW13s1230060717
540419LV00034B/1082/P